D. Olsen.

GUY DE MAUPASSANT

MISS HARRIET

AND OTHER STORIES

TRANSLATED

BY

H. N. P. SLOMAN

PENGUIN BOOKS

HARMONDSWORTH · MIDDLESEX

Penguin Books Ltd, Harmondsworth, Middlesex

U.S.A. : Penguin Books Inc, 3300 Clipper Mill Road, Baltimore 11, Md
Educational Representative:
D. C. Heath & Co., 285 Columbus Avenue, Boston 16, Mass]

AUSTRALIA : Penguin Books Pty Ltd, 200 Normanby Road,
Melbourne, S.C.5, Victoria

AGENT IN CANADA : Riverside Books Ltd, 47 Green Street,
Saint Lambert, Montreal, P.Q.

—

Made and printed in Great Britain by
The Whitefriars Press Ltd, Tonbridge

—

This translation first published 1951

CONTENTS

INTRODUCTION

GUY DE MAUPASSANT was born in 1850 at the Château de Miromesnil, a seventeenth-century mansion situated in a magnificent park in Normandy some six miles south of Dieppe; his father had leased the property for a few years, and it was here first, and later at his mother's house at Étretat, that his son passed his childhood. His parents' married life was unhappy and the boy saw little of his father. He was educated at the seminary at Yvetot and at the private Institution Leroy-Petit – of which latter school we have a picture in this volume in *The Question of Latin* – and then at the Lycée Corneille at Rouen. He entered the Civil Service after a period in the army as a conscript, which coincided with the Franco-Prussian War of 1870, though he saw no actual fighting. He worked in the Ministries of Marine – the scene of *The Legacy* in this volume – and of Public Instruction in Paris for ten years. Thus the background of most of his stories is the France of the early years of the Third Republic from 1870 to 1890. He was encouraged to write by his godfather, the great stylist Flaubert; and in 1880 he published a volume of verse and, in Zola's *Soirées de Médan*, one of his greatest 'nouvelles' or long short stories, *Boule de Suif*. From this date till his early death in 1893 – he died in an asylum for general paralysis of the insane, the result of a venereal disease for which no cure was then known – he lived by his pen, and his output was enormous; in thirteen years he wrote in addition to his verse six full-length novels, three volumes of *Travel Sketches*, four plays and some 300 stories. His verse and his plays have been forgotten and his novels are comparatively little read to-day; it is as a writer of short stories that his immortality is secure, and his influence on other writers in that *genre*, abroad as well as in France, has been marked. To cite only one example, Mr W. Somerset Maugham in the Introduction to the volume of his own collected stories called *Altogether* acknowledges him as his teacher. 'It is natural enough,' he writes, 'that when at that age I began writing stories myself I should unconsciously have chosen these little masterpieces as a model. I might very well have hit upon a worse.' It is surprising that such a master of the short story should have been unsuccessful with the larger canvas of his full-length novels, which are more like strings of short stories, disconnected incidents arbitrarily attached to the characters.

Guy de Maupassant belonged to the Naturalist school, of which Zola and Flaubert were the leaders; these writers carried further the principles of the realist school of Balzac, who had died in 1850. His observation of life is keen and detailed, if sometimes cynical and even coarse; he studied all classes of contemporary France with equal interest and detachment, from the Normandy peasants – whom we meet in this volume in *Uncle Tony* and *The Hautots, Father and Son* – to all ranks of Paris society, prostitutes, civil servants, artists, soldiers, both officers and privates, and members of the old families of the *noblesse* of the *Ancien Régime* as well as of the *petite bourgeoisie*, to which the author himself belonged and in which he was always most at home.

He has often been criticized for painting an unduly low, even sordid picture of human life and its motives, but his picture of the Normandy peasants, as in *Uncle Tony*, is not unsympathetic, though he is well aware of their excessive preoccupation with money. He seldom analyses his characters, though *Miss Harriet*, a study in abnormal psychology, is an exception to this rule; men act but he does not show us why they act. He is not interested, like Joseph Conrad or Chehov, in the analysis of motive for its own sake. He said himself: 'For me psychology in a novel or story consists in this: to show the inner man by his life.' But profitable criticism should not concern itself, mainly at any rate, with the qualities which an author lacks; it is futile to criticize Corneille because he has not the qualities of Shakespeare. Rather we should enjoy and try to understand the qualities which our author has got. And I hope this short collection, containing as it does several of de Maupassant's admitted masterpieces – many critics have rated *The Legacy* top among his 'nouvelles' – as well as some of his less outstanding stories, will enable the reader to form a fair idea of his quality and chief characteristics and, above all, to enjoy what he reads.

Of the very large number of incidents of the Franco-Prussian War which de Maupassant describes, we have here *Prisoners of War*, in which he pokes good-humoured fun at the French National Guard, and *Mademoiselle Fifi* with its savage description of the behaviour of the occupying German officers.

Though wit is common, humour is comparatively rare, as is the case with most French writers, but *The Pool* and *Old Vestey* show genuine humour with no desire to wound. The satire in *Monsieur Bush* and *Cemetery Walkers* is certainly bitter but brilliantly effective. I have included *The Withered Hand* and *Who Knows?* as examples of the *genre macabre* which had a considerable attraction for de Maupassant, though in my opinion other writers have been more successful here.

Monsieur Parent shows our author at his tragic best; there is no relief and the story moves like a Greek play to its inevitable, almost unbearable climax. The unhappiness of de Maupassant's life as a civil servant is reflected in the devastating picture of the Ministry of Marine in *The Legacy;* the petty rivalries and jealousies of the *fonctionnaires*, the struggle to keep up appearances on a miserable salary, the terrible monotony of the whole life, everything is pitilessly described, the atmosphere of the office being conveyed with masterly effect by means of realistic conversations. One is reminded of the early stories of Arnold Bennett and H. G. Wells.

For pure charm it would be hard to beat *Looking Back*, the story of a simple country *curé;* though de Maupassant was a free-thinker in religious matters, his priests are invariably sympathetically drawn. *The Question of Latin* is an attractive piece of sentiment without any hint of satire.

It cannot be denied that our author had a low opinion of women, though he was no misogynist; it has been suggested, and it may well be the truth, that he was obsessed with the physical side of the sex relationship and was therefore incapable of appreciating the spiritual side of love; he admitted that he never understood a woman's mind – but does any man?

While not a great stylist like Flaubert – he wrote too easily and too fast for that to be possible – his prose is clear and straightforward, vivid and forcible; and he is a master of creating atmosphere, sometimes in a few lines as in *The Hautots, Father and Son*, sometimes at greater length as in the first section of *The Legacy* and *Who Knows?*

The stories vary in length from 'contes' of about 2,000 words – of these sketches we have *Looking Back, The Withered Hand* and *Old Vestey* in the present volume – to 'nouvelles' of 15,000 words and upwards, such as *The Legacy* and *Monsieur Parent*. Farce, comedy, tragedy, satire, all are treated with equal mastery. The descriptions of scenery – and here there is a marked contrast to Zola – are always relevant to the plot and the reader is never tempted to skip. It is never easy to translate from a Latin or Slavonic language into English, not because the sense is obscure but because the Latin and the Slav talk about their feelings quite naturally, as we never do. No attempt has been made to transplant de Maupassant's stories into an English setting or into 'period' language; I have merely tried to give the reader simple modern English free from gallicisms, though some of the tricks of style, among which will be noticed the perhaps over-frequent use of three synonyms, have been preserved. Slang, which is bound to 'date', has generally been avoided, except in *The Pool* and *Uncle Tony*, where it is the essence of the story. I have left francs, which in the last quarter of the nineteenth century were worth about 10*d*, so that 100 francs came to about £4, as such.

H. N. P. S.

January, 1951

THE LEGACY

I

THOUGH it was not yet ten o'clock, the members of the staff were streaming up to the main entrance of the Ministry of Marine, flocking in from every corner of Paris, for it was getting near New Year's Day, when everyone was on his best behaviour in the hope of promotion. The noise of hurrying footsteps filled the huge building with its labyrinth of tortuous passages, broken by innumerable doors giving access to the various offices.

Each man entered his own room, shook hands with any colleague who had already arrived, took off his jacket, put on his old working coat and sat down at the table where a pile of papers was awaiting him. Then they went off to the offices near-by in search of news. Enquiries were first made as to whether the Chief had arrived, if he was in a good temper and if the day's mail was heavy.

M. César Cachelin, Personal Assistant in the Department of General Equipment, an ex-N.C.O. of Marines, who had become Permanent Clerk by effluxion of time, was entering in a huge ledger all the documents which the Registry messenger had brought. Facing him the Forwarding Clerk, old Savon, a stupid old man well known throughout the office for his matrimonial troubles, was copying a telegram from the Chief in his laborious handwriting, sitting stiffly with his body sideways, glancing over his shoulder at the original to avoid mistakes.

M. Cachelin, a fat man with short white hair standing straight up from his head, talked all the time as he went on with his routine job: 'Thirty-two telegrams from Toulon. That naval base sends us as much as the other four put together.' Presently he asked old Savon the question he put to him every morning: 'Well, my dear Savon, and how is Madame Savon?'

The old man replied, going on with his work: 'You know quite well, Monsieur Cachelin, that this is an extremely painful subject.'

And the Personal Assistant laughed, as he did every day at the same answer.

The door opened and M. Bunny came in. He was a handsome dark man, unmarried and always overdressed; he regarded himself as socially above his colleagues, his looks and manners being too good for his job. He wore showy rings, an imposing gold watch-chain and a monocle, only because it was the fashion, for he took it out of his eye to work, and he was continually shooting his cuffs to show off his big gold links.

He asked as he came in at the door: 'Is there much to do to-day?' Cachelin replied: 'Lots of stuff from Toulon as usual. It's obvious that New Year's Day is getting near. They want to show how efficient they are down there.'

But another member of the staff, M. Pitolet, a humorous witty fellow, who came in at this moment, retorted with a laugh: 'I suppose that's something we never do here!'

And, looking at his watch, he went on: 'It's seven minutes to ten, and everybody at his desk! Did you ever know anything like it? And I bet His Worship M. Lesable got here at nine, the same time as our noble Chief.'

The Personal Assistant stopped writing and, putting his pen behind his ear and his elbows on the desk, remarked: 'My word! If *he* doesn't get on, it won't be for want of trying!'

M. Pitolet, sitting down on the edge of the table and swinging one leg, rejoined: 'Oh! he'll be all right, my dear Cachelin; you may be sure he'll get on. I bet you ten francs to a sou he'll be the Chief inside ten years.'

M. Bunny, who was rolling a cigarette, as he stood warming the back of his legs at the fire, remarked: 'Damn it all! I'd rather stay at two thousand four hundred all my life than work myself to death as he does.'

Pitolet turned on his heel and said banteringly: 'All the same, my dear fellow, the fact remains that to-day, December 20th, you are here before ten o'clock.'

The other shrugged his shoulders indifferently: 'Of course, I don't want everybody else to get in before me. As you all get here in time to admire the dawn, I do the same, much as I deplore your punctuality. There's all the difference in the world between that and calling the boss "My dear Chief", as he does, and staying on till half-past six and taking work home. Besides I have a lot of social engagements and other things to do that take up my time.'

M. Cachelin had stopped making his entries and was gazing reflectively in front of him. At last he asked: 'Do you think he'll get his rise this year?'

Pitolet cried: 'Of course, he'll get it, I bet you ten to one! He doesn't pull all these strings for nothing.'

So they discussed the eternal question of promotion and bonuses, which had been the sole topic of conversation for a month in this vast hive of civil servants from the ground floor to the top.

The chances were reckoned, the amounts guessed, the claims weighed and anger aroused by the anticipated injustices. The interminable discussions started again, which had been begun the day before and would be repeated to-morrow with the same reasons and arguments and in the same words.

A recently joined clerk entered the room, M. Boissel, a small, pale, unhealthy-looking man, who fancied his life to be as full of melodramatic incidents as a novel by the elder Alexandre Dumas. He was always having unusual experiences and every morning he had stories to tell his neighbour, Pitolet, of the odd people he had met the evening before, dramatic happenings which he imagined in the house where he lived, screams in the street, which had made him open his window at twenty minutes past three in the morning. Every day he had separated men fighting, stopped runaway horses, saved women in distress, and, although he was physically as weak as a kitten, he was always recounting his deeds of daring with an air of conviction in his drawling voice.

As soon as he realized that they were talking of Lesable, he declared: 'I mean to tell that snivelling creature every day what I think of him, and, if he gets in my way, I'll give him such a shaking-up that he won't want to do it again.'

Bunny, smoking all the time, sneered: 'Well then you'd better begin to-day, for I have reliable information that you have been passed over this year in favour of Lesable.'

Boissel raised his hand, saying: 'I swear that if . . . .'

The door had opened again, and a short young man wearing the side whiskers of a naval officer or a lawyer, with a very high stiff collar, entered hurriedly with a preoccupied air; he spoke so fast that his words fell over one another, as if he never had time to finish what he wanted to say. He shook hands all round perfunctorily like a man with no time to waste, and, going up to the Personal Assistant, he said: 'My dear Cachelin, will you give me the Chapelou file, rope-yarn, Toulon, A.T.V., 1875?'

The clerk got up, reached for a file above his head, and took out a sheaf of papers enclosed in a blue jacket, saying, as he handed it: 'Here you are, M. Lesable; you are aware that the Chief took three telegrams out of this file yesterday?'

'Yes, I've got them, thanks.'

And the young man hurried out of the room.

He had hardly shut the door, when Bunny exclaimed: 'What manners, eh! You'd think he was the boss already!'

Pitolet replied: 'You wait and see; he'll get his promotion over all our heads.'

M. Cachelin had not resumed his writing; he seemed to have something on his mind. He went on: 'He's got a great future, that young fellow!'

But Bunny murmured disdainfully: 'For a man who doesn't look beyond the Ministry, that's all right, but for anyone else there's not much in it . . .'

Pitolet interrupted him: 'I suppose you mean to be an ambassador!'

The other made a gesture of impatience: 'It's not what I think. I don't care a damn! But that doesn't alter the fact that being head of a department in a Ministry will never cut any ice in society.'

Old Savon, the Forwarding Clerk, had been going on with his copying all the time. But for the last few minutes he had been dipping his pen over and over again in the inkpot and wiping it carefully on the damp sponge round the opening without making it write a letter. The blue-black fluid ran down to the point of the nib and fell drop by drop on the paper in dark blots. The poor old fellow, not understanding, looked ruefully at his manuscript, which he would have to begin all over again, like so many others recently, and said sadly in a low voice: 'Somebody has been tampering with the ink again.'

A roar of laughter all round greeted his words. Cachelin's stomach made the table shake. Bunny bent double as if he was preparing to go backwards up the chimney; Pitolet stamped his foot, coughed and waved his right hand as if it was wet, and Boissel himself choked with laughter, though he usually took things seriously and could not see a joke.

But old Savon, at last tumbling to it and wiping his pen on the skirt of his frock-coat, went on: 'There's nothing to laugh at. I have to do all my work two or three times over.'

He took another piece of paper out of his writing pad, adjusted the lined sheet under it and began with the first line again: 'Your Excellency and dear colleague . . .' This time the ink stayed on the nib and the letters came out clear. And the old man took up his sideways position again and began his second copy.

The others were still laughing, choking with merriment. They had been playing the same practical joke on the poor old fellow for the last six months or so and he never spotted it. It consisted in pouring a few drops of oil on the damp sponge used for cleaning the pens. So the nib with its coating of grease would not hold the ink; and the Forwarding Clerk spent hours in amazement and irritation, used up whole boxes of nibs and bottles of ink, and finally declared that the stuff now supplied in the office was of wretched quality.

What had started as a joke became an obsession with them in spite of the worry it caused the old man. They mixed gunpowder with his snuff, they drugged the water in the bottle he drank out of from time to time, and they told him that ever since the Commune most of the things in everyday use had been tampered with by the socialists in order to undermine the prestige of the Government and lead to a revolution.

So he had conceived a violent hatred of the anarchists, whom he imagined as lying in wait concealed everywhere, and was haunted by an undefined fear of some terrifying unknown person in disguise.

But a bell in the passage rang sharply. They all recognized the angry ring of the Chief, M. Torchebeuf; and everyone hurried to the door to get back to his own room.

Cachelin went on with his entries, but he soon put down his pen and rested his head in his hands in order to think.

He was working out a plan which had been running in his head for some time. An ex-Marine N.C.O., discharged after being three times wounded, once in Senegal and twice in Cochin China, he had been given as a special favour a post in the Ministry, where he had to put up with a great deal of harsh treatment, bullying and mortification in his long career as a clerk at the very bottom of the ladder; so he had the greatest respect for authority, especially the authority of his official superiors. The head of a department was in his eyes a superman, inhabiting a sphere far above him; and the civil servants whom he heard described as 'smart fellows, marked out for quick promotion', seemed to him beings of another world far superior to him.

Therefore he felt a boundless respect, almost amounting to veneration, for his colleague, Lesable, and he nourished a secret ambition, which persisted, to get him to marry his daughter.

She would be rich one day, very rich. The whole Ministry knew the story; for his sister, Mlle Cachelin, had a million francs in good hard cash; it was whispered that she owed her fortune to love, but she had rendered her wealth respectable by taking to religion, somewhat late in the day.

The old maid, after living the gay life, had retired with half a million francs, which she had more than doubled in eighteen years by stringent economy and by living on a scale which could hardly be called even modest. For many years she had shared a flat with her brother, who had remained a widower with his daughter Coralie; but her contribution to the household expenses was negligible; she saved her money and let it accumulate, continually saying to Cachelin: 'It comes to the same thing; it's all for your daughter, but get her married quickly, because I want to see my grand-nephews. Through her I shall have the satisfaction of holding in my arms one of our own flesh and blood.'

All this was common knowledge at the Ministry; and there was no lack of suitors. It was said that Bunny himself, the good-looking Bunny, the social success of the office, was cultivating old Cachelin with intentions that could not be mistaken. But the ex-sergeant, a wily old 'sweat' who had knocked about all over the world, wanted a son-in-law with a future, one who would be head of a depart-ment, so that he, the ex-N.C.O., would bask in reflected glory. Lesable was just the man he was looking for, and he had long been trying to discover some means of getting him to his house.

Suddenly he sprang up, rubbing his hands. He had got it!

He knew everyone's weak spots. Lesable's vanity, his profes-sional vanity, gave him his chance. He would go and ask for his help, as one goes to a Senator or a Deputy or some very important personage.

As he had not had promotion for five years, Cachelin thought he was pretty sure to get it this year. He would pretend to believe that he owed it to Lesable and would ask him to dinner by way of thanking him.

He had no sooner conceived the idea than he started operations. He took down his city coat from its hook in the cupboard, removed his old jacket and, picking up all the documents that concerned his colleague's department and had been entered up, he made his way to the office which the latter had all to himself as a special favour because of his efficiency and the importance of his work.

The young man was writing at a large table, surrounded by open files and papers scattered about, numbered in red and blue ink.

Seeing the Personal Assistant come in, he asked in a familiar tone but with a hint of respect in his voice: 'Well, my dear Sir, have you got a lot of work for me?'

'Yes, a fair amount. And besides I want a word with you.'

'Sit down, my dear Sir; I am at your service.'

Cachelin sat down, cleared his throat, looked worried and began timidly: 'This is what brings me to you, M. Lesable. I won't beat about the bush. I'll come straight to the point like an old soldier. I want to ask a favour.'

'What?'

'To put it briefly, I must get my rise this year. And I have no one to push my claims; so I thought of you.'

Lesable blushed slightly, surprised and flattered, his confusion mingled with pride. However he replied:

'But, my dear Sir, I have no influence here. I am a much less important person than you, who are going to be a Principal Clerk. I have no pull. I assure you that . . .'

Cachelin interrupted him very respectfully: 'Nonsense! You have the Chief's ear, and, if you put in a word to him on my behalf, I go up. You know I qualify for a pension in eighteen months and I shall lose 500 francs on that, if I don't get a rise this January. I know everybody says: "Cachelin is on a good wicket; his sister has got a million francs." It's quite true, she has, but her million is busy producing interest, she doesn't give any away. It's true too that it will all come to my daughter, but my daughter isn't me. A lot of good it will be to me, if my son-in-law and my daughter drive about in their carriage, while I starve. You appreciate the position?'

Lesable nodded: 'I quite understand your point. Your son-in-law may not hit it off with you. And besides it's always nice not to be beholden to anyone. Anyhow I promise to do all I can; I'll have a word with the Chief and explain the position; if necessary, I'll put it strongly. You can leave it to me.'

Cachelin got up, grasped both his colleague's hands and shook them as they do in the army; and he stammered: 'Thanks ever so much . . . You may be sure that if I ever have the chance . . . if I can ever . . . .' He broke off, unable to finish his sentence, and went out, stamping down the passage like a soldier on parade.

But he heard the angry ringing of a bell in the distance, and, recognizing it, he began to run. It was the Chief, M. Torchebeuf, ringing for his Personal Assistant.

A week later Cachelin found one morning on his desk a sealed letter couched in the following terms:

'My dear Colleague, I am happy to inform you that the Minister, acting on the suggestion of our Director and our Chief, yesterday signed your promotion to Principal Clerk. You will receive official notification to-morrow. Till then you know nothing about it – you understand?

Yours sincerely,
J. L. LESABLE.'

César immediately hastened to his young colleague's office, thanked him, apologized for having bothered him and offered to do anything to show his eternal gratitude.

Next day the news came through that Messrs. Lesable and Cachelin had both got their promotion. The rest of the staff would have to wait for better luck next year and be content with a bonus varying from 150 to 300 francs.

M. Boissel declared that he would lie in wait for Lesable one evening at midnight at the corner of his street and beat him unconscious. The other clerks made no comment.

The following Monday Cachelin went to his patron's office as soon as he arrived, made an impressive entry and said formally: 'I hope you will do us the honour of dining with us during the festive season. Choose your own day.'

The young man, somewhat taken aback, raised his head and looked his colleague straight in the face; then he replied, keeping his eyes fixed on the other's face, trying to read his thoughts: 'But, my dear fellow, the fact is . . . I've not got an evening free for some time.'

Cachelin pressed him with good-humoured insistence: 'I'm sure you won't disappoint us by refusing after the service you have rendered us. I invite you in the name of my family as well as my own.'

Lesable hesitated uncertainly. He had understood but he didn't quite know what to do; he had not had time to think and weigh the pros and cons. At last he reflected: 'I don't commit myself to anything by going to dinner,' and he accepted with pleasure, choosing the following Saturday evening. He added with a smile: 'So that I shan't have to be up early next morning.'

II

M. Cachelin had a small flat in the upper part of the Rue Roche-
chouart on the fifth floor with a balcony commanding a view of the
whole city. It had three bedrooms, one for his sister, one for his
daughter and one for himself; the dining-room was also used as a
sitting-room.

He was busy all the week with preparations for the dinner-party.
The menu was the subject of prolonged discussion; it was to be at
once unpretentious and distinguished. The following was ulti-
mately agreed upon: a clear egg soup, *hors-d'œuvres* consisting of
shrimps and sausage, a lobster, a nice chicken with tinned peas, a
pâté de foie gras, a salad, an ice and dessert.

The *foie gras* came from the pork-butcher near-by, the best
quality being insisted upon; in fact, it cost three and a half francs.
For the wine Cachelin went to the wine-merchant round the corner,
who supplied the red table wine he ordinarily drank. He refused to
go to a big shop. 'The small man,' as he said, 'does not often have
a chance of getting rid of his fine wines; so he keeps them a long
while and they are in first-class condition.'

He came home earlier than usual on the Saturday to make certain
that everything was ready. The servant who opened the door was
as red as a tomato, for she had been standing all the afternoon over
her oven, which had been lighted at midday, so that everything
should be ready in time; moreover she was in a state of nerves over
the party.

He went into the dining-room to check over everything. The
round table made a large white patch in the centre of the small room
brightly lighted by a lamp with a green shade.

By the side of the four plates, which were concealed by napkins
folded in the shape of a mitre by Aunt Charlotte, lay white metal
knives and forks; in front of them stood two glasses, one large and
the other small. César did not consider this sufficiently impressive
and called: 'Charlotte!'

The door on the left opened and an old woman appeared; she
was short and ten years older than her brother, with a narrow face

framed in white curls produced with the help of curl-papers. Her piping voice seemed too weak for her bent body and she dragged one foot a little as she walked; even her gestures seemed tired.

In her youth people had said of her: 'What a sweet little thing!'

Now she was a skinny old woman, still clean in her person from force of habit, self-willed and obstinate, narrow-minded, fussy and easily annoyed. Having become very pious, she had apparently entirely forgotten the irregularities of her early life.

She asked: 'What do you want?'

He replied: 'I feel the table doesn't look well with only two glasses. Why not have some champagne? It won't cost more than three or four francs, and we could put on the champagne glasses straightaway; it would make all the difference to the look of the room.'

Mlle Charlotte retorted: 'It seems to me useless waste of money; but you are paying, so it doesn't make any difference to me.'

He hesitated, wanting to be convinced: 'It really would look much better. And it will make everyone cheery for the Twelfth-Night cake.' This argument clinched the question. He put on his hat and went downstairs again, returning in five minutes with a bottle which had a broad white label with a huge coat-of-arms on its side: 'Vintage Champagne bottled at the Comte de Chatel-Rénovau's vineyard.'

And Cachelin declared: 'It only cost three francs and the man says it's a first-class wine.'

He brought out the champagne glasses himself from the cupboard and put one in front of each place.

The door on the right opened and his daughter came in. She was tall and plump with a fresh complexion, chestnut hair and blue eyes, a fine strong healthy-looking girl. A simple frock showed off the rounded curves of her lithe figure. Her powerful contralto, almost a man's voice, had low appealing notes in it. She cried: 'Good Lord! Champagne! That's great!' clapping her hands like a small child.

Her father said to her: 'Now you must be nice to this man; I owe a lot to him.'

She gave a deep laugh, implying: 'I know all about it!'

The bell rang. Doors were opened and shut and Lesable appeared. He was in evening dress with a white tie and white gloves. The effect was instantaneous. Cachelin had rushed forward, apologetic but delighted: 'But, my dear Sir, it's only a family meal; you see, I haven't changed.'

The young man answered: 'I know, you told me. But I never go out in the evening without dressing.' He bowed, with his opera-hat under his arm and a flower in his buttonhole. Cachelin introduced him: 'My sister Mlle Charlotte – my daughter Coralie – we call her Cora in the family.'

Everyone bowed. Cachelin went on: 'We have no drawing-room. It's rather a nuisance, but we manage.' Lesable replied: 'It's delightful!'

Then they took his hat, which he wanted to keep. And he immediately began to take off his gloves.

They had sat down, watching him across the table, and there was a silence.

Cachelin asked: 'Did the Chief stay late? I left early to give the ladies a hand.' Lesable replied nonchalantly: 'No, we left the office together, because we had to discuss the question of the tarpaulins at Brest. It's a very intricate problem, which won't be easy to settle.'

Cachelin had to enlighten his sister and, turning to her, he said: 'All the difficult questions at the office are given to M. Lesable; he's really the Chief's understudy.'

The old lady bowed politely: 'Oh! I've heard a lot about M. Lesable's ability.'

At this point the maid came in, pushing the door open with her knee and bearing aloft in both hands the large soup-tureen; and the host announced loudly: 'Let's sit down. Will you sit between my sister and my daughter, M. Lesable? I'm sure you're not afraid of ladies!' And the meal began.

Lesable made himself agreeable with an air of assurance almost amounting to condescension, and kept looking at the girl out of the corner of his eye, surprised at the unspoilt charm of her health and freshness. Mlle Charlotte did her best, knowing what was in her brother's mind, and kept the conversation going with tedious commonplaces. Cachelin, in high spirits, talked loud, made jokes and poured out the wine he had bought an hour before at the shop round the corner: 'Have a glass of this humble Burgundy, M. Lesable. I don't say it's a vintage wine, but it's pretty good; it's been years in the cellar, and it's not doctored, I can promise you that. We get it from some friends on the spot.'

The girl said nothing, blushing slightly from nervousness, for she felt uncomfortable next to this man, suspecting what was in his mind.

When the lobster appeared, Cachelin declared: 'Here is a gentleman, whose nearer acquaintance I am most anxious to make!' Lesable, with a smile, quoted the author who had called the lobster 'The Cardinal of the deep', entirely unaware that the creature was black until it was boiled. Cachelin roared with laughter, repeating: 'What a priceless joke!' But Mlle Charlotte was seriously offended and lost her temper: 'I don't see any connection between the two. The remark is in very poor taste. I can see a joke as well as anyone, but I won't have the clergy ridiculed in my presence.'

The young man, wishing to please the old lady, made the occasion an excuse for a profession of faith. He referred to the lack of breeding of those who speak lightly of the eternal verities and he concluded : 'As for me, I regard the religion of my forbears with respect and veneration; I was brought up in it and I shall remain in it till my dying day.'

Cachelin had stopped laughing; he was rolling bread pellets, murmuring: 'Quite so, quite so!' Then he changed the subject which did not interest him, and, with the tendency natural to those who do the same job day in and day out, he reverted to office 'shop' and asked: 'Our Adonis, Bunny, must be furious at not getting his promotion, isn't he?'

Lesable smiled: 'What do you expect? To each man according to his deserts!'

The conversation kept on the Ministry, a subject in which all were deeply interested, for the two women knew the personnel nearly as well as Cachelin himself, as they were discussed every evening. Mlle Charlotte took a special interest in Boissel because of his stories of his adventures and his romantic view of life. Mlle Cora was secretly much intrigued about the good-looking M. Bunny. Of course, neither of the ladies had ever seen the two men.

Lesable affected a tone of superiority, such as a minister might use in speaking of his staff.

They listened to his pronouncements: 'Bunny has a certain amount of ability; but in order to succeed one must work harder than he does. He's too fond of the pleasures of society, and they distract the mind. He won't get very far and he'll have no one to blame but himself. He may become a Deputy Principal, with his influence, but no more. As for Pitolet, he's good at drafting, one must admit; he has an undeniable distinction of style, but he's got no depth; all his goods are in the shop-window. He's a young fellow one couldn't put in charge of an important Department, but an intelligent Chief could make good use of him, if he told him exactly what to do.'

Mlle Charlotte asked: 'And what about M. Boissel?'

Lesable shrugged his shoulders: 'A poor creature, no good! He won't face facts. He's always imagining things and day-dreaming. In the Ministry he's a misfit.'

Cachelin began to laugh and declared: 'Old Savon's the best of the bunch!' and everyone joined in the laugh.

Next they talked of the theatres and the year's successes. Lesable laid down the law just as authoritatively on dramatic literature, arranging the authors in a definite order of merit and indicating the strong and weak points of each with the assurance of one conscious of his own infallibility and encyclopaedic knowledge.

They had finished the chicken. Cachelin was now opening the pot of *foie gras* with extreme care to emphasize the importance of the contents. He remarked: 'I don't know if this will be a good one; they're usually first-class. We get them from a cousin in Strasbourg.'

And everybody slowly savoured the pork-butcher's creation in ts yellow earthenware crock with the respect due to a culinary masterpiece.

There was a catastrophe over the ice. It had melted and was running about in the dish quite liquid like clear soup. The little maid had asked the confectioner's boy, who had brought it an hour before at seven o'clock, to turn it out of its mould himself, being afraid that she would not know how to deal with it.

Cachelin, much distressed, wanted to send it out, but recovered his equanimity at the thought of the Twelfth-Night cake, which he cut with an air of mystery, as if it concealed a secret of the first importance. All eyes were fixed on the symbolic cake, as it was passed round, everyone being warned to shut his eyes, as he took his slice.

Who would get the bean? There was an inane grin on every face. Lesable uttered a little cry of astonishment and held up a fat white bean, still covered with dough, between his finger and thumb. Cachelin began to clap and cried: 'Choose your Queen! Choose your Queen!'

For a moment the 'king' hesitated. Would it not be politic to choose Mlle Charlotte? She would be flattered and pleased; her support would be assured. But he reflected that he had been invited for Mlle Cora and he would look foolish if he chose the aunt. So, turning to his youthful neighbour, he presented the royal bean to her: 'Mlle Cora, allow me to offer it to you.'

'Thank you, Sir', she replied, and accepted the token of her sovereignty.

He was thinking: 'She really is a very pretty girl. She's got magnificent eyes and she's a damned fine wench!'

A pop made the women jump. Cachelin had just uncorked the champagne, which overflowed from the bottle and ran on to the cloth. The glasses were filled with the sparkling wine and the host declared: 'This is good stuff, that's obvious.' But just as Lesable was about to drink to prevent it running over, Cachelin cried: 'The King drinks! The King drinks!' And Mlle Charlotte animatedly repeated in her high-pitched soprano: 'The King drinks! The King drinks!'

Lesable drained his glass with complete assurance, saying as he put it down on the table: 'You see, I know what to do!' and, turning to Mlle Cora, he went on: 'Now it's your turn, Mademoiselle.'

She tried to drink but everybody shouted: 'The Queen drinks! The Queen drinks!' She blushed, began to giggle and put down the glass.

The meal ended in an atmosphere of gaiety, the King being gallantly attentive to his Queen. After the liqueurs Cachelin exclaimed: 'Now we'll have the table cleared, so that we can have room. If it's not raining, we might go out on to the balcony for a minute or two.' He wanted to show the view, though it was quite dark.

The glass door was opened. A breath of damp air came in. It was as warm outside as if it was April. And they all took the step up from the dining-room to the broad balcony. Nothing could be seen but the faint glow over the great city, like the halo over the head of a saint. Here and there the light seemed brighter and Cachelin began to explain the view. 'Look, over there that bright patch is the Eden. There's the line of the Boulevards; it's extraordinary how one can follow them. In the daytime the view from here is superb. You can travel all over the world without finding a finer one.'

Lesable was leaning on the iron rail next to Cora, who was gazing into space, silent and preoccupied, affected by one of those sudden waves of sentimental melancholy which sometimes come over girls. Mlle Charlotte went in for fear of the damp. Cachelin continued talking, pointing out the direction of the Invalides, the Trocadéro and the Arc de Triomphe at the Étoile.

Lesable said in a low voice: 'Do you like the view over Paris from up here, Mlle Cora?'

She gave a start as if he had woken her up and answered: 'I . . . yes, especially at night, I think of everything that is going on below us – all the happiness and all the unhappiness in all those houses. If one could see everything, what a lot one would learn!'

He had moved nearer till their elbows and shoulders were touching: 'By moonlight it must be fairyland.'

She murmured: 'Yes, it is. It's like a Gustave Doré engraving. How wonderful it would be to walk for miles over the roofs!'

He went on to ask questions about her tastes, her dreams, her pleasures; and she answered quite naturally, like an intelligent girl who has thought about things, without being unduly fanciful. He found in her a fund of common-sense and he thought to himself that it would really be delightful to put his arm about the firmly rounded waist and press long slow kisses on this cool cheek, near the ear, where the lamplight fell on it, as one sips old brandy, savouring every drop. He was excited by her proximity and very conscious of her attraction, and he wanted her virgin body, just ripe for love with all the delicate charm of youth. He felt he could have stayed there for hours, nights, weeks, for ever, leaning on the rail by her side, feeling her close to him, captivated by the thrill of her touch. He was stirred, too, by an involuntary wave of poetic feeling before the immensity of Paris spread out before him, with its bright gas lamps and its night life of dissolute pleasure. He dominated the great city, looking down on it like a soaring bird; and he felt it would be wonderful to lean on the railing there every evening by his wife's side; they would make love with passionate kisses and embraces, far above the vast city with its hidden love-life, exalted above all vulgar satisfactions and common joys, close to the stars.

There are some nights when even those least given to poetic feeling begin to dream, as if their souls were growing wings. Possibly he was a little drunk.

Cachelin, who had gone in to fetch his pipe, came back, lighting it: 'I know,' he said, 'you don't smoke; so I'm not offering you a cigarette. This is a marvellous place for a smoke. If I had to live downstairs, I should die. We might do so, for the whole house and those on either side belong to my sister; they bring her in a tidy income. She got the houses for a song years ago.' And turning towards the sitting-room, he shouted: 'How much did you pay for this property, Charlotte?'

The old lady's shrill voice began to speak; Lesable only caught a phrase here and there: ' . . . in 1863 . . . thirty-five francs . . . built later . . . a banker . . . sold again for at least five hundred thousand francs.' She spoke of her fortune with the gusto of an old soldier telling the story of his campaigns. She gave details of what she had bought, of the subsequent offers she had had, how the value had increased, and so on.

Lesable, keenly interested, turned round with his back to the balcony railing. But as he could only catch bits of her explanations, he abruptly deserted his youthful companion and went back into the room, so that he could hear it all; and, sitting down by Mlle Charlotte's side, he had a heart to heart talk with her about the probable increase in the rents, and what the money would bring in, if wisely invested in shares or real estate.

He did not leave till nearly midnight, promising to come again.

A month later the marriage of Jacques Léopold Lesable and Mlle Céleste Coralie Cachelin was the sole topic of conversation at the Ministry.

III

The young couple started their married life on the same floor as Cachelin and Mlle Charlotte in a flat similar to theirs, getting rid of the existing tenant.

One thing, however, worried Lesable. The aunt had refused to leave her fortune to Cora absolutely. But she had consented to swear 'before God' that she had made a will and deposited it with her solicitor, Maître Belhomme. Moreover, she had promised that her whole estate would come to her niece, subject only to one condition. In spite of pressure she had refused to explain the nature of this condition, but she had given the assurance, with a benevolent smile, that it was easy to satisfy.

In view of these explanations and the obstinacy of the pious old lady, Lesable thought himself justified in going ahead, and, being strongly attracted by the girl, he let his inclination overcome his doubts and capitulated before Cachelin's persistent attack.

Now he was happy, though still harassed by a feeling of uncertainty. And he was in love with his wife, who had entirely come up to his expectations. The monotony of his existence went on unruffled. In a week or two he had settled down to married life, while still showing himself the perfect civil servant as before.

The year ended and New Year's Day came round again. To his great surprise he did not get the promotion on which he had counted. Bunny and Pitolet were the only two to get their step up; and Boissel told Cachelin in confidence that he meant to give his two colleagues a thrashing one evening, as they left the office, in front of the main door before everyone. He did not carry out his threat.

For a week Lesable could not sleep from vexation at missing his promotion in spite of all his hard work. He had worked like a galley-slave, doing for an indefinite period the job of the Deputy Director, M. Rabot, who was away ill for nine months every year in the hospital of Val-de-Grâce; he arrived every morning at half-past eight and stayed every night till half-past six. What more could a man do? He had not got recognition for all this hard work and the effort he was making; very well, he would do like everybody else. The labourer is worthy of his hire. How could M. Torchebeuf, who always treated him as a son, have failed him? He wanted an explanation. He would go round and find the Chief and have it out with him.

So one Monday morning, before his colleagues arrived, he knocked at the great man's door.

An irritable voice shouted: 'Come in!' He went in.

M. Torchebeuf was writing, sitting at a big table littered with papers; he was a small man with a large head, which seemed to rest on his writing pad. Seeing his favourite clerk, he said: 'Good morning, Lesable; how are you?'

The young man replied: 'Good morning, my dear Chief; I'm very well, thanks; how are you?'

The Chief stopped writing and swivelled his chair round. His slight, frail, skinny body, clothed in a tight-fitting frock-coat of formal cut, seemed quite out of place in the great high-backed leather chair. His rosette as Officer of the Legion of Honour, bright red and far too big for the wearer, blazed like a red-hot coal on his pigeon chest, which seemed unable to bear the weight of his large head, as if his whole power of growth had gone into a domed top-storey like a mushroom.

The jaw was sharp, the cheeks sunken, the eyes prominent and the broad forehead was covered with a mop of white hair brushed back.

M. Torchebeuf spoke: 'Take a seat, my dear fellow, and tell me what brings you here.'

To all the other clerks he showed a cavalier bluntness, behaving like a captain on his own quarter-deck, for he regarded the Ministry as a great battle-ship, the flag-ship of the Admiral in supreme command of all the French Navy.

Lesable, a little pale and uncomfortable, stammered: 'My dear Chief, I've come to ask you if you have any cause of complaint against me.'

'Of course not, my dear chap! Why do you ask that?'

'The fact is, I'm a bit surprised at not getting my promotion this year, as I have always done before. Let me explain myself, my dear Chief, and I hope you will forgive my plain speaking. I am well aware that I owe to you many unusual favours and unexpected benefits. I know that promotion is normally only given every two or three years; but allow me to put it to you that I give the office about four times the amount of work of an ordinary member of the staff and spend at least twice the number of hours at my desk. If the result of my efforts in terms of work done is weighed against my remuneration therefor, I am sure that the latter cannot be considered adequate to the former.' He had prepared his speech with care and was pleased with the result.

M. Torchebeuf, taken by surprise, hesitated before answering. At last he said in a slightly chilly tone: 'Although in principle a discussion of such a subject is not permissible between a Chief and his subordinate, I am prepared for once in a way to give you an answer in view of your excellent work. I did put forward your name for promotion as in previous years. But the Director passed you over owing to the fact that your marriage has amply provided for your future, assuring you of more than a competence, of a fortune, in fact, to which your humbler colleagues can never aspire. To put

t shortly, it is surely equitable to consider everyone's private cir-
umstances. You will be a rich man, a very rich man, and an extra
hree hundred francs will be nothing to you, while an increase of
hat amount will mean a lot to the rest. That, my dear fellow, is
vhy you were passed over this year.'

Lesable, not knowing what to say, retired in a state of consider-
ble irritation.

That evening he was rude to his wife at dinner. She was usually
n good spirits and not easily annoyed, but she had a will of her
wn, and, when she really wanted anything, she stuck to her guns.
he no longer had for him the physical attraction of their early days,
nd, although he still wanted her, for she was pretty and unspoilt,
e sometimes felt the sense of disillusion, almost amounting to
isgust, which so soon comes to two people living together. The
housand ridiculous trivialities of everyday life, the sloppy clothes
t breakfast, the shabby old woollen dressing-gown, the faded
ath-wrap, for they were not well off, and all the necessary house-
old chores that one cannot get away from in a small flat were
aking the gilt off the charm of marriage, and the bloom of poetry,
o attractive from a distance to an engaged couple, was beginning
o fade.

Aunt Charlotte was also making his life at home unpleasant, for
he was always about; she was constantly interfering, she wanted
o arrange everything and was always criticizing. And, as they were
errified of offending her, they resigned themselves to putting up
vith it all, but their exasperation, though concealed, was growing.

The old woman trailed about the flat, dragging her foot, and was
lways saying in her reedy voice: 'You really ought to do this; you
eally ought to do that.'

When they were alone, Lesable, his patience exhausted, would
ry: 'Your aunt is really getting insufferable. I don't want any more
f her! Do you hear? I don't want any more of her!' And Cora
vould answer calmly: 'Well, what do you expect me to do about
t?'

Then he lost his temper: 'It's intolerable having a family like
his on the top of one!'

And she answered placidly: 'Yes, the family is intolerable, bu the legacy is worth having, isn't it? Don't be a fool. It's you interest as much as mine to keep on the right side of Aun Charlotte.'

This was unanswerable; so he relapsed into silence.

The aunt now began to worry them continually with her mani for a child. She took Lesable into corners and whispered in his ear 'Nephew, I want you to be a father before I die. I want to see m heir. You'll never make me believe that Cora can't be a mother you've only got to look at her. The object of marriage is to foun a family and have issue. Our Holy Church forbids sterile union I know you are not well off and a child is an expense. But after m death, you'll be quite comfortable. I want a little Lesable; I insis do you understand?'

After they had been married fifteen months, as her desire wa still unrealized, she began to get anxious and became more insistent she whispered advice to Cora, the practical advice of a woman wh has known all about such things in the past and can still remembe when she wants to.

One morning she was not well enough to get up. As she ha never been ill in her life, Cachelin in a state of panic came an knocked at his son-in-law's door: 'Run round to Doctor Barbett and tell the Chief, will you, that I shan't be in to-day in view c what has happened.'

Lesable had a bad day; he couldn't work or draft letters, h couldn't concentrate. Surprised, M. Torchebeuf asked: 'You mind's not on what you're doing to-day, M. Lesable; what's th matter?' And Lesable replied nervously: 'I'm dead tired, my dea Chief; I was up all night with our aunt who is seriously ill.'

But his Chief made the chilly comment: 'As M. Cachelin staye with her, that ought to be enough. I can't allow my office routin to be upset for my staff's personal affairs.'

Lesable had put his watch out on the table in front of him an he waited for five o'clock with feverish impatience. As soon as th big clock in the main courtyard struck, he fled, leaving the offic for the first time at the statutory hour.

He even took a cab home, so great was his anxiety, and ran up the stairs.

The maid came to the door and he stammered: 'How is she?'

'Doctor says she's very bad.'

His heart stopped beating; quite dazed, he said: 'Really!'

Was she perhaps going to die?

He dared not enter the sick room now and sent the maid to fetch Cachelin who was sitting with her.

His father-in-law appeared immediately, opening the door quietly. He was wearing his dressing-gown and the smoking-cap he put on when he was spending the evening comfortably at the fireside; and he murmured in a low voice: 'She's bad, very bad; she's been unconscious since four. They administered Extreme Unction during the afternoon.'

Lesable felt his knees go weak and sat down.

'Where's my wife?'

'She's with her.'

'What did the doctor actually say?'

'He says it's a stroke. She may pull through or she may die in the night.'

'Do you need me? If not, I'd rather not go in. It would be very painful to see her in this state.'

'No, go to your flat. If there's any change, I'll have you called at once.'

Lesable went back to his flat. The place seemed changed; it looked larger and brighter. But, as he couldn't stay still, he went out on the balcony.

It was the last week of July and the summer sun, as it went down behind the twin towers of the Trocadéro, was shedding a sunset glory over the sea of roofs.

The sky, crimson on the horizon, melted higher up into pale gold, then yellow, then through all the shades to a pale luminous green, till at last overhead it was pure clear blue.

Swallows were darting about like arrows, hardly visible, the fleeting curve of their wings silhouetted against the crimson back-cloth of the sky. And over the vast mass of houses and the country beyond floated a pink haze of fiery mist, pierced by the spires of the churches and the slender points of the monuments, like some transformation scene. The Arc de Triomphe at the Étoile stood out huge and black against the fiery red of the horizon, and the dome of the Invalides looked like another sun that had fallen from heaven on top of the building.

Lesable, with both his hands on the iron railing, drank in the air, as one drinks wine; he wanted to dance, shout aloud and throw his arms about. A wave of deep triumphant joy swept over him; life was suddenly radiant, his future bright with happiness. What were his plans? And he began to dream.

A noise behind him made him start. It was his wife. Her eyes were red and her face was slightly swollen, and she looked tired. She held out her cheek for his kiss; then she said: 'We're having dinner at father's, so as to be near her. The maid will stay with her while we eat.'

And he followed her into the adjoining flat.

Cachelin was already seated, waiting for his daughter and her husband. A cold chicken, potato salad and a dish of strawberries were on the sideboard and the soup was steaming in the plates.

They sat down. Cachelin declared: 'I'm glad things aren't often like this; it's not very cheerful.' He spoke in an indifferent tone, with a look of satisfaction on his face. And he set to with a good appetite, pronouncing the chicken excellent and the potato salad most refreshing.

But Lesable had no appetite; he was worried and hardly ate anything, listening for any sound from the next room, which remained as silent as if it was empty. Cora wasn't hungry either; she was upset and almost in tears, wiping her eyes from time to time on the corner of her napkin.

Cachelin asked: 'What did the Chief say?'

Lesable had to give all the details, which his father-in-law insisted on having repeated several times, for he wanted to know everything, as if he had been away from the Ministry for a year.

'The news of her illness must have created a sensation.'

He was thinking of his triumphal return after her death and the expression on his colleagues' faces; but, as if troubled by a qualm of conscience, he said aloud: 'It's not that I wish the dear old lady any harm. God knows I would like to have her with me for many years; but all the same it will make an impression. Old Savon will forget about the Commune!'

They were just starting on the strawberries, when the door of the sick room opened a crack. Excitement brought all three diners to their feet with a start. And the little maid appeared, preserving her unruffled air of stolid stupidity. She announced calmly: 'Her breathing has stopped.'

Cachelin, dropping his napkin on top of the dishes, rushed in like a madman; Cora followed with beating heart; but Lesable remained standing near the door, his eyes fixed on the white patch of the bed hardly visible in the half-light at the far end of the room. He saw his father-in-law's back bending over the bed, not moving, as he made his examination; suddenly he heard his voice, which seemed to come from far away, very far away, from the ends of the world, like a voice heard in a dream saying something utterly unexpected. The voice was saying: 'It's all over; there's not a sound.' He saw his wife fall on her knees, burying her face in the bedclothes, sobbing. At last he steeled himself to go in, and, as Cachelin was no longer leaning over the bed, he saw against the white pillow Aunt Charlotte's face with closed eyes, so sunken, so stiff, so pale, that it looked like a wax doll.

He asked anxiously: 'Is it all over?'

Cachelin, whose eyes had also been fixed on his sister, turned to him and they looked each other straight in the face. He answered: 'Yes!' trying to force an expression of sorrow, but the two men had understood each other at a glance, and instinctively, not knowing why, they shook hands, as if grateful for what each had done for the other.

Then, without losing any time, they got busy with all the things that have to be done when someone dies.

Lesable promised to go for the doctor and carry out as quickly as possible the necessary arrangements.

He seized his hat and ran downstairs in his hurry to get into the street, to be alone, to be able to think and savour his good fortune without witnesses.

When his jobs were finished, instead of going home, he made for the Boulevard; he felt an urge to see people, to mingle with the jostling crowd and the cheery night life. He wanted to shout to the passers-by: 'I've got an income of fifty thousand francs a year!' and he walked along with his hands in his pockets, looking at the shop windows with their display of rich materials, jewellery and expensive furniture, thinking happily to himself: 'Now I can afford this sort of thing.'

Suddenly he passed a shop with mourning in the window and the thought flashed across his mind: 'Suppose she isn't dead! Suppose they've made a mistake!'

And he hurried home, unable to get the idea out of his mind.

When he got back, he asked: 'Has the doctor been?'

Cachelin replied: 'Yes; he has pronounced her dead and promised to issue the certificate.'

They returned to the chamber of death. Cora was still crying in the arm-chair, crying quietly, for tears come easily to all women, but no longer bitterly, for she had recovered from her momentary grief.

As soon as they were all three in the room together, Cachelin said in a low voice: 'Now the maid has gone to bed, we can look and see if there is anything hidden in the cupboards and drawers.'

And the two men set to work. They emptied drawers, searched pockets, unfolded the smallest scraps of paper. By midnight they had found nothing of interest. Cora had dropped asleep and was snoring with gentle regularity.

Cachelin asked: 'Have we got to stay here all night?' Lesable wasn't quite sure but thought it was the correct thing to do. His father-in-law without a moment's hesitation said: 'In that case let's get arm-chairs.' So they went and fetched two other upholstered arm-chairs from the young couple's room.

An hour later the three next-of-kin were all asleep and snoring in different keys, while the body lay there frozen into eternal immobility.

They woke at dawn, as the little maid entered the room. Cachelin immediately confessed, rubbing his eyes: 'I got a bit drowsy the last half-hour or so.' But Lesable, wide awake at once, declared: 'So I observed. I never lost consciousness for a moment; I had merely closed my eyes to rest them.'

Cora went back to her flat.

Then Lesable asked with assumed indifference: 'When shall we go to the solicitor for the reading of the will?'

'Well, what about going this morning?'

'Is it necessary for Cora to come with us?'

'I think perhaps it would be as well; after all she's inheriting.'

'In that case I'll go and tell her to get ready.'

And Lesable left the room briskly.

The office of Maître Belhomme, the solicitor, had only just opened its doors when Cachelin, Lesable and his wife presented themselves, in deep mourning, with the correct expression of sorrow.

The solicitor saw them at once and made them sit down. Cachelin acted as spokesman: 'I think you know who I am, Sir. I am Mlle Charlotte Cachelin's brother; this is my daughter and this my son-in-law. My poor sister died yesterday; the funeral will be to-morrow. As she had lodged her will with you, we have come to ask if she expressed any wish with regard to her interment, and if you have any communication to make to us.'

The lawyer opened a drawer, extracted an envelope, tore it open and took out a document, declaring: 'This is a true copy of the will, the contents of which I can let you know at once. The original, of which this is an exact copy, must remain in my hands.' And he began to read: 'The last will and testament of me, the undersigned, Victorine Charlotte Cachelin:

'I bequeath the whole of my fortune, amounting to about one million one hundred and twenty thousand francs, to the children who shall be born of the marriage of my niece, Céleste Coralie Cachelin, the income to remain at the disposal of the parents until the eldest child comes of age.

'The arrangements which follow relate to the share of each

child and that part to be enjoyed by the parents during their life-time.

'In the event of my death occurring before the birth of an heir to my niece, the whole of my estate will remain in the hands of my solicitor for three years, so that my wishes expressed above may be carried out, if a child is born within that period.

'But in the event of Coralie not being blessed by Heaven with issue within three years after my decease, my estate will be distributed through my solicitor among the poor and the charitable institutions in the following list.'

Here followed an interminable catalogue with the names of institutions, figures, instructions and recommendations.

The lawyer handed the document politely to Cachelin, who was speechless with astonishment.

The former even thought it incumbent upon him to add a few words of explanation: 'Mlle Cachelin,' he said, 'when she did me the honour to consult me about her intention to make a will in these terms, stressed her passionate desire to see an heir of her own blood. She countered all my arguments with an increasing emphasis on this desire of hers, founded on religious feelings, for she held that a childless marriage was a sign of divine displeasure. I failed to modify her intentions in a single particular. Believe me, I very much regret it.' But, he added, with a smile at Coralie: 'I have no doubt that the hopes of the deceased will speedily be realized!'

And the three members of the family went away, too frightened to think.

They made their way home side by side in silence, feeling ashamed and furious, as if each had tricked the other out of the money.

Even Cora's grief had suddenly completely evaporated, her aunt's ingratitude having now rendered any appearance of sorrow unnecessary. At last Lesable, whose pale lips were tightly set with vexation, said to his father-in-law: 'Give me this document; I want to see it with my own eyes.' Cachelin passed him the paper and the young man began to read it. He stood there in the middle of the pavement, being bumped into by the passers-by, perusing the words with his sharp practical eye. The other two waited for him a few steps in front, still silent.

Then he gave back the will with the remark: 'There's nothing to be done: she's made us all look pretty silly!'

Cachelin, furious at seeing his hopes dashed, replied: 'It was up to you to have a child, damn it all! You knew perfectly well she had set her heart on it for years.'

Lesable shrugged his shoulders in silence.

When they got home, they found a crowd of people waiting for them, the people whose business it is to deal with corpses. Lesable went back to his flat, refusing to take any further part in the proceedings, and César bullied everybody, shouting that he wanted to be left in peace and get it all over as quickly as possible, complaining that they were taking an unconscionable time to get the body out of the way.

Cora shut herself up in her room and gave no sign of life. But after an hour Cachelin went and knocked at his son-in-law's door: 'I have come, my dear Léopold,' he began, 'to put one or two considerations before you; we've got to come to an understanding. My view is that, in spite of what has happened, we ought not to skimp the funeral, or we shall arouse suspicions at the Ministry. We'll make some arrangement about the expenses. Besides, the position is not hopeless. You've not been married very long and it would be very bad luck if you didn't have children. You must get a move on, that's all. Don't waste any time. Will you make it your business to look in at the Ministry presently? I'll get on with addressing the funeral cards.'

Lesable agreed rather sourly with his father-in-law and they sat down at opposite ends of a long table to address the black-bordered mourning envelopes.

Later they had lunch. Cora reappeared, apparently quite unaffected, as if all this had nothing to do with her; and she made a hearty meal, having eaten nothing the previous day.

Immediately after lunch she went back to her own room. Lesable went out to go to the Ministry and Cachelin settled himself on the balcony with his pipe, sitting astride on a chair leaning over the

back. The oppressive summer sun was blazing straight down on
the myriad roofs so brightly as to dazzle the sight.

Cachelin in his shirt-sleeves, his eyes blinking in the shimmering
haze, gazed at the green hills far, far away beyond the great city and
its dusty suburbs. He reflected that the Seine was flowing, broad,
placid and cool, at the foot of the wooded hills, and that it would
be very much pleasanter to be lying on one's face in the long grass,
close enough to the river to spit into the water, than to be sitting
on the broiling lead of his balcony. He felt quite upset at the
harassing thought, the painful realization of the catastrophe and his
unexpected bad luck, all the more bitter and hard to bear because
their hopes had been so lively for so many years; and he said out
loud, as one does under stress of great emotion or the obsession of
a fixed idea: 'The old cow!'

Behind him in the bedroom he could hear the undertaker's men
moving about and the repeated clang of the hammer, as they fixed
the coffin lid. He had not looked at his sister's body since the visit
to the lawyer.

But gradually the cheerful warmth and the delightful freshness
of the lovely summer day had its effect on his thoughts as well as
on his body, and he reflected that there was still hope. Why
shouldn't his daughter have a child? She hadn't been married two
years yet. His son-in-law seemed vigorous, strong and healthy,
though short. Damn it all! of course, they would have a child. In
fact, they must!

Lesable had entered the Ministry unobtrusively and slipped into
his office. He found a slip of paper on his table with the words:
'The Chief wants you.' His first reaction was a gesture of impatience
and revolt against the tyranny about to close down on him once
more; then he felt the prick of a sudden violent ambition to get on.
He would be head of a department himself, and soon; he would go
even higher.

Without taking off his city frock-coat, he went to M. Torchebeuf's office. He appeared before him wearing the conventional
expression of grief; indeed there was something more in his face,
a trace of genuine heartfelt sorrow, the instinctive depression

which inevitably affects the look of those whose hopes have been rudely dashed.

The Chief's large head, bending as usual over a sheet of paper, was raised, and he asked sharply: 'I've been wanting you all the morning. Why haven't you been here?' Lesable replied: 'My dear Chief, we have had the misfortune to lose my aunt, Mlle. Cachelin; I was on my way to invite you to the funeral, which will be to-morrow.'

M. Torchebeuf's frown immediately cleared and he answered with a hint of sympathy in his tone: 'In that case, my dear fellow, everything is explained. Thank you for the invitation; you can have the day off; you must have a lot to do.'

But Lesable wanted to show his conscientiousness: 'Thanks, my dear Chief; but all the arrangements are made and I shall stay till the usual time.' With that he went back to his room.

The news had got round and people came in from every office to offer what were really congratulations more than condolences; they also wanted to see how he was taking it. He received their conventional expressions of sympathy and their searching glances with an actor's mask of resignation and an unexpected show of proper feeling. Some said: 'He's taking it very well.' And others added: 'He well might, for after all he must be damned glad!'

Bunny, with greater outspokenness than the rest, asked with the casual indifference of a man of the world: 'Do you know exactly how much she left?'

Lesable replied as though it had nothing to do with him: 'No, not exactly. The will mentions about one million two hundred thousand francs. I only know that because the solicitor had to inform us at once of certain clauses affecting the funeral arrangements.'

Everyone imagined that Lesable would leave the Ministry. With an income of 60,000 francs a year one does not stick to quill-driving; one is somebody; one can satisfy one's ambitions. Some thought he was aiming at the Conseil d'État; others that he would go into Parliament. The Chief expected to receive his resignation to lay before the Director-General.

The whole Ministry attended the funeral, which was voted: 'done on the cheap'. But it was whispered: 'That is how Mlle Cachelin wanted it; it was in the will.'

Next day Cachelin was back at the office, and Lesable, after being away sick for a week, reappeared, slightly paler than before but hard-working and efficient as usual. There was no apparent change in their way of life. It was noticed only that they ostentatiously smoked large cigars and were always talking about rates of interest, railway shares and securities, like men who have money invested; and a little later the news spread that they had taken a country place outside Paris for the summer holidays.

People thought: 'They're as close as the old lady; it's a family trait; birds of a feather! Anyhow it's not decent to stay on at the Ministry with a fortune like that.'

Quite soon the incident was forgotten. They were placed, pigeon-holed and dismissed from mind.

IV

As he followed Aunt Charlotte's coffin to the cemetery, Lesable was thinking of the million; he felt a grudge against everybody for his unfortunate situation, devoured by disappointment all the more acute, because it must be concealed.

He also asked himself: 'Why haven't I had a child after being married for two years?' And his heart thumped at the thought that his union might remain childless.

Then, like the small boy who sees the prize waiting to be won at the top of the tall shining greasy pole and swears to himself that he will reach it by his own efforts and will-power, that he has the necessary strength and perseverance, Lesable determined to become a father at whatever cost. So many other men are, why shouldn't he succeed? Perhaps he had been careless, perhaps he hadn't taken enough trouble, perhaps there was something he didn't know, because his heart was not really in it. Having never had any great wish for an heir, he had never really concentrated on the job. In the future he would leave no stone unturned, no expedient untried; and success would crown his efforts, because he willed it so.

But, when he got home, he did not feel well and had to go to bed. The shock of disappointment had been too great; he was suffering from the reaction.

The doctor thought his condition sufficiently serious to order complete rest; and even after this he would have to be careful for a long time. There was danger of brain fever.

However, a week later he was up again and back at work.

But he still did not feel well enough to seek the conjugal couch. He was nervous and hesitated like a general on the eve of a decisive battle. Every night he put it off till the next night, hoping for one of those moments of physical well-being and confidence, when one feels on top of the world. He was continually feeling his pulse and, if he found it weak or irregular, he took tonics, ate raw beef and went for long walks on his way home to get his strength up.

When he did not seem to be recovering as he had hoped, he decided to get out of Paris, till the end of the hot weather. And he had soon convinced himself that the country air would have the desired effect on his nerves. In his condition getting out of Town is always an unfailingly effective specific. This certainty of success in the near future restored his confidence and he said over and over again to his father-in-law in meaning tones: 'When we're in the country, I shall be better and everything will be all right.' The mere word 'Country' seemed to have a mystical significance.

So they took a small house in the village of Bezons and all three moved in there. The two men used to go off every morning across country to Colombes station and walked back home in the evening.

Cora, delighted to be living close to the gently-flowing river, used to sit about on the bank; she picked wild flowers and brought home great bunches of pale feathery nodding grasses.

Every evening they all strolled along the river's edge as far as the Cod Lock, dropping into the Lindens Restaurant for a bottle of beer. The river, dammed by a long line of stakes, forced its way through the chinks over a breadth of a hundred yards, boiling, leaping, foaming; and the thunder of the chute made the earth tremble, while a fine cloud of damp spray floated overhead, rising from the race like a thin mist and carrying with it the reek of churned-up mud, disturbed by the swirling waters.

Darkness would fall and far away in front of them a fiery glare showed where Paris was; Cachelin was moved to repeat every evening: 'Some city, what!' From time to time a train thundered over the iron bridge spanning the extremity of the island and soon disappeared from sight either to the left towards Paris or to the right to the coast.

They walked home slowly watching the moon rise, sitting down on the bank to enjoy a little longer the sight of its pale yellow light falling on the placid stream and appearing to flow with the current, shimmering like flame-coloured shot silk on the broken water. Frogs uttered their staccato metallic note and the cry of night-birds echoed through the air. And sometimes a large silent shadow glided over the water, breaking the calm gleaming surface. It was a poachers' boat; they would make a sudden cast and pull the huge dark net in again to the boat noiselessly with their catch of shining, leaping gudgeon, like a treasure from the depths, a living treasure of silver fish.

Cora, in sentimental mood, leaned affectionately on her husband's arm, whose intentions she had guessed, though not a word had passed between them. They felt it as a sort of engagement period repeated, a second anticipation of the kiss of love. Sometimes he kissed her furtively just below where the ear springs from the neck, that fascinatingly soft spot with its wispy curls. She answered by squeezing his hand; they wanted each other but would not gratify their desires yet, worried and restrained by a more powerful desire for the million, which beckoned them like a ghost.

Cachelin, his anxiety appeased by the hopeful atmosphere about him, enjoyed himself, drank a great deal and ate heartily; in the gloaming he felt surging up in him those waves of poetic emotion and fatuous sentimentality which certain country sights inspire in the most coarse-grained, the deluge of light through the branches, a sunset over the distant hills with purple reflections in the river. He would say: 'The sight of these things make me believe in God.

It gets me here' – and he indicated the pit of his stomach – 'I feel
quite upset and I come over all queer. It's as if I'd been plunged in a
bath and it makes me want to cry.'

But Lesable was feeling better, conscious of the stirring of
passions to which he had long been a stranger; he wanted to gambol
like a young stallion, roll on the grass and shout for joy.

He felt that the time had come. It was a real wedding-night and
they had a second honeymoon, full of endearments and hopes.

But they soon discovered that their efforts had been in vain and
their confidence misplaced.

They were in despair; it was a tragedy. But Lesable did not lose
heart; he made superhuman efforts. His wife, who shared both his
desire and his fears, being more robust physically, responded
willingly to his advances and did all in her power to stimulate his
weakening passion.

They returned to Paris early in October.

Their life was becoming hell. They were always nagging at each
other; and Cachelin, who sensed the position, was always scarifying
them with the poisoned shafts of an old soldier's coarse witticisms.

One thought, the thought of the legacy slipping through their
fingers, never left their minds, tormenting them and stirring up
their mutual rancour. Cora did not conceal her contempt and
bullied her husband; she treated him like a small child, a weakling,
a person of no importance. And Cachelin repeated every evening
at dinner: 'If I'd been well-off, I'd have had lots of kids. But a poor
man has to be careful.' And, turning to his daughter, he would add:
'You must take after me, but there we are . . .' And he cast a meaning look at his son-in-law, accompanied by a contemptuous
shrug.

Lesable made no answer, like a gentleman who finds himself
among boors. At the Ministry they thought him looking ill. Even
the Chief asked him one day: 'You're not ill, are you? You look to
me a bit changed.'

He replied: 'No, my dear Chief. Perhaps I'm a bit tired. I've been
working very hard of late, as you may have noticed.'

He was counting confidently on promotion at the end of the

year, and, with this in view, he had been working like the perfect clerk.

He only got a trifling bonus, less than all the others. His father-in-law, Cachelin, did not get anything at all.

Lesable, bitterly disappointed, went in to find the Chief, and for the first time addressed him as 'Sir': 'What is the use, Sir, of my working as I do, if I don't get anything for it all?'

M. Torchebeuf's broad face showed irritation: 'I have already told you, M. Lesable, that I cannot allow discussion of these matters between us. I repeat that I consider your complaint in bad taste, considering your financial position as compared with the poverty of your colleagues . . .'

Lesable could not contain himself: 'But I've got nothing, Sir! Our aunt left the whole of her fortune to the first child to be born of my marriage. My father-in-law and I are living on our salaries.'

The Chief, in surprise, replied: 'If you've got nothing at the moment, in any case you'll be well-off quite soon. So it comes to the same thing.'

Lesable retired, more depressed at missing his promotion than over the legacy that eluded him.

But just after Cachelin had arrived at the office a few days later, the good-looking Bunny came in with a broad smile on his face, followed by Pitolet with a glint in his eye; soon afterwards Boissel pushed the door open and came in grinning and obviously excited, looking at the others with a conspiratorial air. Old Savon went on with his copying, his clay pipe in the corner of his mouth, sitting on his high chair with his feet on the bars like a small boy.

No one spoke; there was a general air of expectation, while Cachelin went on entering his items, reading them aloud as usual: 'Toulon. Mess-tins for officers for the *Richelieu*. – Lorient. Diving-suits for the *Desaix*. – Brest. Testing sail-cloth from England.'

Lesable appeared. He was now in the habit of coming every morning to fetch the work that concerned him, as his father-in-law no longer took the trouble to send it to him by the messengers.

While he was rummaging about among the papers laid out on

the Personal Assistant's desk, Bunny was watching him out of the corner of his eye rubbing his hands, and lines, indicative of irrepressible amusement, were forming round Pitolet's mouth, while he rolled a cigarette. He turned to the Forwarding Clerk: 'Well, Father Savon, you must have learned a lot in the course of your long life, haven't you?'

The old fellow, thinking that they were going to pull his leg about his wife, did not answer.

Pitolet went on: 'You must have mastered the art of having children, for you have got several, haven't you?'

The old man raised his head: 'You are aware, M. Pitolet, that I am not fond of jokes on this subject. I have had the misfortune to marry an unfaithful wife. As soon as I had proof of her adultery, I left her.'

Bunny asked casually with a serious face: 'You had proof of adultery on several occasions, did you not?'

And old Savon replied gravely: 'Yes, Sir.'

Pitolet went on: 'All the same, you are the father of several children, three or four, I've been told?'

The old fellow, getting very red in the face, stammered: 'You are trying to hurt my feelings, M. Pitolet, but you won't succeed. It is a fact that my wife has had three children; I have reason to believe that the first is mine but I refuse to acknowledge the other two.'

Pitolet continued: 'Yes, everyone says the first is yours. That's enough. It's a fine thing to have a child, a very fine thing, and a great piece of luck. Why, I bet Lesable would be delighted to have one, just one, like you.'

Cachelin had stopped making his entries; he didn't laugh, though old Savon was his usual butt and he had indulged in a whole series of indecent jokes about his matrimonial misfortunes.

Lesable had picked up his papers, but, realizing that an attack was being made on him, he was determined to stay and face it out, for he had his pride, though he was puzzled and annoyed, wondering how they had discovered his secret. Suddenly he remembered what he had said to the Chief and saw at once that he must act with decision, if he did not want to become the laughing-stock of the whole Ministry.

Boissel was walking up and down the room grinning. He imitated the hoarse shout of a street vendor and boomed: 'Infallible recipe for getting children, only ten centimes, two sous! Ask for the infallible recipe for children, revealed by Doctor Savon, with full 'orrible details!'

Everyone except Lesable and his father-in-law joined in the general laugh.

Pitolet, turning to the Personal Assistant, said: 'What's the matter with you, Cachelin? You've lost your usual sense of humour. You don't seem to be amused at the idea of Savon having had a child by his wife. I think it's frightfully funny; it's not everyone who can manage it!'

Lesable went on rummaging among the papers, pretending to be reading and not hearing anything, but he had gone very pale.

Boissel went on in the street vendor's common accent: 'Very useful to enable heirs to claim their legacies, ten centimes, two sous! Buy one to-day!'

Then Bunny, who thought this vulgar joke below him and had a personal grudge against Lesable for robbing him of the hope he had secretly nourished of getting this fortune himself, asked him straight out: 'What's the matter with you, Lesable? You're very pale.'

Lesable raised his head and looked his colleague straight in the eyes. He paused for a moment, his lip quivering, searching for a retort at once cutting and witty, but, not finding what he wanted, he replied: 'I'm all right. I'm only surprised at the delicacy of your question.'

Bunny, still with his back to the fire and holding up the tails of his frock-coat, went on with a laugh: 'One does one's best, my dear fellow! We're all like you, not always successful . . .'

He was interrupted by an explosion of merriment. Old Savon, puzzled, was vaguely aware that the attack was not directed against him, that it was not his leg they were pulling, and remained with his mouth open and his pen poised. And Cachelin was waiting, ready to go for the first person chance put in his way.

Lesable stammered: 'I don't understand. What haven't I succeeded in?'

The good-looking Bunny let go of one side of his coat-tails to curl his moustache and said suavely: 'I know that normally you succeed in everything you undertake. So I was wrong in referring to you. Besides we were discussing Daddy Savon's children, not yours, because you haven't got any. So, as you are invariably successful, it is obvious that, if you have no children, it is because you don't want any.'

Lesable asked rudely: 'What business of yours is that?'

At his offensive tone Bunny in his turn raised his voice: 'Look here, what are you after? Try to be polite or you'll have to give me an explanation.'

But Lesable was shaking with anger and, losing all control, he shouted: 'M. Bunny, I am not like you either a fool or an Adonis. I hope you will never speak to me again. I don't want to have anything to do with you or your friends.' And he looked defiantly at Pitolet and Boissel.

Bunny had suddenly realized that calmness and irony were his most effective weapons; but his vanity had been wounded and he wanted to administer a knock-down blow to his enemy; so, assuming a patronizing tone of fatherly advice but with a glint of anger in his eye, he said: 'My dear Lesable, you are really insufferable. But I quite understand your annoyance. It is most irritating to lose a fortune, and to lose it for so little, for such a simple little thing. . . . Look here, if you like, I'll do the job for you, as friend to friend. It won't take five minutes . . .'

He was still speaking, when he got full in the chest old Savon's inkpot, which Lesable hurled at him. The ink splashed all over his face, blackening him like a nigger in no time. He rushed at Lesable, showing the whites of his eyes, his fists raised. But Cachelin covered his son-in-law, grappling with the tall Bunny, and hustled and pushed him back, pounding him with his fists, till he hurled him against the wall. Bunny wrenched himself free, opened the door, shouted to the two men: 'You will hear from me again', and disappeared.

Pitolet and Boissel followed him. The latter explained that he had been afraid of killing someone and so had refrained from taking an active part in the tussle.

As soon as he got back to his office, Bunny tried to clean himself but without success; he was stained with an indelible violet ink, advertised as impossible to erase. He stood disconsolately in front of his glass, raging, rubbing his face furiously with his towel screwed up into a ball. He only turned a richer black with a reddish tinge, where the blood came to the surface of the skin.

Boissel and Pitolet had followed him and offered their advice. The former suggested washing his face in pure olive oil, the latter thought ammonia would be more effective. The office boy was sent to a chemist for advice. He brought back a bottle of yellow liquid and a bit of pumice-stone. The result was entirely negative.

Bunny sat down discouraged and declared: 'Now I must consider the question of honour. Will you act as my seconds and go and demand from M. Lesable either a full apology or satisfaction by arms?'

Both accepted and discussed the steps to be taken. They knew nothing about affairs of honour but did not wish to admit it; being most anxious to do the right thing, they hesitantly made different suggestions. It was decided to consult a Naval Commander, seconded to the Ministry in charge of the supply of coal. He was equally ignorant. After reflection, however, he advised them to go and find Lesable and ask him to put them in touch with two friends of his.

On the way to their colleague's office, Boissel suddenly stopped: 'Surely we ought to be wearing gloves?'

Pitolet, after a moment's hesitation, answered: 'Yes, perhaps we ought.' But to get gloves they would have to go out and the Chief was particular about such things. So they sent the office boy to fetch an assortment from the haberdasher's. There was a long discussion over the colour. Boissel thought they should be black; Pitolet considered this colour inappropriate in the circumstances. They finally chose mauve.

When he saw the two men come in, gloved and solemn, Lesable looked up and asked sharply: 'What do you want?'

Pitolet replied: 'Sir, we are instructed by our friend, M. Bunny, to demand from you either a full apology or satisfaction by arms for the assault perpetrated by you upon him.'

But Lesable, still in a furious temper, shouted: 'What! He insults me and now he wants to challenge me. Tell him that I despise him, that I don't care what he does or says.'

Boissel took a step forward melodramatically, saying: 'In that case, Sir, you will force us to publish in the papers an account of the incident, which will be most unpleasant for you.'

And Pitolet added mischievously: 'And which will reflect seriously on your honour and prejudice your future career.'

Dumbfounded, Lesable looked at them. What was he to do? He must gain time: 'Gentlemen, you shall have my answer in ten minutes. Will you wait in M. Pitolet's office?'

As soon as he was alone, he looked round the room, seeking advice and protection.

A duel! He was going to be involved in a duel!

He sat still, breathing hard, terrified; he was a peace-loving man, who had never envisaged such a possibility; he had never prepared himself to face such risks, such emotions; he had never screwed up his courage to confront the prospect of such a formidable eventuality. He tried to get up but sank back into his chair with beating heart and trembling knees. His anger and his strength had suddenly evaporated. But the thought of public opinion in the Ministry and the talk that the incident would cause in every office roused his weakening pride and, unable to make up his own mind, he went to consult the Chief.

M. Torchebeuf was surprised and nonplussed. He saw no need for a duel, reflecting that this would disorganize his routine even further. He repeated: 'I can give you no advice. It is a question of honour which does not concern me. Shall I give you a line to

Captain Bouc? He knows all about such matters and will be able to put you wise.'

Lesable accepted the offer and went to see the Captain, who consented to act as second; he got his Deputy Head Clerk to act with him.

Boissel and Pitolet were waiting for them, still gloved. They had borrowed two chairs from the office next door so as to have four seats.

The four men bowed gravely to each other and sat down. Pitolet spoke first, explaining the position. The Captain, after listening, replied: 'This is a serious matter, but there seems to me a way out. Everything turns on the motive.' He was a crafty old sailor and was much amused by the whole thing.

A long discussion began: all four in turn drafted letters, apologies being due from both sides. If M. Bunny admitted that his insult had not been the result of malice aforethought, M. Lesable would be prepared to admit in principle that he had been wrong to hurl the inkpot and would apologize for his unpremeditated assault.

Then the four emissaries returned to report to their principals.

Bunny was now sitting at his table, disturbed at the possibility of a duel, though expecting his opponent to climb down; he was examining his cheeks, one after the other, in one of the little metal mirrors, which all the clerks kept in their drawers, so that, before leaving in the evening, they could comb their beards and hair and straighten their ties.

He read the letters submitted to him and declared with obvious satisfaction: 'This seems to satisfy my honour. I am prepared to sign.'

Lesable for his part had accepted his seconds' suggestion without discussion, declaring: 'If this is what you advise, I can only agree.'

The four envoys met again. The letters were exchanged; they bowed formally to each other and, the matter now being settled, separated.

There was extraordinary excitement in the office. All the clerks were in search of the latest developments, going from door to door and accosting each other in the passages.

There was a general feeling of anticlimax, when it was known that the matter had been settled. Somebody said: 'But Lesable is no nearer getting his child!' The gibe was taken up; one clerk turned it into a limerick.

But, just as everything seemed settled, a difficulty arose when Boissel asked: 'What was to be the attitude of the two adversaries when they met? Would they bow or would they cut each other?' It was arranged that they should meet, as if by accident, in the Chief's office and exchange a few polite words in M. Torchebeuf's presence.

This ceremony was immediately carried out; after which Bunny, sending for a cab, drove home to try and get his face clean.

Lesable and Cachelin, in a very bad temper, went home together in silence, each feeling as if what had happened had been the other's fault. As soon as he got back to his flat, Lesable, throwing his hat violently on the sideboard, shouted at his wife: 'I'm about fed up! Now I've got a duel on my hands over you.'

She looked at him in surprise, ready to lose her temper: 'A duel! Why?'

'Because Bunny insulted me about you.'

She took a step towards him: 'About me? How?'

He had thrown himself into an arm-chair; he repeated: 'He insulted me . . . I need not go into details.'

But she wanted to know: 'I insist on your telling me what he said about me.'

Lesable blushed and stammered: 'He said . . . he said . . . it was about your not having children.'

She started; then she lost her temper and burst out, her father's coarseness showing through her feminine delicacy: 'Me! I'm barren, am I? What does he know about it, the blighter? Barren with you, yes, because you're not a man; if I'd married a man, anybody you like, I'd have had children, let me tell you. You're one to talk! I'm paying for having married a weakling like you . . . and what, pray, did you say to this swine?'

Lesable, terrified at this outburst, stammered: 'I . . . I boxed his ears!'

She stared at him in amazement: 'And what did he do then?'

'He sent his seconds to me. There you are!'

She now began to take an interest in the affair, attracted as all women are by anything dramatic, and she asked, suddenly mollified and feeling for the first time a certain admiration for this man, who was going to risk his life: 'When are you going to fight?'

He answered calmly: 'We're not fighting. The matter has been arranged by the seconds. Bunny has apologized.'

She looked him up and down with withering contempt: 'So I was insulted in your presence, and you did nothing – you're not going to fight. So you're a coward too! That's the last straw!'

He couldn't swallow that: 'Don't say another word. I can look after my honour better than you. Besides here's Bunny's letter; read it and you'll see.'

She took the letter, glanced at it, guessed everything and said with a sneer: 'Did you write a letter too? You were each afraid of the other. What cowards men are! In your place any woman . . . Anyhow the insult was directed at me, and you're satisfied with that. I'm no longer surprised you can't get a child. It's all of a piece; you're as . . . impotent with women as you are with men. I married a weakling with no spunk in him!'

Her voice and gestures were Cachelin to the life, an old soldier's vulgar gestures and a man's bass voice.

Standing in front of him, arms akimbo, tall, powerful, strongly built, with full breasts, her face red, her voice deep and ringing, the blood rushing to her fresh young cheeks, she looked down on the man sitting in front of her, this insignificant little man, slightly bald, clean shaven except for a barrister's short whiskers, and she could have strangled him, throttled him with her bare hands.

And she repeated: 'You're no good, no damned good! You even let everyone else at the office get promotion before you.'

The door opened and Cachelin appeared, attracted by the sound of voices; he asked: 'What's up?'

She turned round: 'I'm telling this milksop some home truths.'

And Lesable, looking up, saw the likeness between the two. A curtain seemed to be rising and he was seeing them for the first time as they really were, father and daughter, of the same blood, of the same common vulgar stock; he saw himself wasting his life, condemned to live for ever between the two of them.

Cachelin remarked: 'It's a pity you can't get a divorce. It's no fun being married to a bullock!'

Lesable leapt up, trembling with fury, unable to contain himself at this insult. He took a few steps towards his father-in-law, stammering: 'Get out of here ... get out! This is my house, do you hear? I won't have you here.' And he seized a bottle of sedative water from the sideboard and brandished it like a club.

Cachelin, intimidated, retreated, murmuring: 'What's come over him?'

But Lesable's anger was still at boiling point; this was beyond bearing. He turned to his wife, who was still looking at him, rather surprised at his violence, and, after putting down the bottle on the sideboard, he shouted: 'As for you ... as for you ...' but having nothing to say and no explanation to give, he stood there facing her, his face working and his voice breaking.

Suddenly she began to laugh.

At this merriment, which was a further insult, he saw red, rushed at her and, seizing her by the throat with his left hand, he boxed her ears again and again with his right. She staggered backwards, dumbfounded and choking. She came up against the bed and fell back on to it. He kept his hold and went on striking her. Presently he straightened himself and, suddenly ashamed of his violence, he stammered: 'There ... that's what we've come to!'

But she lay perfectly still, as if dead. She was lying on her back at the edge of the bed, covering her face now with both hands. He went up to her awkwardly, wondering what would happen next and waiting for her to uncover her face in order to see what was going on in her mind. After a minute or two, with growing anxiety, he murmured: 'Cora, say something, Cora dear!' She did not answer or move. What was the matter with her? What was she doing? Above all, what was she going to do next?

His anger having evaporated as quickly as it had boiled up, he hated himself and felt like a criminal. He had struck a woman, his own wife, and he was normally a man of good behaviour, self-controlled, well brought up and always amenable to reason. And with the remorse that follows rage he wanted to go down on his knees and beg pardon, to kiss the cheek red from his slapping. Very gently, with the tip of his finger he touched one of the hands which hid her face. She appeared not to feel his touch. He stroked her, caressingly, as one caresses a dog after a scolding. She took no notice. He repeated: 'Cora, listen, dear; I'm sorry; do listen!' She might have been dead. Then he tried to raise one hand; it came easily away from the face and he saw one eye open, looking at him with a fixed stare that was acutely disturbing.

He went on: 'Listen, Cora, I lost my temper. What your father said was more than I could bear. There are some things a man can't swallow.'

She did not answer, seeming not to hear. He did not know what to say or do. He kissed her under the ear and, as he straightened himself, he saw a tear in the corner of her eye, a big tear, which welled out and ran down her cheek; the eyelid trembled and closed again after each tear.

He was seized with a sense of guilt and deeply moved, and, putting his arms round her, he lay down on top of his wife. He moved the other hand away with his lips and kissed her face all over, begging: 'My poor darling, forgive me, please forgive me!'

She went on crying, quite quietly, without sobs, as one weeps in real trouble.

He held her tight in a close embrace, stroking her face and whispering in her ear all the endearments he could think of. But she remained unresponsive. However her tears stopped. They stayed a long time, lying side by side in each other's arms.

Night was coming on and the little room grew dim; and, when it was quite dark, he was emboldened to seek her forgiveness in a manner calculated to revive their hopes.

When they got up he had recovered his composure and his voice was normal, as if nothing had happened. She seemed on the contrary more affectionate and her tone was gentler than usual; she looked at her husband with a submissive, almost caressing expression, as if the unexpected punishment she had received had relieved some nervous tension and softened her heart. He said quietly: 'Your father must be getting bored all alone in his flat. You ought to go and fetch him. Besides, it's dinner-time.' She went out.

It was in fact seven o'clock and the little maid announced the soup. Cachelin appeared with his daughter, calm and smiling. They sat down, and the conversation that evening was more cordial than it had been for a long time, as if they had all had a piece of good fortune.

v

But their hopes, constantly revived and as often dashed, came to nothing. As month followed month, their repeated disappointments, in spite of Lesable's perseverance and his wife's co-operation, kept them in a state of nervous anxiety. Each blamed the other for their failure, and the husband, now in despair and getting worn and tired, had in particular to endure the coarse gibes of Cachelin, who in the course of the continual sparring that went on in the house always referred to him as 'Mr Bull', no doubt in allusion to the day when he had nearly received a bottle in the face for using the word 'bullock'.

His daughter and he, natural allies, irritated by the ever-present thought of the great fortune that was so close but continually eluded them, taxed their ingenuity to humiliate and wound the weakling to whom their misfortune was due.

As they sat down, Cora would say every day: 'There's not much for dinner. It would be quite different if we were well off. It's not my fault.'

When Lesable was starting for the office she shouted to him from her room: 'Don't forget your umbrella or you'll come home covered with mud like the wheel of an omnibus. After all, it's not my fault that you have to go on quill-driving.'

When she was going out herself she never failed to remark: 'Of course, if I'd married anybody else I should have a carriage of my own.'

Every hour, on every occasion, this thought was in her mind; she was always wounding him with some reproach or lashing him with some insult, blaming him alone and making him solely responsible for the loss of the money that she should have enjoyed.

At last one evening his patience was exhausted and he cried: 'Damn it all! Do shut up! In the first place, it's your fault, entirely your fault, let me tell you, that we've got no child, because I've already had one.'

This was a lie but he preferred anything to the constant reproach and shame of appearing impotent.

She stared at him, taken aback for a moment, trying to read the truth in his eyes; then she understood and retorted contemptuously: 'So, you've had a child, have you?'

He replied brazenly: 'Yes, an illegitimate boy, who is being brought up at Asnières.'

She answered calmly: 'We'll go and see him to-morrow; I'm curious to see what he's like.'

He blushed up to the ears and replied: 'As you like.'

Next morning she got up at seven and, when he expressed surprise, she said: 'I thought we were going to see your child! You promised I should yesterday evening. Perhaps he has disappeared in the night!'

He jumped out of bed: 'It's not my child we're going to see but a doctor; he'll tell you some home truths!'

She replied with complete assurance: 'I'm quite agreeable.'

Cachelin promised to report at the Ministry that his son-in-law was ill; and husband and wife, on the advice of a neighbouring doctor, at one o'clock sharp knocked at the door of Dr Lefilleul, who had written several works on the scientific aspects of procreation.

They entered a waiting-room, papered in white with a gold stripe and badly furnished, which felt bare and unlived-in in spite of the number of chairs. They sat down, Lesable was nervous and uncomfortable and rather ashamed too. When their turn came, they went into a sort of consulting-room, where they were received by a tubby little man with a formal chilly manner.

He waited for their explanation; but Lesable's courage failed him and he blushed up to the ears. So his wife took the plunge, and, in the level tones of one determined to shrink from nothing to attain her end, said: 'We have come to consult you, Sir, because we have no children. A great deal of money depends on our having them.'

The consultation was long, detailed and painful. Cora alone did not seem worried and submitted to the doctor's careful examination with the air of a woman sustained and encouraged by some higher purpose.

After an examination of both of them lasting more than an hour, the specialist refused to commit himself.

'I find nothing,' he said, 'nothing out of the ordinary, nothing unusual. Moreover cases of this kind are not uncommon. It is the same with the physical constitution as with the psychological. When we see so many marriages broken up by incompatibility of temperament, it is not surprising to find others barren from physical incompatibility. Madame seems to me particularly well formed and fitted to have children; whereas Monsieur, while presenting no physical malformation, seems in a somewhat debilitated condition, due possibly to his excessive desire to become a father. Will you let me sound you?'

Lesable, considerably disturbed, took off his waistcoat, and the doctor made a lengthy auscultation of the clerk's chest and back; after that he tapped him all over from the stomach to the throat and from the kidneys to the neck.

He found a slight irregularity in the first beat of the heart and even a threatening of trouble in the region of the lungs.

' You must be careful of yourself, Sir, very careful. It is a case of anaemia, general debility, nothing else. These symptoms, trivial to-day, might quickly develop into something very serious.'

Lesable, pale with anxiety, asked what he was to do. The doctor prescribed a complicated regimen. Iron, red meat, soup between meals, exercise, rest and a holiday in the country in the summer. Then he gave them both advice for the time when he should be better. He prescribed practical measures, which had often proved successful in such cases.

His fee was forty francs.

When they got out into the street, Cora, boiling with suppressed indignation and foreseeing the future, declared: 'This is awfully nice for me, I must say!'

He made no answer. He walked on in a pitiable state of panic, going carefully over every word the doctor had said. Had he told him the truth? Had he not really considered his case hopeless? He hardly thought of the legacy now or of the child. It was a matter of his own life or death.

He thought he detected a whistle in his lungs and an acceleration of the heart. As they were crossing the Tuileries he felt faint and had to sit down. His wife, exasperated, remained standing near him to make him feel a fool, looking him up and down with contemptuous pity. He was breathing painfully, exaggerating the breathlessness really due to his anxiety; and, with the fingers of his left hand on the pulse in his right wrist, he counted the beating of his heart.

Cora, who was fidgeting impatiently, asked: 'Is all this nonsense finished yet? When will you be ready to go on?' He got up with the air of a victim being led to the slaughter and walked on without a word.

When Cachelin heard the result of the consultation, his anger knew no bounds; he shouted: 'Now we're in the soup, properly in the soup!' And he glared at his son-in-law fiercely, as if he would have liked to eat him.

Lesable heard nothing, took nothing in; he could only think of his own health and the threat to his life. They could shout as they liked; they were not in his skin, and that was what he wanted to save.

He had a whole chemist's shop at his place at every meal and measured his doses with great care under his wife's smiles and his father-in-law's loud guffaws. He was always looking at himself in the glass and putting his hand on his heart to count the beats; he also had a bed made up for himself in a little dark room, which was used as a cupboard, being afraid of the physical proximity of Cora.

She now inspired him with definite hatred, mingled with fear, contempt and disgust. All women indeed appeared to him as monsters, dangerous wild animals whose object was to kill men; he thought of Aunt Charlotte's will only as one thinks of an accident in the past, which nearly proved fatal.

Month followed month. There was now only a year left before the final date.

Cachelin had hung up a huge calendar in the dining-room and every morning he crossed off one day. Exasperation at his helplessness, despair at feeling this fortune slipping from his grasp from week to week, the maddening thought that he would have to go on slaving at the office and then live on a miserable pension of 2,000 francs till he died, all this drove him to a violence of language, which on the slightest excuse would have been translated into action.

He could not look at Lesable without a wild desire to strike him, strangle him, trample on him. He was eaten up with a passionate hatred of the man. Every time he saw him open the door and come in, it was as if a thief was entering his house, who had robbed him of some sacred possession, some family heirloom. He hated him more fiercely than one hates a mortal enemy and at the same time he despised him for his impotence and, even more, for his cowardice in giving up the pursuit of their common hope, because he was afraid of his health.

In fact Lesable was now living more completely apart from his wife than if there had been no bond between them. He never went near her now, never touched her; he even avoided her eye as much from shame as fear.

Every day Cachelin asked his daughter:

'Well, has your husband made up his mind to do anything?'

She replied: 'No, Daddy.'

Every evening at dinner there were painful scenes. Cachelin was always saying: 'When a man isn't a man, he'd do better to kick the bucket and make room for somebody else.'

And Cora would add: 'The fact is some people are entirely useless and only get in the way. I can't see what good they do in the world; they're just a burden to everyone.'

Lesable went on taking his medicine in silence. At last, one day his father-in-law shouted at him: 'Look here, you, if you don't change your ways now that you're better, I know what my daughter will do!'

His son-in-law looked up with a questioning glance in anticipation of some fresh insult. Cachelin went on: 'Why, she'll get somebody else. You're damned lucky she hasn't done so before this. When a girl is married to a whistlecock like you, anything is excusable.'

Livid with rage, Lesable retorted: 'I'm not preventing her following your excellent advice.'

Cora had lowered her eyes. And Cachelin, vaguely aware that he had said too much, looked rather uncomfortable.

VI

At the Ministry relations between the two men remained outwardly friendly. They had a kind of tacit agreement to conceal the bickering that went on at home from their colleagues. They called each other 'my dear Cachelin' – 'my dear Lesable'; they even pretended to have their little jokes, to be entirely happy and contented, as if they enjoyed living together. Lesable and Bunny, for their part, treated each other with the formal politeness of adversaries who have only just avoided fighting. The duel, which had not come off but had caused them deep alarm, produced in both an exaggerated politeness and elaborate courtesy; it was also perhaps the cause of a secret desire to make friends, which sprang from a subconscious fear of fresh complications. Their colleagues noted this with approval as the attitude of men of the world who have had an affair of honour.

They bowed to each other from a distance with unsmiling formality, taking off their hats with a most dignified sweep.

They did not speak, neither being willing, or not daring, to be the first to begin.

But one day Lesable, on an urgent summons from the Chief, was

unning, in order to advertise his efficiency, and round a corner in
the passage he crashed full tilt into the stomach of a clerk coming
in the opposite direction. It was Bunny. They both staggered back
and Lesable asked with polite embarrassment:

'I do hope I haven't hurt you, Sir!'

The other replied: 'Not in the least, Sir!'

After this they thought it good form to exchange a few words
when they met. Soon, neither wishing to be outdone by the other
in courtesy, they were doing little things to oblige each other, and
from this there soon developed a certain familiarity, followed soon
by a sort of shy friendliness, the friendliness that comes after
mutual misunderstanding but is still held in check by hesitant
timidity; finally, after much formal politeness and frequent visits to
each other's room, they became close friends.

Now they often had a chat together, when they met in the
Personal Assistant's office in search of the latest gossip. Lesable had
lost the arrogance of the subordinate sure of his promotion and
Bunny no longer made a show of his society manners; Cachelin,
too, would join in the conversation, seeming to be interested in
their growing friendship. Sometimes, when the good-looking clerk
had left the room, holding himself straight and almost touching the
lintel of the door with his head, he murmured with a glance at his
son-in-law: 'He's a fine figure of a man anyhow!'

One morning when all four of them were there, for old Savon
never left his copying desk, the Forwarding Clerk's chair collapsed
under him, some practical joker, no doubt, having sawn through
one of the legs, and the old fellow fell to the ground with a cry of
alarm.

The other three rushed to him. The Personal Assistant attributed
the accident to the sinister designs of the Communists and Bunny
was anxious to examine the bruised portion of his anatomy.
Cachelin and he even tried to take off his clothes to dress the wound
as they said. But he resisted desperately, crying that he was all right.

When their merriment had exhausted itself, Cachelin suddenly
exclaimed: 'Look here, M. Bunny, now that we're all friends, you
really ought to come to dinner with us at home on Sunday. It

would give us all great pleasure, my son-in-law, myself and my daughter, who knows you well by name, for we often talk about the office. You'll come, won't you?'

Lesable backed up his father-in-law's invitation, though without much warmth: 'Yes, do come, we'd all like it.'

Bunny hesitated, in some embarrassment, smiling at the recollection of all the rumours current at the office.

Cachelin pressed his invitation: 'That's a date, then?'

'Very well, I accept with pleasure.'

When her father told her on his return: 'You'll never guess who's coming to dinner on Sunday – M. Bunny,' Cora, first of all surprised, stammered: 'M. Bunny . . . well, I never!'

And she blushed up to the roots of her hair, without knowing why. She had so often heard about him, his perfect manners and his success with women, for at the Ministry he was considered a lady killer and quite irresistible, and she had long wanted to meet him.

Cachelin went on, rubbing his hands: 'You'll see, he's a fine figure of a man and so good-looking. He's as tall as a guardsman, a very different sort of person from your husband.'

She made no reply, as if her father had guessed her dreams about him. Preparations for this dinner were made as carefully as they had been for Lesable long ago. Cachelin discussed the dishes and insisted on everything being just right; he seemed more cheerful, as if he felt some undefined, subconscious confidence which he would not admit and as if some mysterious power of foreseeing the future had allayed his anxiety.

All Sunday he fussed about supervising the arrangements, while Lesable dealt with a piece of urgent work he had brought home from the office the night before. It was already the first week of November and New Year's Day was not far off.

At seven o'clock M. Bunny arrived in great spirits. He was entirely at home and presented Cora with a large bunch of roses with a well-turned compliment. He added confidentially, with the assurance of a man accustomed to society: 'I feel, Madame, that I already know you a little and that I have known you since you were a child, for your father has talked to me about you for years.'

When Cachelin saw the flowers he cried: 'You see, he knows his manners!' and his daughter remembered that Lesable had not brought any when he paid his first visit. The handsome clerk seemed in excellent form; he laughed like a good-natured schoolboy coming for the first time to the house of old friends, and he paid Cora discreet compliments which brought the blood to her cheeks.

He thought her luscious. She found him devastating. When he had gone Cachelin remarked: 'He's a good chap, what! What a kid he'd father! No woman can resist him, they say.'

Cora, less enthusiastic, admitted nevertheless that she had found him quite nice and not as affected as she had anticipated.

Lesable, who seemed less tired and depressed than usual, agreed that he had been mistaken about him in the beginning.

Bunny came back, at first at discreet intervals, later on more frequently. They all liked him. They pressed him to come and spoiled him. Cora made his favourite dishes for him and the three men soon became inseparable. Their new friend took the family to the theatre in a box obtained on Press tickets.

They walked home in the dark through the crowded streets to the door of the Lesables' flat. Bunny and Cora walked in front, in step, shoulder to shoulder, swinging along rhythmically, like two people born to march through life side by side. They were talking in a low voice with subdued laughter, for they got on admirably together; from time to time the young woman turned to glance at her father and her husband.

Cachelin kept a benevolent eye on them, often declaring, without thinking that he was addressing his son-in-law: 'They're a good-looking pair and no mistake; it's a joy to see them together.'

Lesable replied calmly: 'They're about the same height,' and, happy to know that his heart was more regular, that he did not get so out of breath walking fast and that he felt better all round, he gradually let his bitterness against his father-in-law subside; moreover the latter had recently given up poking ill-natured fun at him.

On New Year's Day he was appointed Assistant Principal. He was so pleased at this that he kissed his wife when he got home for the first time for six months. She seemed taken aback and confused, as if he had done something tactless; and she looked at Bunny, who had come to offer his respects and good wishes for the New Year. Even he seemed embarrassed and turned towards the window so as not to see.

But Cachelin soon became irritable and ill-tempered again and began to be facetious at his son-in-law's expense. Sometimes he was even rude to Bunny, as if he considered him, too, partly responsible for the catastrophe hanging over them, for the inevitable date was drawing nearer and nearer every day.

Cora was the only one who appeared completely unconcerned, completely happy, completely blooming; she had apparently forgotten the dreadful time-limit now so near.

March arrived. All hope seemed lost; for by July 20th it would be three years since Aunt Charlotte's death.

Spring was early and everything was growing. One Sunday Bunny suggested to his friends a walk along the Seine to pick violets in the woods.

They went off by an early train and got out at Maisons-Lafitte. The bare branches were still shivering in the chilly wind, but the young grass in its fresh green was already starred with white and blue flowers; and the fruit-trees on the hillsides seemed garlanded with roses, their slender boughs clothed with bursting blossom.

The sluggish Seine flowed, grim and muddy from the recent rains, between banks which showed the erosion of the winter floods, and all the countryside, soaking wet as if emerging from a bath, gave off the warm smell of moist earth heated by the first days of sunshine.

They got lost in the park. Cachelin gloomily prodded the clods of earth with his stick, more depressed than usual that day by the bitter thought of their misfortune so soon to be complete. Lesable, also glum, was afraid of getting his feet wet in the grass, while his wife and Bunny were trying to make a nosegay. Cora had seemed out of sorts for several days, languid and pale.

She suddenly felt tired and wanted to turn back for lunch. They made their way to a small restaurant built against an old ruined mill; and the traditional lunch of Parisians out for the day was soon served in an arbour on a wooden table with two napkins for a cloth, quite close to the river.

They had finished the crisp fried gudgeon, chewed the beef with its ring of potatoes and were just passing round the salad bowl full of fresh lettuce, when Cora suddenly got up and began to run towards the bank, holding her napkin pressed to her mouth with both hands.

Lesable asked anxiously: 'What's the matter with her?' Bunny blushed in some confusion and stammered: 'I ... I don't know ... she was all right just now!' And Cachelin paused in alarm, his fork poised in the air with a lettuce leaf on the end of it.

He got up, looking after his daughter. As he leant forward, he saw her with her head against a tree, being sick. A sudden suspicion made his knees weak and he sank back on his chair, with frightened glances at the two men who now seemed equally uncomfortable. He scanned their faces anxiously, not daring to speak, torn between hope and fear.

A quarter of an hour passed in complete silence. Then Cora reappeared, rather pale, walking with difficulty. No one asked what had happened; they all seemed to guess at a happy event that was hard to speak about, though they were at once burning to know and afraid to ask. Cachelin was the only one who enquired: 'Are you better?' She replied: 'Yes, thank you; it was nothing; but let's go home soon. I've got a bit of a headache.'

When they started home, she took her husband's arm with the air of one in possession of a mysterious secret that may not yet be revealed.

They parted at the Gare Saint-Lazare. Bunny, pretending to remember an engagement, went away after bowing and shaking hands.

As soon as Cachelin was alone with his daughter and son-in-law, he asked: 'What was the matter with you at lunch?'

At first Cora did not answer; then after a short pause she said: 'It was nothing; I was feeling rather sick.'

She was walking slowly with a smile on her lips. Lesable was anxious and worried, the victim of confused contradictory emotions; there was his longing for the comforts that money can buy, and at the same time suppressed anger and a feeling of shame that he would not admit and the jealousy of a coward. As a result he did what sleepers do, who shut their eyes in the morning so as not to see the ray of sunshine coming in through a crack in the curtains and throwing a line of light across the bed.

As soon as he got home he said he had some work to finish and shut himself up in his room.

Immediately Cachelin, putting both his hands on his daughter's shoulders, said: 'You're going to have a baby, aren't you?'

She stammered: 'Yes, I think so. I've thought so for two months.'

Before she had finished speaking he was jumping for joy; then he began to dance a real music-hall fling round her, reminiscent of his army days. He threw up his heels and leapt into the air in spite of his paunch, shaking the whole flat. The furniture rocked and the glasses on the sideboard clinked against each other, while the hanging lamp swung and shook like a ship's lantern.

After that he took his beloved daughter in his arms and kissed her wildly; and, giving her an affectionate little dig in the stomach, he said: 'Well, there we are at last! Have you told your husband?'

She murmured, suddenly frightened: 'No, not yet, I was waiting.'

But Cachelin exclaimed: 'All right; I expect you feel shy about telling him. Wait a minute and I'll do it.'

And he rushed into his son-in-law's flat. Seeing him come in, Lesable, who was doing nothing, got up; but Cachelin did not give him time to collect himself: 'Do you know your wife is in the family way?'

The husband, taken aback, changed colour and his cheeks flamed: 'Eh? What? Cora? Do you mean it?'

'I tell you she's in the family way, do you hear? What a bit of luck!'

In his excitement he seized his hands and shook them violently, as if to convey his congratulations and thanks; he kept repeating:

'There we are at last! It's all right, it's all right! Just think of it, the money's ours!' And, unable to contain himself, he threw his arms round him.

He was shouting all the time: 'More than a million, just think of it, more than a million!' He began to dance again but broke off crying: 'But come along, she's waiting for you; come and give her a kiss, that's the least you can do,' and, putting his arms round him, he shoved him forward and projected him with a push into the room where Cora was standing, listening anxiously.

As soon as she saw her husband she took a step back, choking, with emotion.

He stopped in front of her, pale and strained; he looked like a judge facing a criminal in the dock.

At last he said: 'I gather you are going to have a baby!'

She stammered in a shaking voice: 'It looks like it.'

But Cachelin caught both of them by the neck and pushed their faces together, shouting: 'You might give each other a kiss, damn it all, it's worth it!'

And, letting them go, he declared, bubbling over with irrepressible joy; 'At last the game's in our hands! Look here, Léopold, we'll buy a country place straightaway; that will set you up anyhow!'

The idea was a shock to Lesable. His father-in-law went on: 'We'll invite M. Torchebeuf and his missus there and, as the Deputy Director is quite near the end of his time, you'll be able to succeed him. That's the first step.'

Lesable saw the whole picture as Cachelin talked; he saw himself receiving the Chief at the door of a nice little white house near the river; he was in a duck coat with a panama.

A great weight was lifted from his mind at the prospect; something warm and comforting seemed to permeate his whole being; he felt light as air and better already.

He smiled but said nothing.

Cachelin, intoxicated with hope and carried away by his imagination, went on: 'Who knows? We shall become people of importance in the neighbourhood. Perhaps you'll enter Parliament. In any

case we'll get into county society and we can afford luxuries.
You'll have a pony and dog-cart to drive to the station every
morning.'

Pictures of luxury, refinement and prosperity rose up before
Lesable's mind. The thought that he would drive a smart carriage,
like the rich people whose lot he had so often envied, completed
his satisfaction. He couldn't refrain from saying: 'Yes, it'll be
wonderful!' Cora, seeing the battle won, was smiling too, affectionate and thankful, and Cachelin, feeling all obstacles cleared
away, declared: 'Let's go and dine at a restaurant. Damn it all,
we'll treat ourselves to a cheery evening!'

They were all three a little drunk when they got home, and
Lesable, who was seeing double and whose brain was all muzzy,
couldn't find his dark bedroom. He went to bed, perhaps by
mistake, perhaps out of forgetfulness, in the empty bed to which
his wife would come presently. And all night he felt as if the bed
was rolling like a boat, pitching and tossing and turning turtle. He
was even a little seasick.

He was very much surprised, when he woke up, to find Cora in
his arms. She opened her eyes, smiled and kissed him with sudden
violence, full of gratitude and affection. Then she said in the
wheedling tone which all women use to get their own way: 'If you
want to be nice to me, you won't go to the office to-day. You
needn't be so particular now that we're going to be so well off.
Let's go out into the country again, just us two alone.'

He was rested, full of that indolent happiness that follows the
exhaustion of excess and enervated by the warmth of the bed. He
felt slack and wanted to stay where he was for hours, just doing
nothing but lying there in placid indolence. He felt a paralysing,
overpowering urge to be lazy, such as he had never known before;
he didn't want to think or move. And at the back of his mind there
was always the serene, blissful thought that he was going to be rich
and independent.

But suddenly a disquieting thought occurred to him and he asked
in a whisper as if the walls had ears: 'Are you quite sure you are
going to have a baby?'

She reassured him at once: 'Oh, yes, of course! I'm not making any mistake.'

And he stroked her gently, still a little anxious, running his hand over her swollen belly. He declared: 'Yes, it's quite true, but the baby won't be born before the date. Perhaps they'll contest our claim.'

She was furious at the very idea – 'No, we aren't going to be done out of it now, after all our anxiety, our perseverance and our efforts, I should think not indeed!' She had sat up in the violence of her indignation.

'Let's go and see the lawyer straightaway,' she said.

But he thought it would be wise to get a doctor's certificate first; so they went back to Doctor Lefilleul.

He recognized them at once and asked: 'Well, have you been successful?'

They both blushed up to the ears and Cora, in some confusion, stammered: 'I think so, Sir.'

The doctor rubbed his hands: 'I quite expected it, I quite expected it! The steps I recommended never fail unless there is some radical incapacity in one of the spouses.'

After examining the young woman he declared: 'It's quite all right – well done!'

And he wrote on a sheet of paper: 'I the undersigned, doctor of medicine of the University of Paris, certify that Madame Léopold Lesable, formerly Cachelin, has all the symptoms of a pregnancy of about three months.'

Then, turning to Lesable, he added: 'And you? What about that chest and heart?' He sounded him and pronounced him entirely cured.

They went off arm-in-arm, blissfully happy, walking on air. On the way Lesable had an idea: 'Perhaps you would do well to put a towel or two round your waist before going to the lawyer; it will catch the eye and impress him. He won't think we're trying to gain time.'

So they went back home and he undressed his wife himself to put her false figure in place. He changed the position of the towels a dozen times, stepping back to observe the effect, in order to ensure a lifelike result.

When he was satisfied they set out again, and in the street he seemed proud to be walking beside this pregnant womb, the evidence of his virility.

The solicitor received them warmly. He listened to their explanation, glanced at the doctor's certificate and, when Lesable pressed him to read it, he said: 'Anyhow, Sir, one look at her is enough to convince anybody,' as he noted the young woman's distended swollen figure.

They waited anxiously as the lawyer went on: 'Quite so. Whether the child is born or not yet born, it is there and it is alive. Therefore we will postpone execution of the will till Madame's time is up.'

As they left the office they kissed on the stairs in the exuberance of their joy.

VII

After this happy discovery perfect peace reigned in the household. All three were gay, good-tempered and considerate. Cachelin had recovered all his old geniality and Cora spoiled her husband. Lesable too seemed a different man, always happy and cheerful as never before.

Bunny came less often and now seemed uncomfortable in the family circle; his reception was always cordial but slightly less warm, for happiness makes people self-centred and outsiders are in the way.

Cachelin himself appeared to be feeling a secret antipathy to the good-looking clerk, whom he had been so anxious, only a few months earlier, to introduce to the family. It was he who informed this friend of Cora's pregnancy. He announced it curtly: 'You know my daughter is going to have a baby!'

Bunny, affecting surprise, replied: 'Indeed! You must be delighted.'

'Indeed we are!' answered Cachelin, observing that his colleague, unlike himself, did not appear very pleased. Men do not like seeing women to whom they are attached in this condition, whether it is their fault or not.

Every Sunday, however, Bunny still dined at the flat. But the evenings were becoming difficult, though no serious difference had arisen between them; and this embarrassment increased from week to week. One evening, when he had just left, Cachelin actually exclaimed angrily: 'That fellow's getting on my nerves!'

And Lesable replied: 'The fact is, he doesn't improve on acquaintance.' Cora had lowered her eyes. She offered no opinion, but she always seemed uncomfortable in the presence of the tall Bunny, who wore an almost shamefaced air when near her, no longer smiling at her as he used to do; he no longer took them to the theatre and appeared to feel that what had been a cordial friendship was now an irksome duty.

But one Thursday at dinner-time, when her husband came in from the Ministry, Cora kissed his whiskers more affectionately than usual and whispered in his ear:

'Perhaps you'll be cross with me?'

'Why?'

'Well, the fact is M. Bunny has just been in to see me. I don't want people talking scandal about me, so I asked him not to come again, when you were out. He seemed rather hurt.'

Lesable asked in surprise:

'Well, what did he say?'

'Oh! He didn't say much, but I didn't like it all the same and I asked him not to come again. You know, it was Daddy and you who brought him: he's not my friend. So I was afraid you might be annoyed at my forbidding him the house.'

A wave of gratitude and joy swept over her husband.

'You were quite right, quite right; I'm more than thankful you've done so.'

She went on to define clearly the position between the two men, about which she had made up her mind in advance: 'At the office you'll pretend to know nothing and you'll talk to him as before; but he's not to come here any more.'

Lesable, embracing his wife tenderly, showered butterfly kisse
on her eyes and face, repeating: 'You're an angel!' And he fel
against his body the pressure of the child, already growing stron,
in her womb.

VIII

Cora's pregnancy ran its normal course.

She gave birth to a daughter towards the end of September
The child was called Désirée, but, as they were anxious to make
big affair of the baptism, it was decided to postpone it till th
following summer at the country house they intended to buy.

They chose a place at Asnières on the hill above the Seine.

A great deal happened during the winter. As soon as they ha
got the legacy, Cachelin had claimed his retiring pension, whic
was immediately granted, and had left the office. He now spent hi
spare time in cutting up the lids of cigar-boxes with a fine mecha
nical saw. He made clocks, little boxes, flower-stands and all sort
of dolls' furniture. He was passionately keen on this hobby, th
idea having been suggested by the sight of a pedlar doing this kin
of work with pieces of wood in the Avenue de l'Opéra. Every da
he produced intricate new patterns, ingenious but useless, and hel
them up for universal admiration.

He was always impressed by his own handiwork and he used t
say: 'It's amazing what one can make!'

The Deputy Director, M. Rabot, having at last died, Lesab
took on his work, though without the title, as the statutory interv
had not elapsed since his last promotion.

Cora had become an entirely different woman, quieter and mo
refined in manner, for she realized instinctively the change necess
tated by their new financial standing.

On New Year's Day she paid a call on the Chief's wife, a port
lady, who had remained provincial in spite of having lived in Par
for thirty-five years, and begged her with such irresistible char
to be the child's godmother, that Madame Torchebeuf could n
refuse. Grandfather Cachelin was the godfather.

The ceremony took place on a blazing Sunday in June. All the ffice was invited except the good-looking Bunny, whom they ever saw nowadays.

At nine o'clock Lesable was waiting at the station for the Paris ain, while a groom in livery with large gilt buttons was standing t the head of a sleek pony in a brand new dog-cart, holding the ein.

The engine whistled in the distance and soon came into sight ith its train of carriages, which disgorged a flood of passengers.

M. Torchebeuf alighted from a first-class carriage with his wife a striking costume, while Pitolet and Boissel got out of a second-lass compartment. They had not dared to invite old Savon, but it as understood that they would meet him by accident in the after-oon and take him back to dinner with the Chief's consent.

Lesable hurried to meet his superior, who came towards him, a ny figure in his frock-coat, wearing the big rosette of the Legion f Honour like a huge red rose in the lapel. His enormous head, urmounted by a broad-brimmed top-hat, seemed too heavy for is frail body, so that he looked like a freak at a show; and his wife, y raising herself ever so little on tiptoe, could easily see over his ead.

Lesable, in the seventh heaven of delight, bowed and expressed is thanks. He handed them into the dog-cart, then, running to-ards his two colleagues who were following modestly in the rear, e shook hands, apologizing for not being able to take them in his arriage, as it was too small: 'Follow the river and you'll come to he gate of my house, Villa Désirée, the fourth house after the urning. Don't be too long.'

And, getting into his carriage, he seized the reins and drove ff, while the groom jumped smartly on to the little seat at the ack.

The ceremony went off splendidly. Afterwards they went back o the house for lunch. Each guest found under his napkin a resent, nicely adapted to the recipient's importance. The god-nother received a massive gold bracelet, her husband a ruby ie-pin, Boissel a Russia leather wallet and Pitolet a magnificent

meerschaum pipe. These were called Désirée's presents to h
new friends.

Madame Torchebeuf, blushing with embarrassment and pleasur
put the gold bangle on her fat forearm, and, as the Chief w.
wearing a narrow black tie which would not take a tie-pin, he stu
the jewel into the lapel of his frock-coat below the Legion
Honour, as if it was the insignia of some lesser order.

Through the window the great ribbon of the river was visib
flowing down from Suresnes between banks bordered with tree
The sun, blazing down on the water, transformed it into a river
fire. The beginning of the meal was formal with the seriousness d
to the presence of Monsieur and Madame Torchebeuf. Later on th
ice was broken. Cachelin made some jokes of an equivocal natur
feeling that his wealth was sufficient excuse, and everybod
laughed. They would have been shocked if Pitolet or Boissel ha
ventured on anything of the sort.

During dessert the infant had to be brought in to be kissed by a
the guests. Swathed in snowy lace, it gazed at each one with blu
eyes, expressionless and unthinking, turning its disproportionate
big head from time to time as if beginning to take in what
saw.

Pitolet, amid the hum of the general conversation, whispered
Boissel, who was next to him: 'It looks just like a little Bunn
rabbit!'

The jest went the round of the Ministry next day.

By now, however, two o'clock had struck; the liqueurs had bee
drunk and Cachelin suggested an inspection of the estate and
walk along the river bank afterwards. The guests moved in proces
sion through the rooms from attic to cellar; then they went roun
the garden, tree by tree and plant by plant, and finally broke u
into two parties for their walk.

Cachelin, whose style had been somewhat cramped by th
presence of the ladies, dragged Boissel and Pitolet off to the rive
side cafés, while Mesdames Torchebeuf and Lesable with thei
husbands walked up the other bank, as the ladies could not mi
with the common herd of Sunday holiday makers. They strolle

long the tow-path, followed by the two men in earnest conversa-
on on office business.

On the river rowing boats were passing, propelled by the sweep-
ng strokes of bare-armed oarsmen, their muscles rippling under
heir tanned skin. Their girl companions, lolling at full length on
vhite or black fur rugs, steered, dozing in the sun and holding over
heir heads silk sunshades, red, yellow or blue, like enormous
owers on the water. There were noisy exchanges between the
oats, shouted conversations and vulgar abuse; and the hum of
oices in the distance, indistinguishable and continuous, betrayed
he presence of the seething holiday crowd.

Rows of men fishing were sitting motionless all along the bank,
vhile almost naked bathers were standing up in heavy fishermen's
raft, diving in and scrambling back into their boats and jumping
n again.

Madame Torchebeuf regarded the scene with surprise. Cora told
her: 'It's always like this on Sundays. It quite spoils the lovely
ountryside for me.'

A boat approached slowly. Two women were rowing two
thletic young men, who were stretched at full length in the bottom
of the boat. One of them shouted towards the bank: 'Hullo! You
adies! I've got a man for sale, quite cheap; any offers?'

Cora, turning away in disgust, took her guest's arm, saying:
One really can't stay even here; let's go. These people are too
awful!'

And they moved away. M. Torchebeuf was saying to Lesable:
It's all fixed up for January 1st; the Director has given a definite
promise.'

And Lesable answered: 'I don't know how to thank you, my
dear Chief.'

When they got back they found Cachelin, Pitolet and Boissel
laughing till they cried, almost carrying old Savon, whom they had
discovered, they said jokingly, with a lady of easy virtue.

The old fellow kept saying: 'It's not true, no, it's not true! You
oughtn't to say so, Monsieur Cachelin, you really oughtn't.'

And Cachelin, choking with laughter, cried: 'You like your little

bit of fun, don't you? You were calling her "your little bit of fluff"
we caught you out, you naughty old man!'

Even the ladies began to laugh, the old fellow looked so take
aback.

Cachelin went on: 'With M. Torchebeuf's permission, we'll hol
him prisoner, and as a punishment he shall have dinner with us.'

The Chief graciously consented, and they went on laughing
over the lady deserted by the old man, who continued to protest
taking this vulgar jest quite seriously.

The incident proved an inexhaustible source of jokes, some o
them of a doubtful nature, till the evening.

Cora and Madame Torchebeuf, sitting under an awning on the
terrace, watched the reflections of the sunset. A crimson ligh
poured through the leaves; not a breath was stirring the branches
the windless, fiery sky shed a serene restfulness over the scene. A
few boats were still passing, returning to the boathouse more
slowly than the rest.

Cora asked: 'Is it true that this poor M. Savon married a bac
lot?'

Madame Torchebeuf, who knew all the scandal of the office
replied: 'Yes, a girl much too young for him, who had lost her
parents and who was unfaithful to him with some scamp and finally
ran away with him.' The portly lady added: 'I call him a scamp bu
I really know nothing about him. They were said to have been
madly in love with each other. In any case old Savon isn't precisely
attractive.'

Madame Lesable replied sententiously: 'That is no excuse. One
can't help being sorry for the old man. The same thing happened
to our next-door neighbour M. Barbou. His wife fell in love with
a painter of some sort, who used to come here for the summer, and
she went off with him abroad. I can't understand a woman falling
so low. I consider that there ought to be a special punishment for
immoral women of that kind, who bring shame on their families.'

The nurse appeared at the end of the garden path, carrying
Désirée in her lace robe. The child was brought towards the two
women, her face tinted with the golden crimson of the sunset. She

was gazing at the fiery sky with the same expressionless, hazy-eyed look of surprise with which she looked at people.

All the men, who were chatting further away, approached, and Cachelin, seizing his grand-daughter, lifted her up at arms' length, as if he wanted to raise her to the sky. She was silhouetted against the bright backcloth of the horizon, with her white robe falling to the ground.

And the grandfather cried: 'That's the best sight in the world, eh, father Savon?'

The old man made no answer, not knowing what to say or perhaps having too much to think about.

A man-servant opened the door on to the terrace and announced: 'Madame, dinner is served.'

UNCLE TONY

I

Uncle Tony, known also as Fatty Tony, Three-star Tony, Tony Chewbread, otherwise Tony Punch, the inn-keeper of Windbreak, was a familiar figure for thirty miles around.

He had brought fame to the village which was buried in a valley sloping down to the sea, a poor country village in the Normandy style, surrounded by ditches and trees.

There they were, those houses, nestling in a grassy, furze-covered ravine, behind a bend which had given the place the name of Windbreak. Like birds hiding in the furrows on a stormy day, they seemed to have sought shelter in this hollow from the high winds, the bitter, salty winds blowing off the open sea, as biting and searing as fire, as parching and withering as a winter frost.

The whole village seemed to belong to Antony Chewbread, or Punch, who was just as often called Tony or Three-star Tony, because of the expression he was always using: 'My Three-star is the best in France.'

His 'Three-star' was his brandy, of course.

For twenty years he had quenched the thirst of the place with his Three-star and his Punch; for, every time anybody asked him: 'What shall we have, Uncle Tony?' he invariably answered: 'A tot of Punch, son-in-law; that warms the guts and clears the head; there's nothing better for a fellow.'

He was in the habit of calling everybody 'son-in-law', although he had never had a daughter, married or marriageable.

Ah, yes! we all knew Tony Punch, the fattest man in the parish, and even in the whole county. His little house seemed ludicrously small and low for a man of his size and, whenever one saw him standing at his door, where he spent whole days, one wondered how he ever got inside. He always went in with every client, for Three-star Tony was invariably invited as of right to join in the first round at the visitor's expense.

His inn had on its sign 'The Friends' Retreat', and Uncle Tony really was the friend of the whole countryside. People came from Fécamp and Montvilliers to see him and have a good laugh at his stories, for the fat old man would have made an effigy on a tomb-stone laugh. He had a way of pulling people's legs without giving offence and he conveyed much more than he said by a wink; he would slap his thigh in an access of merriment, which made you helpless with laughter at every slap. It was worth a visit just to see him drink; he put down as much as he was stood, no matter what it was, his sly glance revealing his pleasure at two things, first the joy of having a drink, and secondly of making money out of it. The local wits were always asking him: 'Why don't yer get down to drinkin' the sea, Uncle Tony?' And he would reply: 'There's two reasons why I doesn't, first it's salt and secondly it'd have to be in bottle, 'cos my belly ain't made to bend down so far.'

It was worthwhile, too, hearing him scrap with his wife; it was an entertainment in itself well worth paying for. During their thirty years of married life they had had a regular set-to every day. The only difference was that Tony enjoyed every minute of it, while his wife lost her temper. She was a tall peasant-woman, who walked with the long strides of some wading bird and had the face of an angry screech-owl. She spent her time looking after her hens in a tiny yard behind the inn, and she had a great reputation for fattening poultry.

When a dinner-party was being given in the most exclusive circles of Fécamp society, the meal was not considered complete without one of Auntie Tony's nurselings.

But she had been born in a bad temper and nothing was ever quite right for her. The whole world was her enemy, and she had her knife particularly into her husband. His cheeriness, his popu-larity, his robust health and his portliness got on her nerves. She regarded him as a good-for-nothing creature who made his money without working, and as a glutton, because he ate and drank enough for ten; and not a day passed without her declaring furiously: 'The right place for a pot-belly like 'im is naked in a pig-sty. It makes yer fair sick to see fat like 'is.'

And she would scream at him: 'Just you wait a bit and we'll see what'll 'appen. 'E'll bust one day like a corn-sack, the great bloated oaf!'

Tony would roar with laughter and, patting his stomach, reply: 'Well, old hen, you bag of bones, try and fatten yer poultry like me – you just try!'

And, rolling up his sleeve to show his huge forearm, he went on: 'There's a nice little wing for you, old lady, aye, it's a good 'un!'

And all the men in the bar banged with their fists on the tables, roaring with laughter; they stamped on the earth floor and spat in the exuberance of their merriment. The old woman, furiously angry, would go on:

'You just wait a bit; we'll see what'll 'appen; 'e'll bust like a corn-sack.'

And she would go off in a rage amid the laughter of the men drinking.

Tony was really an astonishing sight, he had got so fat and bloated, so red in the face and so short of breath. He was one of those enormous men whom it seems to amuse Death to play with; the slow process of dissolution is rendered irresistibly comic with humorous cunning and deceptive light-heartedness. Instead of revealing his approach, as with most people, by hair going white, wasting and increasing weakness, symptoms which excite the terrified comment: 'Good God! How he's changed!' Death amused himself by increasing Tony's girth, making him a caricature of obesity, flushing his face with red and purple blotches, inflating him and giving him an appearance of abnormally robust health; all the usual deformities of mankind, which herald the approach of death, in him were laughter-provoking, droll, amusing, instead of being grim and arousing pity.

'Just you wait a bit and we'll see what we shall see,' repeated Auntie Tony.

II

One day Tony had a stroke and fell down paralysed. They put the giant to bed in the little room behind the partition of the bar-parlour, so that he could hear what was said in the next room and chat with his friends. His brain had remained clear, while his huge frame, which was too heavy to move or lift, was smitten with complete paralysis. At first they hoped that he would recover the power of movement in his immense legs, but this hope soon disap-peared and Three-star Tony lay day and night on a bed, which was made only once a week with the help of four neighbours, who lifted the inn-keeper by his arms and legs, while the mattress was turned.

But he kept his spirits, though his cheerfulness was not quite the same as before; now he was more timid, more humble, more afraid of his wife, like a little child. She still screamed at him all day:

'Look at the great fat toad, 'e's good for nothing! Look at 'im, 'e can't work, the drunkard. It's a pretty kettle of fish, and no mistake!'

Nowadays he made no answer; he just winked behind the old woman's back and turned over, which was as much as he could do. He called this change of position 'doing a tack to the North' or 'a tack to the South'.

His one amusement now was listening to the talk in the bar-parlour and joining in through the wall, when he recognized a friend's voice. He would shout:

'Hullo! son-in-law, is that you, Célestin?'

And Célestin Maloisel would reply:

'Yes, it's me all right, Uncle Tony. Are you 'oppin' about again, old man?'

Three-star Tony answered:

''Oppin' about, you say? No, not yet, but I'm not losing weight; my stomach's all right.'

Soon he had his closest friends into his room and he wasn't so lonely, though he was miserable, when he saw them drinking with-out him. He used to say over and over again:

'Damn it all! What 'urts, son-in-law, is not being able to taste my brandy! I don't care a 'oot about the rest of it, but it's cruel 'ard not to be able to drink.'

And the owl-like face of Auntie Tony appeared at the window and she shouted:

'Just look at 'im, the great fat useless 'ulk, what 'as to be fed and washed and cleaned out like a pig.'

When the old woman had gone, a cock with red feathers sometimes hopped up on to the window-sill, peered into the room with a round enquiring eye and crowed loudly. Sometimes, too, one or two hens would flap in as far as the foot of the bed, looking for crumbs on the floor.

Three-star Tony's friends soon deserted the bar-parlour and dropped in every afternoon for a chat at the fat man's bedside. Though bed-ridden, Tony still amused them with his jokes; the humorous old fellow would have made the devil laugh. There were three of them who came in every day, Célestin Maloisel, a tall thin man with a body gnarled like an old apple-tree, Prosper Horslaville, a dried-up little man with a ferret's nose, sly and cunning as a fox, and Césaire Paummel, who never said a word but enjoyed himself all the same. They brought in a board from the yard, laid it on the edge of the bed and played dominoes; they had great games lasting from two to six.

But Auntie Tony soon got beyond anything; she couldn't endure the way her great useless hulk of a husband went on enjoying himself, playing dominoes in bed; and, as soon as she saw a game begun, she rushed up in a violent temper, upset the board, seized the pieces and carried them back into the bar-parlour, declaring that it was quite enough to feed the great greasy swine without seeing him amusing himself, as if in defiance of the wretched people who had to work all day.

Célestin Maloisel and Césaire Paummel bent their heads before the storm, but Prosper Horslaville egged on the old woman, whose tantrums amused him.

One day, seeing her more exasperated than usual, he said to her:

'Look 'ere, Auntie, d'you know what I'd do, if I was you?'

She waited for him to explain himself, fixing him with her owl-like stare.

He went on:

"E's as 'ot as a oven, your old man, and 'e never gets out of bed. Well, Auntie, I'd use 'im to 'atch eggs.'

She stood there not understanding, thinking he was pulling her leg, her eyes fixed on the skinny sly face of the peasant, who went on:

'I'd put five eggs under one arm and five under t'other, the same day as I put a clutch under a 'en; they'd 'atch out together. When they comed out, I'd give yer 'usband's chicks to the 'en for 'er to mother. That 'ud give yer more pullets, eh, Auntie?'

The old woman asked in amazement:

'Could it be did?'

The man replied:

'O' course it can! Why wouldn't it work? Yer can 'atch eggs in a warm box, yer can 'atch 'em in a bed.'

This argument impressed her and she went away to think it over quietly.

A week later she came into Tony's room with her apron full of eggs and said:

'I'se just put the yaller 'en on the nest with ten eggs. 'Ere's ten for you, and don't yer go and break 'em.'

Tony, bewildered, asked:

'What d'yer want me to do?'

She replied:

'I want yer to 'atch 'em, you good-for-nothing.'

At first he laughed; then, as she insisted, he got annoyed and resisted, firmly refusing to have the eggs put under his fat arms to be hatched out.

But the old woman exclaimed angrily:

'Yer won't get no stew till yer takes 'em. We'll see what we shall see.'

Tony, worried, said nothing.

When he heard twelve o'clock strike, he called out:

"Ullo, Missus, be the soup ready?'

She shouted back from the kitchen:

'There ain't no soup for you, you great lazybones!'

He thought she was joking and waited; then he begged and prayed and swore, made desperate tacks to North and South, banged on the wall with his fists, but in the end he had to allow the five eggs to be put inside the bed against his left side. After which he got his soup.

When his friends arrived they thought he was feeling ill, he seemed so strange and uncomfortable.

Presently they began their usual game, but Tony didn't seem to enjoy it a bit, stretching out his hand very slowly and carefully.

''Ave yer got yer arm tied up?' asked Horslaville.

Tony replied:

'My shoulder's a bit stiff.'

Suddenly they heard steps in the bar-parlour and the domino-players stopped talking.

It was the Mayor and his deputy. They called for two brandies and began to discuss village business. As they were talking in a low voice, Tony wanted to put his ear close to the partition and, forgetting the eggs, he made a sudden tack to the North and found himself lying on an omelette.

He swore aloud and his wife rushed in and, guessing at the accident, tore back the bedclothes roughly. For a moment she stood there motionless, too angry to utter a word, before the glutinous yellow poultice sticking to her husband's side. Then, quivering with rage, she fell upon the paralytic and began to pommel his stomach as hard as she could, as if she was beating her dirty linen on the edge of the pond. The blows fell with a dull thud one after the other like the drumming of a rabbit.

Tony's three friends were helpless with laughter, coughing, sneezing, snorting, while the fat man, terrified, tried to defend himself against his wife's onslaught, taking great care, however, not to break the eggs on his other side.

III

Tony was beaten. He had to act as an incubator and give up his games of dominoes; indeed he had to give up all movement, for his old wife cut off his food remorselessly every time he broke an egg.

There he lay on his back without moving, gazing at the ceiling, his arms spread out like wings, warming the embryo chicks inside the white shells close against his body.

He only spoke in a whisper, as if he was as much afraid of noise as of movement, and he took a great interest in the yellow sitting hen, who was engaged on the same job as himself in the hen-run.

He was always asking his wife:

"As that yaller 'en taken 'er food to-night?'

And the old woman was kept on the go between her husband and her hens and back again; her anxiety over the chicks which were developing in the bed and the nest became a positive obsession.

When the neighbours heard the story they came to ask after Tony with eager curiosity. They entered the room on tiptoe as one enters a sick room and asked with keen interest:

'Well! 'Ow's things to-day?'

Tony answered:

'Oh! champion, but I gets that het up I don't know where I is; I twitches all over.'

One morning his wife came in a great state of excitement and declared:

'The yaller 'en's got seven out; there was three eggs addled.'

Tony's heart beat fast; how many would he hatch?

He asked:

'I won't be long now, will I?' – with all the anxiety of a woman about to give birth.

The old woman answered crossly, tortured by fear of failure:

'I jolly well 'opes not.'

They waited. His friends, who had been warned that the time was getting near, came to see him in a state of nervous expectation themselves.

The subject was discussed in the cottages; people went to their neighbours for the latest news.

About three o'clock Tony fell into a doze. Nowadays he slept half the day. Suddenly he was woken up by a strange tickling sensation under his right arm. He immediately felt there with his left hand and found a downy yellow chick, which wriggled in his hand.

His excitement was such that he called out and let go the chicken, which ran over his chest. The bar-parlour was crowded. The whole lot leapt to their feet and rushed into the bedroom, forming a circle as if round an acrobat at a fair. The old woman, arriving on the scene, picked up the little creature, which had taken cover under her husband's beard, with the greatest care.

No one spoke. It was a hot April day. Through the open window could be heard the clucking of the yellow hen as she called her brood.

Tony, sweating with excitement and anxious anticipation, whispered:

'I'se got another now under the left arm!'

His wife thrust her long skinny hand into the bed and brought out a second chick with all the precaution of a midwife.

The neighbours all wanted to see it. It was passed round from hand to hand as if it was something abnormal.

For twenty minutes no more came out; then four hatched out all together. There was a buzz of conversation in the room. And Tony smiled, delighted with his achievement and beginning to take real pride in this new line in paternity. Anyway, there weren't many men like him! He was something out of the ordinary!

He announced:

'That makes six. Good God! What a christenin' we'll 'ave!'

Everyone in the room laughed. The bar-parlour was crowded, too. People asked: "Ow many 's 'e got?'

"E 've got six.'

Auntie Tony took this addition to her brood out to the hen, who clucked distractedly, bristling up her feathers and spreading her wings to shelter her rapidly increasing brood.

''Ere's another,' cried Tony.

He was wrong; there were three! It was a triumph! The last hatched out at seven o'clock in the evening. All the eggs were good. Tony, in an ecstasy of delight, proud of his task accomplished, kissed the tiny chick on its back, till he nearly suffocated it. He wanted to keep this last one in his bed all night, so strong was his maternal feeling for the frail creature, which owed its life to him; but his wife took it away like the rest, deaf to her husband's entreaties.

The audience went away delighted, discussing the incident, and Horslaville, who was the last to leave, asked:

'Look 'ere, Uncle Tony, you'll invite me to yer first chicken stew, won't yer?'

At the idea of chicken stew, Tony's face lit up and he replied:

'O' course, you shall be there, son-in-law.'

WHO KNOWS?

I

THANK God! At last I've made up my mind to put my experiences on record! But shall I ever be able to do it, shall I have the courage? It's all so mysterious, so inexplicable, so unintelligible, so crazy!

If I were not sure of what I've seen, certain that there has been no flaw in my reasoning, no mistake in my facts, no gap in the strict sequence of my observations, I should consider myself merely the victim of a hallucination, the sport of some strange optical delusion. After all, who knows?

To-day I am in a Mental Home, but I went there of my own free will as a precaution, because I was afraid. Only one man knows my story, the House Doctor. Now I'm going to put it on paper, I really don't quite know why. Perhaps in the hope of shaking off the obsession, which haunts me like some ghastly nightmare.

Anyhow, here it is:

I have always been a lonely man, a dreamer, a kind of solitary, good-natured, easily satisfied, harbouring no bitterness against mankind and no grudge against Heaven. I have always lived alone, because of a sort of uneasiness, which the presence of others sets up in me. How can I explain it? I can't. It's not that I shun society; I enjoy conversation and dining with my friends, but when I am conscious of them near me, even the most intimate, for any length of time, I feel tired, exhausted, on edge, and I am aware of a growing and distressing desire to see them go away or to go away myself and be alone.

This desire is more than a mere craving, it is an imperative necessity. And if I had to remain in their company, if I had to go on, I do not say listening to, but merely hearing their conversation, I am sure something dreadful would happen. What? Who knows? Possibly, yes, probably, I should simply collapse.

I am so fond of being alone that I cannot even endure the proxi-

nity of other human beings sleeping under the same roof; I cannot
live in Paris; to me it is a long drawn-out fight for life. It is spiritual
death; this huge swarming crowd living all round me, even in their
sleep, causes me physical and nervous torture. Indeed other
people's sleep is even more painful to me than their conversation.
And I can never rest, when I know or feel that there are living
beings, on the other side of the wall, suffering this nightly suspen-
sion of consciousness.

Why do I feel like this? Who knows? Perhaps the reason is quite
simple: I get tired very quickly of anything outside myself. And
there are many people like me.

There are two kinds of human beings. Those who need others,
who are distracted, amused, soothed by company, while loneliness,
such as the ascent of some forbidding glacier or the crossing of a
desert, worries them, exhausts them, wears them out: and those
whom, on the contrary, the society of their fellows wearies, bores,
irritates, cramps, while solitude gives them peace and rest in the
free world of phantasy.

It is, in fact, a recognized psychological phenomenon. The
former are equipped to lead the life of the extrovert, the latter that
of the introvert. In my own case my ability to concentrate on things
outside myself is limited and quickly exhausted, and as soon as this
limit is reached, I am conscious of unbearable physical and mental
discomfort. The result of this has been that I am, or rather I was,
very much attached to inanimate objects, which take on for me the
importance of human beings, and that my house has, or rather had,
become a world in which I led a lonely but purposeful life, surrounded by things, pieces of furniture and ornaments that I knew
and loved like friends. I had gradually filled my home and decorated
it with them, and in it I felt at peace, contented, completely happy
as in the arms of a loving wife, the familiar touch of whose caressing
hand has become a comforting, restful necessity.

I had had this house built in a beautiful garden, standing back
from the roads, not far from a town, where I could enjoy the social
amenities, of which I felt the need from time to time. All my servants slept in a building at the far end of a walled kitchen-garden.

In the silence of my home, deep hidden from sight beneath th
foliage of tall trees, the enveloping darkness of the nights was s
restful and so welcome that every evening I put off going to bed fo
several hours in order to prolong my enjoyment of it.

That evening there had been a performance of *Sigurd* at the loc
theatre. It was the first time I had heard this beautiful fairy pla
with music and I had thoroughly enjoyed it.

I was walking home briskly, with scraps of melody running i
my head and the entrancing scenes still vivid in my memory. It wa
dark, pitch dark, and when I say that I mean I could hardly see th
road and several times I nearly fell headlong into the ditch. Fron
the toll-gate to my house is a little more than half a mile or abou
twenty minutes slow walking. It was one o'clock in the morning
one o'clock or half-past one; suddenly the sky showed slightl
luminous in front of me, and the crescent moon rose, the melan
choly crescent of the waning moon. The moon in its first quarter
when it rises at four or five o'clock in the evening, is bright, witl
cheerful, silvery light; but in the last quarter, when it rises afte
midnight, it is copper-coloured, suggesting gloomy foreboding, a
real Witches' Sabbath moon. Anyone given to going out much a
night must have noticed this. The first quarter's crescent, ever
when slender as a thread, sheds a faint but cheering gleam, at whicl
the heart lifts, and throws clearly defined shadows on the ground
the last quarter's crescent gives a feeble, fitful light, so dim that i
casts almost no shadow.

The dark silhouette of my garden loomed ahead and for som
reason I felt an odd disinclination to go in. I slackened my pace
The night was very mild. The great mass of trees looked like a
tomb, in which my house lay buried.

I opened the garden gate and entered the long sycamore drive
leading to the house with the trees meeting overhead; it stretched
before me like a lofty tunnel through the black mass of the trees and
past lawns, on which the flower-beds showed up in the less intense
darkness as oval patches of no particular colour.

As I approached the house I felt curiously uneasy. I paused
There was not a sound, not a breath of air stirring in the leaves

What has come over me?' I thought. For ten years I had been coming home like this without the least feeling of nervousness. I was not afraid. I have never been afraid in the dark. The sight of a man, a thief or a burglar, would merely have thrown me into a rage and I should have closed with him unhesitatingly. Moreover, was armed; I had my revolver. But I did not put my hand on it, or I wanted to resist this feeling of fear stirring within me.

What was it? A presentiment? That unaccountable presentiment which grips a man's mind at the approach of the supernatural? Perhaps. Who knows?

As I went on, I felt shivers running down my spine, and when I was close to the wall of my great shuttered house I felt I must pause or a few moments before opening the door and going in. So I sat down on a garden seat under my drawing-room windows. I stayed here, my heart thumping, leaning my head against the wall, staring into the blackness of the foliage. For the first few minutes I noticed nothing unusual. I *was* aware of a kind of rumbling in my ears, but hat often happens to me. I sometimes think I can hear trains passing, bells ringing or the tramp of a crowd.

But soon the rumbling became more distinct, more definite, more unmistakable. I had been wrong. It was not the normal hrobbing of my arteries, which was causing this buzzing in my ears, but a quite definite, though confused, noise coming, without any question, from inside my house. I could hear it through the wall, a continuous noise, a rustling rather than a noise, a faint stirring, as of many objects being moved about, as if someone were shifting all my furniture from its usual place and dragging it about gently.

Naturally, for some time I thought I must be mistaken. But after putting my ear close to the shutters in order to hear the strange noises in the house more clearly, I remained quite firmly convinced that something abnormal and inexplicable was going on inside. I was not afraid, but – how can I express it? – startled by the sheer surprise of the thing. I did not slip the safety-catch of my revolver, somehow feeling certain it would be of no use. I just waited.

I waited a long while, unable to come to any decision, with my mind perfectly clear but deeply disturbed. I waited motionless listening all the time to the growing noise, which swelled at times to a violent crescendo before turning into an impatient, angry rumble, which made me feel that some outburst might follow at any minute.

Then suddenly, ashamed of my cowardice, I seized my bunch of keys, picked out the one I wanted, thrust it into the lock, turned it twice, and pushing the door with all my force hurled it back against the wall inside.

The bang echoed like a gunshot and immediately the crash was answered by a terrific uproar from cellar to attic. It was so sudden, so terrifying, so deafening, that I stepped back a few paces and, though I realized it was useless, I drew my revolver from its holster.

I waited again, but not for long. I could now distinguish an extraordinary sound of trampling on the stairs, parquet floors and carpets, a trampling not of human feet or shoes, but of crutches, wooden crutches and iron crutches, that rang with the metallic insistence of cymbals. Suddenly, on the threshold of the front door, I saw an arm-chair, my big reading chair, come waddling out; it moved off down the drive. It was followed by others from the drawing-room; next came the sofas, low on the ground and crawling along like crocodiles on their stumpy legs, then all the rest of my chairs, leaping like goats, and the little stools loping along like rabbits.

Imagine my feelings! I slipped into a clump of shrubs, where I crouched, my eyes glued all the time to the procession of my furniture, for it was all on the way out, one piece after the other, quickly or slowly according to their shape and weight. My piano, my concert grand, galloped past like a runaway horse with a faint jangle of wires inside; the smaller objects, brushes, cut-glass and goblets, slid over the gravel like ants, gleaming like glow-worms in the moonlight. The carpets and hangings crawled away, sprawling for all the world like devil-fish. I saw my writing-desk appear, a rare eighteenth-century collector's piece, containing all my letters, the whole record of anguished passion long since spent. And in it were also my photographs.

Suddenly all fear left me; I threw myself upon it and grappled with it, as one grapples with a burglar; but it went on its way irresistibly, and, in spite of my utmost efforts, I could not even slow it up. As I wrestled like a madman against this terrible strength, I fell to the ground in the struggle. It rolled me over and over and dragged me along the gravel, and already the pieces of furniture behind were beginning to tread on me, trampling and bruising my legs; then, when I let go, the others swept over me, like a cavalry charge over an unhorsed soldier.

At last, mad with terror, I managed to drag myself off the main drive and hide again among the trees, watching the disappearance of the smallest, tiniest, humblest pieces that I had ever owned, whose very existence I had forgotten.

Presently I heard, in the distance, inside the house, which was full of echoes like an empty building, a terrific din of doors being shut. They banged from attic to basement and last of all the hall door slammed, which I had foolishly opened myself to allow the exodus.

At that I fled, and ran towards the town and I didn't pull myself together till I got to the streets and met people going home late. I went and rang at the door of a hotel where I was known. I had beaten my clothes with my hands to shake the dust out of them, and I made up a story that I had lost my bunch of keys with the key of the kitchen-garden, where my servants slept in a house by itself, behind the garden wall which protected my fruit and vegetables from thieves.

I pulled the bed-clothes up to my eyes in the bed they gave me; but I couldn't sleep and I waited for dawn, listening to the violent beating of my heart. I had given orders for my servants to be informed as soon as it was light, and my valet knocked at my door at seven o'clock in the morning. His face showed how upset he was.

'An awful thing has happened during the night, Sir', he said.

'What is it?'

'All your furniture has been stolen, Sir, absolutely everything, down to the smallest things.'

Somehow I was relieved to hear this. Why? I don't know.

I had complete control of myself; I knew I could conceal my feelings, tell no one what I had seen, hide it, bury it in my breast like some ghastly secret. I replied:

'They are the same people who stole my keys. The police must be informed at once. I'm getting up and I'll be with you in a few minutes at the police station.'

The enquiry lasted five months. Nothing was brought to light. Neither the smallest of my ornaments nor the slightest trace of the thieves was ever found. Good Heavens! If I had told them what I knew. . . . If I had told . . . they would have shut up, not the thieves, but me, the man who could have seen such a thing.

Of course, I knew how to keep my mouth shut. But I never furnished my house again. It was no good. The same thing would have happened. I never wanted to go back to it again. I never did go back. I never saw it again. I went to a hotel in Paris and consulted doctors about the state of my nerves, which had been causing me considerable anxiety since that dreadful night.

They prescribed travel and I took their advice.

II

I began with a trip to Italy. The sun did me good. For six months I wandered from Genoa to Venice, from Venice to Florence, from Florence to Rome, from Rome to Naples. Next I toured Sicily, an attractive country, both from the point of view of scenery and monuments, the remains left by the Greeks and the Normans. I crossed to Africa and travelled at my leisure through the great sandy, peaceful desert, where camels, gazelles and nomad Arabs roam and where in the clear, dry air no obsession can persist either by day or night.

I returned to France via Marseilles and, in spite of the gaiety of Provence, the diminished intensity of the sunlight depressed me. On my return to Europe I had the odd feeling of a patient who thinks he is cured, but is suddenly warned by a dull pain that the source of the trouble is still active.

I went back to Paris, but after a month I got bored. It was autumn, and I decided to take a trip, before the winter, through Normandy, which was new ground to me.

I began with Rouen, of course, and for a week I wandered about, intrigued, charmed, thrilled, in this mediaeval town, this amazing museum of rare specimens of Gothic art.

Then one evening, about four o'clock, as I was entering a street that seemed too good to be true, along which flows an inky black stream called the Eau de Robec, my attention, previously centred on the unusual, old-fashioned aspect of the houses, was suddenly arrested by a number of second-hand furniture shops next door to one another.

They had, indeed, chosen their haunt well, these seedy junk dealers, in this fantastic alley by the side of this sinister stream, under pointed roofs of tile or slate, on which the weather-vanes of a vanished age still creaked.

Stacked in the depths of the cavernous shops could be seen carved chests, china from Rouen, Nevers and Moustiers, statues, some painted, some in plain oak, crucifixes, Madonnas, Saints, church ornaments, chasubles, copes, even chalices, and an old tabernacle of gilded wood, now vacated by its Almighty tenant. What astonishing store-rooms there were in these great, lofty houses, packed from cellar to attic with pieces of every kind, whose usefulness seemed finished and which had outlived their natural owners, their century, their period, their fashion, to be bought as curios by later generations!

My passion for old things was reviving in this collector's paradise. I went from shop to shop, crossing in two strides the bridges made of four rotten planks thrown over the stinking water of the Eau de Robec. And then – Mother of God! My heart leapt to my mouth. I caught sight of one of my finest cabinets at the edge of a vault crammed with junk, that looked like the entrance to the catacombs of some cemetery of old furniture. I went towards it trembling all over, trembling to such an extent that I did not dare touch it. I stretched out my hand, then I hesitated. It *was* mine, there was no question about it, a unique Louis XIII cabinet, unmistakable to anyone who had ever seen it. Suddenly, peering further into the sombre depths of this gallery, I noticed three of my arm-chairs covered with 'petit point' embroidery, and farther off my two Henri II tables, which were so rare that people came specially from Paris to see them.

Imagine, just imagine my feelings!

Then I went forward, dazed and faint with excitement, but I went in, for I am no coward; I went in like a knight in the dark ages entering a witches' kitchen. As I advanced, I found all my belongings, my chandeliers, my books, my pictures, my hangings and carpets, my weapons, everything except the writing-desk containing my letters, which I could not discover anywhere.

I went on, downstairs, along dark passages, and up again to the floors above. I was alone. I called but there was no answer. I was alone; there was no one in this huge winding labyrinth of a house.

Night came on and I had to sit down in the dark on one of my own chairs, for I wouldn't go away. At intervals I shouted: 'Hullo! Hullo! Anybody there!'

I had been there, I am sure, more than an hour, when I heard footsteps, light, slow steps; I could not tell where they came from. I nearly ran away, but, pulling myself together, I called again and I saw a light in the next room.

'Who's there?' said a voice.

I answered:

'A customer.'

The answer came:

'It's very late, we're really closed.'

I retorted:

'I've been waiting for you an hour.'

'You could have come back to-morrow.'

'To-morrow I shall have left Rouen.'

I did not dare to move and he did not come to me. All this time I saw the reflection of his light shining on a tapestry, in which two angels were flying above the dead on a battlefield. That, too, belonged to me.

I said:

'Well, are you coming?'

He replied:

'I'm waiting for you.'

I got up and went towards him.

In the centre of a large room stood a very short man, very short and very fat, like the fat man at a show, and hideous into the bargain. He had a sparse, straggling, ill-kept, dirty-yellow beard, and not a hair on his head, not a single one! As he held his candle raised at arm's length in order to see me, the dome of his bald head looked like a miniature moon in this huge room stacked with old furniture. His face was wrinkled and bloated, his eyes mere slits.

After some bargaining I bought three chairs that were really mine and paid a large sum in cash, merely giving the number of my room at the hotel. They were to be delivered next morning before nine o'clock. Then I left the shop. He showed me to the door most politely.

I went straight to the Head Police station, where I told the story of the theft of my furniture and the discovery I had just made.

The Inspector telegraphed, on the spot, for instructions to the Public Prosecutor's Office, where the investigation into the theft had been held, asking me to wait for the answer. An hour later it was received, completely confirming my story.

'I'll have this man arrested and questioned at once,' he said, 'for he may have become suspicious and he might move your belongings. I suggest you go and dine, and come back in two hours' time; I'll have him here and I'll put him through a second examination in your presence.'

'Excellent, Inspector! I'm more than grateful to you.'

I went and dined at my hotel, and my appetite was better than I should have thought possible. But I was pretty well satisfied. They had got him.

Two hours later I was back at the Police Station, where the officer was waiting for me.

'Well, Sir,' he said, when he saw me, 'we haven't got your friend. My men haven't been able to lay hands on him.'

'Do you mean . . . ?'

A feeling of faintness came over me.

'But . . . you *have* found the house?' I asked.

'Oh yes! And it will, of course, be watched and guarded till h
comes back. But he has disappeared.'

'Disappeared?'

'Yes, disappeared. He usually spends the evening with his nex
door neighbour, a queer old hag, a widow called Mme Bidoin,
second-hand dealer like himself. She hasn't seen him this evenin
and can't give any information about him. We shall have to wa
till to-morrow.'

I went away. The streets of Rouen now seemed sinister, with th
disturbing effect of a haunted house.

I slept badly, with nightmares every time I dropped off.

As I didn't want to seem unduly anxious, or in too much of
hurry, I waited next morning till ten o'clock before going round t
the Police Station.

The dealer had not reappeared; his shop was still closed.

The Inspector said to me:

'I've taken all the necessary steps. The Public Prosecu
tor's Department has been informed; we'll go together to th
shop and have it opened; you can show me what belongs t
you.'

We drove to the place. Policemen were on duty, with a lock
smith, in front of the door, which had been opened.

When I went in I saw neither my cabinet nor my arm-chairs no
my tables, not a single one of all the contents of my house, though
the evening before I could not take a step without running into
something of mine.

The Chief Inspector, in surprise, at first looked at m
suspiciously.

'Well, I must say, Inspector, the disappearance of this furnitur
coincides oddly with that of the dealer,' I commented.

He smiled:

'You're right! You made a mistake in buying and paying fo
your pieces yesterday. It was that gave him the tip.'

I replied:

'What I can't understand is that all the space occupied by my furniture is now filled with other pieces.'

'Oh well!' answered the Inspector, 'he had the whole night before him, and accomplices, too, no doubt. There are sure to be means of communication with the houses on either side. Don't be alarmed, Sir, I shall leave no stone unturned. The thief won't elude us for long, now we've got his hide-out.'

*

My heart was beating so violently that I thought it would burst.

*

I stayed on in Rouen for a fortnight. The man did not come back. God knows, nobody could outwit or trap a man like that!

Then on the following morning I got this strange letter from my gardener, who was acting as caretaker of my house, which had been left unoccupied since the robbery:

DEAR SIR,

I beg to inform you that something happened last night, which we can't explain, nor the Police neither. All the furniture has come back, absolutely everything down to the smallest bits. The house is now just as it was the evening before the burglary. It's it to send you off your head. It all happened on the night between Friday and Saturday. The paths are cut up as if everything had been dragged from the garden gate to the front door. It was just the same the day it all disappeared.

> I await your return and remain,
>
> Yours respectfully,
>
> PHILIP RAUDIN.

No! No! No! I will *not* return there!

I took the letter to the Chief Inspector of Rouen.

'It's a very neat restitution,' he said. 'We'll lie doggo and we'll nab the fellow one of these days.'

*

But he has not been nabbed. No! They've never got him, and now I'm afraid of him, as if a wild animal were loose on my track. He can't be found! He'll never be found, this monster with the

bald head like a full moon. They'll never catch him. He'll never g[ ]
back to his shop. Why should he? Nobody but me *can* meet hi[m]
and I won't. I won't! I won't! I won't!

And if he does go back, if he returns to his shop, who will [be]
able to prove that my furniture was ever there? There's only m[y]
evidence and I've a feeling that is becoming suspect.

No! My life was getting impossible. And I couldn't keep th[e]
secret of what I had seen. I couldn't go on living like everyone els[e]
with the fear that this sort of thing might begin again at an[y]
moment.

I went and consulted the doctor who keeps this Mental Hom[e]
and told him the whole story.

After putting me through a lengthy examination, he said:

'My dear Sir, would you be willing to stay here for a time?'

'I should be very glad to.'

'You're not short of money?'

'No, Doctor.'

'Would you like a bungalow to yourself?'

'Yes, I should.'

'Would you like your friends to come and see you?'

'No, Doctor, no one. The man from Rouen might venture [to]
follow me here to get even with me.'

*

And I have been here alone for three months, absolutely alon[e]
I have practically no anxieties. I am only afraid of one thing. . .
Supposing the second-hand dealer went mad ... and suppose [he]
was brought to this Home. ... Even prisons are not absolute[ly]
safe ...

THE HAUTOTS, FATHER
AND SON

I

THE house, half farm, half manor, was one of those country places neither one thing nor the other, which were once almost noblemen's mansions and are now occupied by farmers in a big way. In front of the door the dogs, tied up to the apple-trees in the courtyard, were yelping and barking at the sight of the game-bags carried by the keeper and some small boys. In the large room which served as both kitchen and dining-room, the two Hautots, father and son, M. Bermont, the collector of taxes, and M. Mondaru, the lawyer, were having a snack and a glass of wine before starting out, for it was the opening of the shooting season.

Hautot senior, proud of everything he owned, was already boasting of the game which his guests would find on his estates. He was a stalwart Norman, one of those powerful, full-blooded, large-boned men who can lift an apple-cart on their shoulders. Half peasant, half gentleman, rich, respected, influential, used to getting his own way, he had kept his son, César Hautot, at school till he reached the third form, so that he should not be illiterate, before taking him away for fear of his becoming a gentleman with no interest in the land.

César Hautot, nearly as tall as his father but slighter, was a model son, obedient, always cheerful and full of admiration, respect, and deference for his father's wishes and opinions.

M. Bermont, the collector of taxes, a portly little man whose red cheeks were streaked with thin purple veins like the tributaries, and the winding course of rivers on maps, asked:

'And what about hares? Are there any?'

Old Hautot replied:

'As many as you like, especially down in Puysatier Bottom.'

'Where do we start?' enquired the lawyer, a fat pasty-faced man who did himself well and was beginning to develop a paunch; he was wearing a brand new shooting suit bought in Rouen the week before, which was rather tight.

'Oh! over there, in the low-lying ground; we'll drive the partridges out into the open and shoot from higher up.'

Old Hautot got up. The others followed suit, picked up their guns which were standing in the corners of the room, examined the hammers, stamped their feet in order to get comfortable in their boots which were a bit hard, not yet softened by the heat of the foot, and went out; the dogs, straining at their leash, barked shrilly, beating the air with their forepaws.

They started for the low ground. It was a small valley or rather an undulating stretch of poor country, left uncultivated, intersected with ravines full of bracken, affording excellent cover.

The guns spaced themselves out with old Hautot on the right and his son on the left and the two guests in the centre of the line. The gamekeeper and the boys carrying the game-bags followed behind. It was the solemn moment of waiting for the first shot, when the heart beats a little faster and the finger is nervously feeling the trigger.

Suddenly a shot rang out. Old Hautot had fired. They all halted and saw a partridge break away from a covey in full flight and fall into a ravine full of dense scrub. In his excitement the old man broke into a run, plunging forward, tearing away the brambles that stood in his way, and presently disappeared in the undergrowth in search of his bird.

Almost immediately a second shot was heard.

'Ah! the cunning old dog!' cried M. Bermont, 'he must have started a hare down there.'

Everyone waited, their eyes glued to the impenetrable tangle of branches.

The lawyer, using his hands like a megaphone, shouted: 'Have you got them?' There was no answer from old Hautot; and César, turning to the gamekeeper, said: 'You go and help him, Joseph; we must keep in line, we'll wait.'

And Joseph, a dried-up old man like a gnarled tree-trunk, whose

nts all stood out like knobs, went quietly off, down into the
vine, threading his way carefully through the breaks in the scrub
e a fox. Suddenly he shouted:

'Come, quick! there's been an accident.'

They all ran forward and plunged into the undergrowth. Old
Hautot was lying on his side unconscious, holding his stomach
th both hands, while a stream of blood was pouring on to the
ass through his linen jacket where it had been torn by the shot.
e had let go of his gun to pick up the dead partridge within reach
his hand and the shock of its fall had discharged the second barrel
ll into his stomach. They lifted him out of the ditch and took off
s clothes, and found a gaping wound with his entrails hanging
t. After bandaging him as best they could, they carried him home
d waited for the doctor, who had been sent for with a priest.

When the doctor came, he shook his head gravely and, turning
young Hautot who was sobbing in a chair, he said:

'My poor boy, things look pretty bad.'

But when the dressing was finished, the wounded man's fingers
itched; he opened his mouth, then his eyes, and looked round
e room with a blank unseeing gaze, as if searching in his memory
recall and realize what had happened; and he murmured:

'My God! my number's up!'

The doctor was holding his hand.

'Not a bit of it, not a bit of it! A few days in bed and you'll be as
as a fiddle!'

But Hautot went on:

'No, my number's up! My stomach's shot away; I know all
out it.'

Then he added suddenly:

'I want to talk to my son, if I've got time.'

Young Hautot could not restrain his sobs and kept repeating like
small child: 'Daddy, Daddy, poor Daddy!'

His father went on in a stronger voice:

'Come along now, stop crying; it's not the time for tears; I want
talk to you. Sit here quite close to me; it won't take long and I
all get a weight off my mind. Will you all leave us, please?'

They all went out, leaving father and son together.

As soon as they were alone, the old man said:

'Listen, my son; you are twenty-four and one can tell yo
things. In any case there's not really as much mystery about it
we are accustomed to pretend. You know your mother died seve
years ago and I am only forty-five now, as I married at ninetee
You know that?'

The son stammered:

'Yes, I know.'

'Your mother died seven years ago and I was left a widowe
Well, a man like me can't live alone at thirty-seven. See?'

'Yes, I see.'

The father, breathing with difficulty, his pale face twisted wi
agony, went on:

'My God, this pain! Well, you know what I mean. A man isn
made to live like a monk, but I wouldn't marry again —
had promised your mother that. So . . . you understand what
mean?'

'Yes, father.'

'Well, I found a girl in Rouen, Rue de l'Éperlan, number eig
teen, third floor, second door — I'm telling you everything, don
forget it — a girl who couldn't have been nicer to me, affectionat
loving, a real good wife to me, in fact. You're taking in what I'
telling you, my boy?'

'Yes, father.'

'So, if I die, I owe her something, something substantial that sh
can live on. You understand?'

'Yes, father.'

'I tell you, she's a good girl, a real good sort and, if it hadn't bee
for you and the memory of your mother and this house where we a
three lived together, I should have brought her here and marrie
her, I promise you. Listen . . . listen, my boy . . . I might have ma
a will, but I haven't . . . I wouldn't do it . . . some things . . . thing
like this oughtn't to be put in writing . . . it's too painful for th
family . . . it causes all sorts of trouble . . . and everybody
unhappy. Legal documents are no good; never use them. If I'

rich to-day, it's because I've never used them all my life. You understand, my son?'

'Yes, father.'

'There's something else . . . listen carefully. Well, I've not made a will, I wouldn't . . . and I know you, you've got a good heart, you're generous and free with your money . . . see? I said to myself that before I died I would tell you everything and ask you not to forget the girl – Caroline Donet, Rue de l'Éperlan number eighteen, third floor, second door . . . don't forget – and there's something more; go there as soon as I am gone – and see to it that she has no cause to regret my memory. You have the means, you can do it, I'm leaving you enough . . . oh! listen . . . during the week you won't find her, she works at Mme Moreau's, Rue Beauvoisine. Go on Thursday, that's the day she expects me; Thursday has been my day with her for six years. Poor little girl, won't she cry just! . . . I'm telling you all this, because I know you well, my son. These are things one doesn't tell everyone, one doesn't tell a lawyer or a priest. Everybody does them and everybody knows about them, but they aren't mentioned, except when it can't be avoided. So no outsider must be let into the secret, only the family, because the family is really one person. See?'

'Yes, father.'

'You promise?'

'Yes, father.'

'You swear?'

'Yes, father.'

'I beg and implore you, son, don't forget. It's my dearest wish.'

'I won't forget, father.'

'You'll go yourself. I want you to do the whole thing yourself.'

'Yes, father.'

'And then you'll see . . . you'll see . . . she'll explain everything. I can't tell you any more. You've sworn?'

'Yes, father.'

'All right, my son. Kiss me. Good-bye. I'm going to turn up my toes, I'm quite certain of it. Tell them to come in.'

Young Hautot kissed his father with tears in his eyes; then, obedient as always, he opened the door and the priest entered in his white surplice, bearing the holy oils.

But the dying man had closed his eyes and refused to open them again; he refused to answer or show even by a sign that he was conscious.

He had said all he had to say and, strong as he was, he was exhausted. Moreover he felt at peace with the world and wanted to be left alone to die undisturbed. Why should he confess to God's deputy, when he had just made his confession to his son, who was one of the family?

The last rites were administered, he was sprinkled with holy water and given absolution surrounded by his farm-hands on their knees, but not a movement of his features revealed that he was still alive.

He died about midnight after four hours of convulsive twitching, indicative of intense suffering.

II

The funeral took place on Tuesday, the shooting season having opened on Sunday. When he got home after driving his father to the cemetery, César Hautot spent the rest of the day in tears. He hardly slept at all the following night and felt so depressed when he woke up, that he wondered how he could go on living.

All day, however, he kept on thinking that, to carry out his father's dying wish, he must go to Rouen next day and see this girl, Caroline Donet, who lived at number 18 Rue de l'Éperlan, third floor, second door. He had repeated under his breath, as one mumbles a prayer, the name and address over and over again in order not to forget them, till, in the end, he couldn't stop muttering the words mechanically again and again or turn his mind to anything at all, his tongue and his thoughts being obsessed by the phrase.

Accordingly next morning about eight o'clock he ordered Barleycorn to be put in the gig and set off at a brisk trot behind the powerful Percheron down the main road from Ainville to Rouen. He was wearing his black frock-coat with his big top-hat on his head and his trousers with under-straps. In the circumstances he had been unwilling to put on over his best suit the blue blouse which bellies out in the wind and protects the black broad-cloth from dust and spots and which is hurriedly slipped off on arrival, as soon as the wearer has alighted from the vehicle.

He got into Rouen as ten o'clock was striking, stopped, as he always did, at the Good Companions Hotel in the Rue des Trois Mares and had to endure the effusive condolences of the host, his wife and his five sons, for the sad news had spread; after that he had to give full details of the accident, which made him cry; he refused the help which they were all eager to offer, knowing that he was now a rich man, and declined lunch at the hotel, which offended them.

After dusting his hat, brushing his frock-coat and cleaning his boots, he went off to look for the Rue de l'Éperlan, not daring to ask anyone the way for fear of being recognized and arousing suspicion.

Finally, not being able to find it, he saw a priest and enquired of him, trusting to the professional discretion of the Church.

He had only a hundred yards to go – it was the second turning on the right.

Then he hesitated. Up to this point he had obeyed the dead man's wishes blindly like an animal. Now he felt all upset, uncomfortable, humiliated at the prospect of finding himself, the legitimate son, face to face with the woman who had been his father's mistress. All the accumulation of moral prejudices stored up in his subconscious mind by centuries of traditional teaching, all that he had learnt from the days of his catechism about these immoral creatures, the instinctive contempt of every man for the whole sex, even if he marries one of them, his peasant's narrow puritanism, all these feelings stirred in him, holding him back, making him ashamed and bringing a blush to his cheek.

But he reflected: 'I promised father; I must keep my word.' So he pushed the door of number 18 which was ajar, revealing a dark staircase; he went up three flights, saw a door, then a second, found a bell-rope and pulled it.

The tinkle of the bell in a near-by room made him shiver. The door opened and he found himself face to face with a young woman, nicely dressed, dark with a fresh complexion, who looked at him in surprise.

He did not know what to say to her and she, not suspecting anything and waiting for him to speak, did not ask him in. They looked at one another in silence for half a minute:

At last she asked:

'What can I do for you, Sir?'

He murmured:

'I am young Hautot.'

She started, turned pale and stammered, as if she had known him for years:

'M. César Hautot?'

'Yes.'

'Well . . .?'

'I've got a message from my father.'

She exclaimed: 'Oh, my God!' and drew back so that he could come in. He shut the door and followed her.

He noticed a little boy of four or five, sitting on the floor playing with a cat in front of a range, from which rose the steam of food keeping hot.

'Sit down,' she said.

He sat down. . . . She asked: 'Well . . .?'

He sat there not daring to begin his story, his eyes fixed on the table in the centre of the room, laid for three, one place being for a child. He looked at the chair with its back to the fire, the plate, the napkin, the glasses, a bottle of red wine partly drunk and a bottle of white wine unopened. It was his father's place, with his back to the fire! Everything was ready for him. It was his father's piece of bread that he saw and recognized by the side of the fork, for the crust had been removed because of the bad state of Hautot's teeth. Then, raising his eyes, he noticed on the wall his father's portrait,

he large photograph taken in Paris in the Exhibition year, the same
one that hung over the bed in his room at Ainville.

The young woman broke the silence:

'Well, M. César . . . ?'

He looked at her. Anxiety had made her pale as death and she
waited, her hands trembling with apprehension.

At last he took the plunge.

'Well, Mam'zelle, Daddy died on Sunday, the opening day of the
shooting season.'

She was so flabbergasted that she did not move. After a few
seconds' silence she murmured in an almost inaudible voice:

'It can't be true!'

And suddenly tears started to her eyes and, raising her hands, she
covered her face and began to sob.

The child looked round and, seeing his mother in tears, began to
howl. Presently, realizing that this strange man was the cause of the
sudden outburst, he rushed at César and, seizing his trousers with
one hand, he pounded his leg with the other as hard as he could.
And César, not knowing what to do and deeply moved, sat there
between the woman weeping for his father and the child defending
his mother. His eyes filled with tears and he felt he was going to cry:
so, to recover his self-possession, he began to talk.

'Yes,' he said, 'the tragedy occurred on Sunday morning about
eight o'clock. . . .' And he told the story, as if she was capable of
taking it in, not omitting anything, with a peasant's meticulous
accuracy of detail. And the child went on attacking him all the time,
now kicking at his ankles.

When he came to the moment when old Hautot had spoken
of her, she caught her own name, and, uncovering her face,
asked:

'I'm sorry, I wasn't listening and I want to know everything . . .
I wonder if you would mind beginning again.'

He began again, repeating the same phrases: 'The tragedy
occurred on Sunday morning about eight o'clock . . .'

He told the whole story at great length, with pauses, full stops
and reflections of his own from time to time. She listened eagerly,

appreciating with a woman's intuition all the painful details, starting with horror and constantly ejaculating: 'Oh, my God!' The child, thinking she had calmed down, had stopped striking César to hold his mother's hand and he was listening too, as if he could understand.

When the story was over, young Hautot went on:

'Now we'll fix up between ourselves how to carry out his wishes. Listen, I'm not hard up, he left me quite well off. I don't want you to have any cause to complain.'

But she interrupted quickly:

'Oh! M. César, M. César, not to-day! My heart is broken . . . another time, another day, not to-day! If I accept, please understand it's not for myself . . . No, no, no, I swear it, it's for the child. Anyhow the money must be settled on him.'

In a flash César, startled, guessed the truth and stammered:

'So the child's his?'

'Yes, of course!'

And young Hautot looked at his little half-brother, conscious of strong, somewhat painful feelings which he could not define.

After a long silence, for she was in tears again, César went on in a state of acute embarrassment:

'Well, in that case, Mam'zelle Donet, I'll be getting along. When would it suit you to discuss the matter?'

She exclaimed:

'Oh no! Don't go, don't go, don't leave me alone with Émile! I should die of misery. I've got no one left now, no one except my boy. It's a grim prospect for me, M. César. Look here, sit down. You've got lots more to tell me. You must tell me everything he did at home all the week.'

And César, obedient as always, sat down again.

She pulled up another chair for herself close to his in front of the range, where the dishes were still simmering, took Émile on her knee and plied César with questions about his father, little intimate revealing questions, so that he could not fail to realize instinctively how completely the poor girl had given her whole heart to Hautot.

And following the natural train of his thought, always limited, he came back to the accident, which he described again with all the same details.

When he said: 'He had a hole in his stomach you could have put your two fists into,' she uttered a stifled cry and tears started from her eyes again. César began to cry, too, for tears are infectious, and, as weeping always makes one sentimental, he leant over towards Émile, whose forehead was within reach of his mouth, and kissed him.

His mother, recovering herself, murmured:

'He's a poor little orphan now!'

'So am I,' said César.

Nothing more was said.

But suddenly the young woman's practical instincts as a house-wife, who has to think of everything, were aroused.

'You've probably had nothing to eat this morning, M. César?'

'No, Mam'zelle.'

'Oh! You must be hungry; you must have something to eat!'

'Thank you,' he said, 'I'm not hungry, I've been too miser-able.'

She replied:

'However unhappy one is, one has got to go on living; I know you won't refuse! Besides, you must stay a little longer. When you've gone, I don't know what I shall do.'

He gave way after a half-hearted resistance and, sitting opposite her with his back to the fire, he ate a plate of tripe which was crackling in the oven and drank a glass of red wine. But he would not let her open the white wine.

Several times he wiped the child's mouth, when he got gravy all over his chin.

As he got up to go, he asked:

'When shall I come back to discuss business, Mam'zelle Donet?'

'Thursday next, if that suits you, M. César. Then I shan't lose any working time. I always have Thursdays off.'

'Next Thursday will suit me fine.'

'You'll come to lunch, of course?'

'Oh! I won't promise that!'

'One can talk much better over a meal. And it will give us more time.'

'Right you are! I'll be here at twelve o'clock.'

And he went away, after kissing Émile again and shaking hands with Mlle Donet.

III

The week passed slowly for César Hautot. He had never been alone before and the loneliness seemed unbearable. Up to now he had always lived with his father, following him to the fields like his shadow, seen to it that his orders were carried out, and, if he was away from him for a few hours, they met again at dinner. They spent the evenings smoking their pipes opposite one another, talking horses, cows and sheep, and the handshake they exchanged every morning seemed the symbol of the deep bond of family affection which united them.

Now César was alone. He went the round of the autumn ploughing, always expecting to see the silhouette of his father, gesticulating, rise up on the far side of a level stretch of field. To kill time, he dropped in on his neighbours and told the story of the accident to everyone who had not heard it and sometimes repeated it to those who had. Then, having finished his work and come to the end of his ideas, he would sit down on the side of the road and wonder if life would go on like this always.

He often thought of Mlle Donet. He had liked her. He had found her refined and gentle, in fact the good sort his father had described. Yes, she certainly came up to his idea of a good sort. He had made up his mind to act generously and give her an income of 2,000 francs a year, settling the capital on the child. He was even conscious of a feeling of pleasure at the prospect of seeing her again on Thursday and making arrangements with her. And the idea of this brother of his, this little fellow of five, who was his father's son, though it affected him unpleasantly, at the same time warmed his heart. It was a kind of family he had in this illegitimate little boy, who would never bear the name of Hautot, a family that he could recognize or not as he pleased but which would remind him of his father.

So, when he found himself on the Rouen road on Thursday morning, with Barleycorn's rhythmical trot carrying him towards the town, he felt more lighthearted and at peace with the world than at any time since the tragedy.

Entering Mlle Donet's room, he found the table laid as it had been the week before, the only difference being that the crust had not been cut off the bread.

He shook hands with the young woman, kissed Émile on both cheeks and sat down feeling quite at home, though still sad at heart. He thought Mlle Donet looking a little thin and pale. She must have been crying a great deal. She now seemed a little uncomfortable in his presence, as if she had realized something which she had not felt the week before in the first shock of her grief; and she treated him with exaggerated politeness and in the humility of her sorrow she waited upon him with touching solicitude as if to make up by constant attention for all the kindness he had shown her. They dallied over lunch, talking of the business that had brought him. She did not want to accept so much money. It was too much, far too much. She earned enough to live on herself; all she wanted was that Émile should have something behind him when he grew up.

César insisted and even added a present of a thousand francs for herself to cover her mourning.

After he had finished his coffee, she asked:

'Do you smoke?'

'Yes, I've got my pipe.'

He felt in his pocket. Good Heavens! he had forgotten it! He was quite unhappy, till she offered him a pipe of his father's, which she had got locked up in a cupboard.

He accepted, took it, recognized it, sniffed it, proclaimed it in excellent condition with a quiver in his voice, filled and lighted it. Then he took Émile on his knee and made him 'ride a cock-horse' while she cleared away and put the dirty plates at the bottom of the dresser to wash up when he had gone.

About three o'clock he got up regretfully, quite sad at the idea of going.

'Well, Mam'zelle Donet, I must be saying "Good afternoon" – delighted to have made your acquaintance like this!'

She stood in front of him, blushing, deeply moved, and looked at him, thinking of his father.

'Won't you be coming here again?' she said.

He answered simply:

'Certainly, Mam'zelle, if you'd like me to.'

'Of course, M. César! Would next Thursday suit you?'

'Yes, Mam'zelle Donet.'

'Of course, you'll come to lunch?'

'But . . . well, I will, if you like.'

'That's a date then, M. César; next Thursday at twelve, like to-day.'

'Right, Mam'zelle Donet, Thursday, at twelve.'

MADEMOISELLE FIFI

MAJOR GRAF VON FARLSBERG, the Prussian Commanding Officer, was finishing reading his correspondence, lolling in an upholstered arm-chair with his field boots on the elegant marble mantelpiece, in which, during the three months that he had been in occupation of the Château d'Uville, his spurs had dug two holes which grew deeper every day.

A cup of coffee was steaming on a round marquetry table, stained with liqueurs, charred by cigars and hacked by the penknife of the victorious officer, who would often stop sharpening a pencil to scratch figures or patterns according to the whim of the moment on the polished surface.

When he had finished his letters and glanced through the German newspapers which the quartermaster had just brought in, he got up and went over to the window after throwing three or four huge green logs on the fire, for these gentry were gradually denuding the park of its trees in order to keep warm.

The rain was coming down in sheets, as it only rains in Normandy, just as if an angry god had turned on a tap; the thick curtain of driving rain formed an oblique wall of water, lashing, splashing, drowning everything, the sort of downpour common round Rouen, the shower-bath of France.

The officer looked out for some time over the park, flooded from the swollen Andelle in the distance which had burst its banks. He was drumming a German waltz on the window-pane, when a sound made him turn round; it was his second-in-command, Acting-Captain Baron von Kelweingstein.

The Major was a broad-shouldered giant, with a long full beard flowing over his chest; his whole appearance suggested a martial peacock with the tail on his chin. His eyes were blue and his expression was placid and unemotional; one cheek bore the scar of a sword-cut received in the Austrian War. He had the reputation of being a good sort as well as a good officer.

The Captain, a stout, red-faced little man, bursting out of his uniform, wore his flaming red hair closely trimmed, so that in certain lights his face seemed to give off a phosphorescent glow. Owing to the loss of two teeth, which had been knocked out on festive evening – he could never remember exactly how it happened – he hissed his words thickly, so that sometimes he was hard to understand; and he had a bald patch just on the top of his head like a monk's tonsure, with a fringe of little light auburn curls round a circle of bare skull.

The Major shook hands and swallowed his cup of coffee – the sixth since the morning – at one gulp, as he listened to his subordinate's report on routine matters; then they both went over to the window, declaring that things were pretty grim. The Major, who was placid by nature and had a wife at home, took life as it came, but Captain Baron von Kelweingstein, a confirmed Don Juan, who frequented brothels and was mad on girls, was furious at being cooped up in compulsory chastity for three months in this remote spot.

In answer to a timid knock on the door the Major barked: 'Come in!' and one of the robot batmen appeared in the open door, indicating merely by his presence that lunch was ready.

In the dining-room they found the three subalterns, Lieutenant Otto von Grossling and two Second-Lieutenants, Fritz Scheunaubourg and Marquis Wilhelm von Eyrik, a very short fair young man, overbearing and harsh with the men, hard on the defeated French and explosive as a firearm.

Since he had been in France his friends had always called him Mademoiselle Fifi. This nickname was the result of his ladylike appearance, his slim figure – he looked as though he wore corsets – his pale face with only the suggestion of a sprouting moustache and also the habit he had acquired of expressing his sovereign contempt for people and things by using on every possible occasion the French expression 'Fi, fi donc!' which he articulated with a slight hiss.

The dining-room of the Château d'Uville was a magnificent long room: the antique cut-glass chandeliers, now starred with bullet marks, and tall Flemish tapestries, now slashed with sword-cuts and hanging in rags, revealed the way Mademoiselle Fifi spent his time, when he had nothing to do.

On the walls three family portraits, a knight in armour, a cardinal and a president, had now been given long porcelain pipes, while in a frame whose gold had faded with the years a noble lady in a tight-fitting gown proudly sported a huge moustache in charcoal.

There was little conversation during the officers' lunch in this wrecked room which was darkened by the rain and had a depressing air of defeat about it and an old oak floor as solid as the boards of an inn.

When the pipes were lit and they began to drink after the meal, the talk as usual turned on their boredom. Brandy and liqueurs were passed round and they all tilted back their chairs, sipping their drinks and keeping all the time in the corner of their mouth the long curved stem, which ended in a porcelain bowl painted in a style calculated to please a Hottentot.

As soon as their glasses were empty, they refilled them with an air of weary resignation. But Mademoiselle Fifi always broke his, whereupon a soldier immediately placed another before him.

They were enveloped in a cloud of acrid smoke and seemed to be sinking into a depressed state of alcoholic somnolence, the sullen intoxication of people with nothing to do.

But suddenly the Baron sat up. He could stand it no longer; he swore: 'Damn it all! This can't go on; we must think of something amusing.'

Lieutenant Otto and Second Lieutenant Fritz, who both had typically German heavy features and no sense of humour, replied in unison: 'What, Sir?'

He thought for a moment and then answered: 'What? Well, with the C.O.'s permission, we'll organize a party.'

The Major took his pipe out of his mouth: 'What sort of a party, Captain?'

The Baron went over to him: 'I'll make all the arrangements, Sir. I'll send the Factotum into Rouen to collect ladies; I know where to find them. We'll have the dinner here; we've got everything we want and at least we'll make a night of it.'

The Graf von Farlsberg shrugged his shoulders with a smile: 'You're crazy, old man!'

But all the officers had got up and crowded round the C.O., urging him to agree:

'Do let Captain Kelweingstein fix it up; it's so depressing here.'

At last the Major gave way: 'All right!' he said, and immediately the Baron sent for the Factotum; he was an old N.C.O., who had never been known to laugh but who always carried out his superior officers' orders to the letter, whatever they were.

Standing to attention with an expressionless face, he took the Baron's orders; then he went out and five minutes later a big four-horsed waggon from the baggage train, covered with a miller's dome-shaped tilt, was being driven at full gallop through the pelting rain.

Immediately everyone seemed to wake up; they no longer lolled sleepily in their chairs; the universal look of boredom disappeared and conversation became general.

Although the storm showed no sign of abating, the Major declared that it was getting lighter and Lieutenant Otto stated categorically that the sky was on the point of clearing. Even Mademoiselle Fifi could not sit still, continually getting up and sitting down again. His steely blue eye looked round for something to break. Suddenly his glance fell upon the moustached lady and the blond young beast drew his revolver. 'Anyhow, you shan't see our party,' he cried and without getting up he took aim. Two successive shots pierced the eyes of the portrait.

Then he cried: 'Let's lay a mine!' And there was a sudden silence as if some exciting new interest was occupying the attention of the whole company.

Laying a mine was his own invention, his pet way of breaking things for fun.

On leaving the Château, its lawful owner, Count Fernand d'Amoys d'Uville, had not had time to take away or hide anything, except the silver, which he had buried in a hole in the wall. As he was very rich and lived in princely style, the great drawing-room, which opened out of the dining-room, had looked like a museum gallery before its master's precipitate flight.

There were pictures on the walls, drawings and valuable water-colours, while cabinets on the tables and glass-fronted cases, with countless nicknacks, statuettes, Dresden figures, Chinese grotesques, old ivories and Venetian glass, filled the huge room with a priceless accumulation of collector's pieces.

Now there were hardly any left. Not that they had been looted; that Major Graf von Farlsberg would never have allowed, but from time to time Mademoiselle Fifi used to lay a mine; when that happened, all the officers had five minutes of real fun.

The little Marquis went into the drawing-room to get the materials. He brought back an egg-shell teapot, Chinese 'famille rose', which he filled with gunpowder, delicately inserting a long fuse through the spout; after putting a match to it, he ran back with the infernal machine into the adjoining room.

He was back in a few seconds, shutting the door behind him. All the Germans stood up and waited with an inane smile of childish expectation. As soon as the detonation had shaken the Château, they rushed in together.

Mademoiselle Fifi, who led the rush, clapped his hands in an ecstasy of delight before a terra-cotta Venus, whose head had at last been blown off; and everyone picked up bits of china, studying with interest the strange shapes of the jagged fragments, examining the fresh damage done, disqualifying some pieces as the remains of the previous explosion. The Major cast a fatherly eye over the huge salon littered with broken artistic treasures, as if some Nero had turned a machine-gun on to the room. He went out first, saying good-humouredly: 'To-day's mine has been a great success.'

But such a cloud of smoke had belched into the dining-room, mingling with the tobacco smoke, that no one could breathe. The Major opened the window and all the officers, who had come back for a last glass of brandy, crowded round it.

A gust of damp air came in, bringing with it the dank smell of flooded fields and a mist of moisture which settled on their beards.

They watched the tall trees bending before the storm, the broad valley shrouded in fog, as the dark low clouds discharged their burden, and in the far distance the church spire standing up in the torrential rain like a grey needle.

Its bell had not rung since their arrival; the silence of the bell-tower was the only resistance the invaders had met. The curé had made no difficulty about billeting and feeding the Prussian soldiers; indeed he had several times accepted an invitation to join him over a bottle of beer or claret from the enemy commander, who often used him as a friendly liaison agent. But he refused to allow any ringing of his bell; he would have let himself be shot sooner. It was his form of protest against the invasion, a passive silent protest, the only one a priest could make, being a man of peace and not of blood, as he put it. And everybody for thirty miles round was proud of the heroic stand made by the Abbé Chantavoine, who had the courage to emphasize and proclaim the public mourning by the obstinate silence of his church bell.

The whole village, inspired by this passive resistance, was ready to support their priest to the full and face the consequences, considering this mute protest as a vindication of the national honour. The peasants felt that they had deserved better of their country than Belfort and Strasbourg, that they had set as noble an example and that the name of their hamlet would be immortalized. Apart from this they complied with all the demands of the Prussian conquerors.

The Major and his officers used to laugh together over this innocuous exhibition of defiance; and, as the whole countryside proved amenable and obedient, they made no bones about putting up with this conspiracy of patriotic silence.

The little Marquis Wilhelm was the only one who would have liked to insist on the bell being rung. He was furious at the politic consideration of his superior officer for the priest's feelings; and every day he begged the Major to let him ring the bell just once, only just once, for fun. He made his request with the insinuating appeal of a cat and with all the wiles of a woman and the persuasive soft-voiced insistence of a mistress determined to get her way.

But the Major stuck to his guns and Mademoiselle Fifi had to lay mines in the Château d'Uville to console himself.

The five men stood close together by the open window for several minutes, breathing the damp air. At last Lieutenant Fritz remarked with a hoarse laugh: 'The ladies won't have nice weather for their drive!'

Then the party broke up, each one going on duty, while the Captain had a great deal to see to in preparation for the dinner.

When they met again at nightfall, they all laughed at the general smartness; their buttons were polished as if for a ceremonial parade, their hair was oiled and scented, and they had all had a bath. The Major's hair seemed less grey than in the morning and the Captain had shaved, only keeping his moustache like a line of fire on his upper lip.

They left the window open in spite of the rain; and from time to time someone would go and listen. At ten minutes past six the Baron reported a rumbling in the distance. They all crowded to the window; and soon the heavy waggon drove up at full gallop, the four horses plastered with mud, steaming and panting.

Five women got out on the terrace, five good-looking girls carefully picked by one of the Captain's friends, to whom the Factotum had delivered his officer's card.

They had made no difficulties about coming, sure of being well paid; moreover, they had got to know the Prussians during the three months that they had had dealings with them, putting up with the men as they put up with the general situation. 'It's all in the day's work,' they had told each other, as they drove out, no doubt in order to stifle any qualms of conscience that remained.

They went straight to the dining-room. With the lamps lit, its dilapidated appearance was even more depressing than usual; the table loaded with food and the expensive china and silver, which had been found in the wall where the owner had hidden it, made the place look like a robbers' den prepared for supper with the loot from a successful raid. The Captain, beaming, took charge of the girls with an expert's assurance, appraising them, kissing them, sniffing them, assessing their value from a professional point of view. And, when the three younger officers were anxious to choose one each, he refused firmly to allow it, insisting on allotting them fairly according to rank, so as to preserve official army precedence.

In order to avoid all discussion or dispute and all suspicion of favouritism, he sized them as if on parade, and addressing the tallest he barked: 'Your name?'

She answered, raising her voice: 'Pamela.'

He announced: 'Number one, by name Pamela, allotted to the Commanding Officer.'

Next, after kissing the second one, Blondine, to indicate that she was his property, he offered Lieutenant Otto the stout Amanda; he gave Eva, the Tomato, to Second Lieutenant Fritz, and Rachel, the shortest of all, who was very young and dark, with coal-black eyes, a Jewess, whose snub nose was the exception that proves the rule that all the Chosen Race have hooked noses, he assigned to the most junior officer, the slim Marquis Wilhelm von Eyrik.

The three younger officers were eager to take their girls off upstairs at once, on the pretext of offering them brushes and soap, to repair the ravages of the drive. But the Captain wisely refused to allow this, saying that they were tidy enough to sit down and that those who went up would want to change partners, when they came down, and that would upset the pairing. They bowed to his superior experience and contented themselves with plenty of anticipatory kisses.

Suddenly Rachel choked, coughing till she cried and blowing smoke out of her nose. The Marquis, pretending to kiss her, had blown a puff of smoke into her mouth. She did not protest and said nothing, but she glared at her partner with a glint of anger in her dark eyes.

They all sat down; even the Major seemed to be enjoying himself thoroughly; he put Pamela on his right and Blondine on his left, saying as he unfolded his napkin: 'This was a capital idea of yours, Captain Kelweingstein.'

Lieutenants Otto and Fritz made their partners quite nervous with their society manners; but the Baron von Kelweingstein, with the assurance of his wide experience of women, was in great form, using obscene words, as if lit up by his mop of flaming hair. He made love in his guttural French, and his coarse compliments, hissed through the hole where his two teeth were missing, reached the girls in a cloud of saliva.

Anyhow they didn't follow what he said; they only showed a flash of comprehension when he spat out some obscenity or some coarse vulgarism, mutilated by his accent. Then suddenly, with one consent, in a burst of wild laughter, they collapsed into their partner's arms, repeating the words which the Baron went on mispronouncing intentionally, in order to make them repeat the obscenities. The first few bottles of wine had gone to their heads and they shouted out the bawdy phrases with gusto; and, dropping into their normal behaviour by force of habit, they kissed the moustaches of their neighbours to right and left, pinched their arms and uttered shrill screams. They drank out of anyone's glass, singing French catches and bits of German songs which they had picked up in the course of their daily dealings with the enemy.

Soon the men themselves, intoxicated by all these women's bodies exposed to their gaze, asking to be pawed, lost all control, shouting and breaking the crockery, while behind their chairs the soldiers waited on them with expressionless faces.

The Major was the only one who behaved like a gentleman.

Mademoiselle Fifi had taken Rachel on his knee and with cold passion first of all kissed madly the ebony curls on the back of her neck, savouring the exciting warmth and scent of her body in the opening between her dress and her skin; after that he pinched her hard through her clothes till she screamed, with sadistic pleasure, unable to resist the urge to hurt something. Often, too, throwing his arms round her, he crushed her body to his own, pressing his mouth on the moist lips of the Jewess and kissing her till he had to stop for want of breath; suddenly he bit her so hard that blood ran down the girl's chin and dropped on to her frock.

Again she looked him straight in the eyes and, mopping the place, she murmured 'I'll make you pay for this.' He laughed a cruel laugh: 'I'll pay all right!'

They reached dessert and champagne was served. The Major

rose and, with the solemnity with which he would have proposed the health of the Empress Augusta, he gave the toast: 'To our ladies!' This was the first of a series of toasts, given in the language of drunken soldiers, full of bawdy jokes, that sounded even worse in their bad French. They got up one after the other, making great efforts to be witty and amusing; the girls, now so drunk that they could not stand, their eyes misty and their lips slobbering, applauded each sally vigorously. The Captain, wishing, no doubt, to give the drunken orgy an air of gallantry, raised his glass again and cried: 'To our conquest of hearts!'

After that Lieutenant Otto, a regular Black Forest bear, rose to his feet, excited and hopelessly drunk, and, in a sudden fit of alcoholic patriotism, shouted: 'To our conquest of France!'

Intoxicated as they were, the girls received this toast in dead silence and Rachel turned to him, quivering with anger: 'Look here, I know some Frenchmen before whom you wouldn't say that!'

But the little Marquis, who still had her on his knee, laughed with drunken cheerfulness: 'Well, anyway, I've never seen them; as soon as we appear, they clear out.'

The girl in her fury hissed: 'You're a dirty liar!'

For a second he fixed his blue eyes on her as he fixed them on the pictures, when he was shooting holes in the canvas, and began to laugh: 'Well, let's discuss the point, darling; after all, should we be here if they could fight?' And, warming to his subject, he went on: 'We are their masters; France is ours.'

She jumped up from his knee and collapsed on to her own chair; he got up, raised his glass and, leaning forward over the table, repeated: 'France is ours, with the people, the woods, the fields and the houses.'

The others, all quite drunk, in a sudden fit of the brutal enthusiasm of soldiers, seized their glasses and shouted: 'Long live Prussia!' and emptied them at one gulp.

The girls did not protest, silent now and terrified. Even Rachel said nothing, not knowing what to say.

Next the little Marquis balanced his champagne glass, refilled, on he Jewess' head: 'All the women in France are ours, too,' he houted.

She leapt to her feet, so that the glass upset and poured the olden wine over her black hair, like the water at a baptism; it fell o the floor and broke. With trembling lips she glared at the officer, who was still laughing, and stammered, her voice hoarse with nger: 'That's a lie! By God, you'll never have the women of rance.'

He sat down in order to laugh more at his ease and with an ttempt at a Parisian accent said: 'That's good, very good; in that ase, why are you here, darling?'

She was silenced for a minute, not understanding, for her brain vas clouded with the wine; but, as his meaning dawned on her, she ung at him in a fury of indignation: 'Me, me, I'm not a woman, 'm a whore; that's good enough for Prussians!'

She had hardly got the words out, when he boxed her ears oundly, but, as he raised his hand to do it again, mad with rage, he seized a little silver dessert knife off the table and, so quickly hat no one saw what she was doing, plunged it into his neck in the ollow just by the collar-bone.

The word that he was uttering was cut short in his throat and he emained with his mouth open, staring horribly.

There was a general uproar as everybody sprang to their feet; ut, thrusting her chair between Lieutenant Otto's legs so that he neasured his length on the floor, she dashed to the window, flung t open before anyone could get to her and disappeared in the larkness through the rain, which was still falling.

In two minutes Mademoiselle Fifi was dead. Fritz and Otto drew heir swords and wanted to kill the girls, who were clinging to their nees. The Major prevented the massacre with some difficulty and ad the girls shut up in a room guarded by two soldiers; next, as if e was deploying his troops in battle, he organized the pursuit of he fugitive, having no doubt that she would be caught.

Fifty men combed the park, under threats, if they didn't find er; two hundred others searched the woods and the houses in the alley.

The dinner-table was immediately cleared and the body laid out upon it; the four officers, sobered by the shock, stood stiffly near the window with the stern expression of soldiers on duty, peering into the darkness.

The torrential downpour went on. The night was full of the gurgle of water falling and water flowing, pouring down and splashing up.

Suddenly a shot rang out, followed by a second a long way off; for four hours shots were heard at intervals, sometimes close, sometimes far away, and shouts as the sections rallied, strange words shouted by guttural voices as passwords.

In the morning all the soldiers returned. Two men had been killed and three others wounded by their comrades in the excitement of the chase and the confusion of pursuit in the darkness.

Rachel had not been found.

Stern measures were taken against the inhabitants; houses were searched, the whole countryside was combed, gone through, turned upside down. The Jewess seemed to have disappeared into thin air.

The General on being informed gave instructions that the affair must be hushed up to avoid giving a bad example to the army, and he took disciplinary measures against the Major, who passed them on to his subordinates. The General had said: 'One doesn't make war in order to have a good time and make love to prostitues.' And the Graf von Farlsberg in his annoyance determined to have his revenge on the local inhabitants.

As he wanted a pretext to justify severity, he sent for the priest and ordered him to have the church bell rung at the funeral of the Marquis von Eyrik.

Quite unexpectedly the priest raised no objection and obeyed the order humbly. And, as the body of Mademoiselle Fifi left the Château on the way to the cemetery, borne by soldiers with an escort marching with rifles loaded before, behind and on both sides of the coffin, for the first time the church bell rang a funeral peal quite cheerfully, as if a friendly hand was caressing it.

It rang again in the evening, and next day, too, and every day it seemed to enjoy ringing. Sometimes it rang even at night, all by itself, sending out two or three soft notes in the darkness, as if waking up and chuckling to itself at some mysterious joke.

All the peasants thought it was bewitched and no one except the priest and the sexton would go near the belfry.

Actually, a poor prostitute was living up in the tower, all by herself, in constant fear, being fed secretly by the two men.

She stayed there till the Germans left. Then one evening the priest borrowed the baker's cart and himself drove his prisoner to the gate of Rouen. There he kissed her; she got out and hurried back on foot to the brothel, whose owner had given her up for dead.

Some time afterwards she was taken out by a patriot, who had no prejudices and loved her for her brave deed; later he became fond of her for herself and married her, making an honest woman of her, as good as many another.

OLD VESTEY

AT the office old Vestey was considered a bit of a character. He wa
a simple, good-natured old clerk, who had been out of Paris only
once in his life.

It was towards the end of July and every Sunday we all went ou
into the country round to lie about on the grass or bathe. Asnières,
Argenteuil, Chatou, Bougival, Maisons, Poissy, each had its
regular visitors, who all swore by their own particular place. The
attractions and advantages of all these famous beauty-spots, so
beloved of Parisian clerks, were the subject of passionate argument

Old Vestey was always declaring:

'You fellows follow one another like so many sheep. Wonderful
place, your country, I don't think!'

We asked him:

'So, Vestey, you never go out, do you?'

'Excuse me. I do my outings in a bus. After a leisurely lunch in
the wine-merchant's shop on the ground floor, I make out my route
with a map of Paris and a time-table of the bus routes that gives the
connections. Then I climb up on to the top, open my sunshade and
off we go. The things I see! Far more than you ever do. I visit
different quarters. It's as good as a journey round the world; the
inhabitants of one street aren't a bit like those of another. Nobody
knows Paris as well as I do. And there's nothing so entertaining as
the first-floor windows. The things you see in those rooms, as you
pass, you'd never guess. You can imagine the domestic rows just
from the look on the face of a man who has raised his voice; you
roar with laughter as you drive past, at the sight of barbers gazing
out into the street, oblivious of their customer's nose plastered with
soap. You return the glad eye of the girls in dress-shops, just for
fun, because you don't have time to get off. You see all manner of
amusing things!

'It's as good as a play, the simple genuine drama of real life,
as you see it from behind a pair of trotting horses. By Jove, I

wouldn't exchange my bus rides for all your stupid walks in the woods!'

We suggested:

'Just try it, Vestey; come out for once into the country and see what it's like.'

He replied:

'I did once, twenty years ago, and I'm not going to be caught again.'

'Tell us about it, old man!'

'Right you are! This is what happened. You knew Boivin, the clerk who used to vet all the letters; we called him Boileau?'

'Yes, quite well!'

'He worked in the room with me. The old rascal had a house at Colombes and he was always asking me to come out to his place one Sunday; he used to say:

' "Do come, Pantaloon — that was the nickname he gave me as a joke — you'll see what a lovely walk we'll have."

'Well, like a fool, I fell into the trap and set out one morning by the eight o'clock train. I arrived at a sort of town, a town in the country, where it's impossible to find the way about, and finally I discovered at the end of an alley between two walls an old wooden door with an iron bell.

'I rang; after a long wait the door was opened. What was it that opened the door? At first sight I didn't know whether it was a woman or a monkey. She was old and ugly and her clothes were in rags; she seemed dirty and bad-tempered; there were feathers in her hair and she looked as though she would have liked to eat me.

'She demanded:

' "What do you want?"

' "M. Boivin."

' "What do you want M. Boivin for?"

'I felt uncomfortable under the cross-questioning of this fury; I stammered: "But . . . he's expecting me."

'She went on:

' "Oh! you're the bloke who's coming to dinner?"

'I answered with a hesitant "yes".

E 2

'Then, turning round, she shouted into the house in a furious voice:

' "Boivin, here's your guest!"

'This was my friend's wife. Boivin, poor little man, immediately appeared at the door of this lath-and-plaster shack with a corrugated iron roof, which was like a Black Hole. He had on white duck trousers, much stained, and a filthy Panama hat.

'After shaking hands, he took me into what he called his garden; it was at the end of another passage, surrounded by high walls, a little plot about the size of a pocket-handkerchief, shut in by houses so high that the sun only reached it for two or three hours a day. There were pansies, pinks, wallflowers and a few rose-bushes, all struggling to live at the bottom of this airless well, that was like an oven from the heat reflected from the roofs.

' "I've not got any trees," remarked Boivin, "but the walls of the next-door houses do as well; I get as much shade as if I was in a wood."

'He took me by the lapel of my coat and said in a whisper:

' "I want you to do something for me. You've seen my old woman. She's a bit of a Tartar, what! To-day, as you were coming, she's given me clean togs, but, if I get dirty, there'll be the devil to pay. I'm counting on you to water my flowers."

'I agreed, and took off my coat. I turned up my shirt-sleeves and set to work like a black at a kind of pump, which puffed, panted and wheezed like a consumptive and finally only produced a trickle of water like the jet of a drinking fountain. It took ten minutes' hard work to fill a water-can. It made me sweat like a pig. Boivin showed we what to do.

' "Here – this plant – a little more – that's enough; now this one."

'The watering-can had a hole in it and leaked and my feet got more water than the flowers. The bottom of my trouser legs got soaked and plastered with mud. And the process had to be repeated twenty times; I got my feet wet again, I sweated again, as I worked the creaking pump-handle. And, when I was exhausted and wanted to stop, old Boivin pulled me by the arm and begged:

' "One more can – only one more – that'll finish it."

' To show his gratitude he gave me a rose, a fine bloom, but I had hardly put it in my buttonhole when all the petals dropped, leaving me with nothing in my coat but a small green head as hard as a stone; I was dumbfounded but I said nothing.

'Mme Boivin's voice was audible in the distance:

' "When are you coming in? I've told you dinner's ready."

'We made our way to the Black Hole.

'If the garden was in the shade, the house on the contrary was in the blazing sun, and the second sweating room in a Turkish bath isn't nearly as hot as my friend's dining-room.

'Three plates, with badly washed white-metal forks by the side, were sticking to a table of grained wood. In the centre stood an earthenware dish containing boiled beef done up with potatoes, We sat down.

'A large jug of water, just coloured with wine, caught my eye. Boivin, in some confusion, said to his wife:

' "Look here, my dear, just for once won't you let us have some wine without water?"

'She glared at him angrily:

' "So that you can both get drunk, I suppose, and stay in my house all day making a nuisance of yourselves. Just for once, indeed!"

'He subsided. After the stew she served another dish of potatoes, this time with bacon. The second course having been eaten in dead silence, she announced:

' "That's all; now clear out!"

'Boivin looked at her in amazement:

' "But the pigeon . . . the pigeon you were plucking this morning?"

'She stood up with arms akimbo:

' "You've not had enough, I suppose. Because you invite people in that's no reason for eating up everything in the house. What am I going to have this evening?"

'We got up and Boivin whispered in my ear:

' "I'll be with you in a moment and we'll get along."

'He went into the kitchen to which his wife had retired, and I heard the following dialogue:

' "Give me a bob, darling."

' "What do you want a bob for?"

' "One never knows what may happen; it's awkward having no money."

'She raised her voice, meaning me to hear:

' "No, you can't have any money. You've given this fellow dinner; the least he can do is to pay for you the rest of the day."

'Old Boivin came back to me. As I wanted to show that I knew my manners, I bowed to my hostess and stammered:

' "Thank you, Madame, . . . for your kind hospitality."

'She replied:

' "That's all right. But don't bring him home tight, or I shall want to know the reason why."

'We started off.

'We had to cross a level stretch of country as bare as the back of your hand, without any shade. I tried to pick a plant by the side of the path and uttered a cry of pain; it had stung my hand badly – they call the damned things nettles. And there was a stink of manure everywhere, enough to make you sick.

'Boivin kept on saying:

' "Stick to it! We'll be at the river in no time."

'In fact we did reach the river, where there was a vile smell of mud and dirty water, and the sun was blazing down on the water, till my eyes ached.

'I begged Boivin to go in somewhere; he took me to a sort of shack, packed with people, a tavern frequented by riverside watermen. He said:

' "It's not much to look at but they do you well here."

'I was hungry and ordered an omelette. But, lo and behold! Boivin's second glass of wine went to his head, silly fool, and I realized why his wife only let him have wine and water.

'He got up and talked at the top of his voice; he wanted to do conjuring tricks and tried to stop a row between two drunk men who were fighting; we should both have got laid out if the proprietor hadn't intervened.

'I dragged him away, holding him up as you do with intoxicated people, as far as the nearest shade and made him lie down. I lay down beside him and I must have dropped off myself.

'We must have slept a good long time, for it was dark when I woke. Boivin was snoring at my side. I shook him and he got up, but he was still drunk, though not so drunk as before.

'We set off again in the dark across the flat country. Boivin insisted that he knew the way. He made me turn left, then right, then left again. We couldn't see the sky or the ground in front of us, and we got lost in the middle of a forest of poles nose-high; apparently it was a vineyard with the vine-props standing. Not a street-lamp in sight! We walked round in circles, perhaps for an hour or two, turning round, stumbling, feeling our way, at our wits' end, without finding the way out, for we were always having to retrace our steps.

'Finally Boivin fell over a sharp stake, which cut his cheek, and remained, quite contentedly sitting on the ground, giving vent to long loud shouts with all the force of his lungs, while I kept crying "Help!" at the top of my voice and lighting wax vestas to show our rescuers where we were and to keep my pecker up.

'At last a belated peasant heard us and put us on our way. I took Boivin along as far as his house. But, as I was on the point of leaving him at the entrance to his garden, the door burst open and there was his wife, with a candle in her hand. I was terrified.

'As soon as she saw her husband, whom she must have been waiting for since it got dark, she bellowed, making towards me: "You wretched blighter, I knew you'd bring him home tight!"

'You bet I ran for it! And I went on running till I got to the station, where I locked myself in the lavatory, for I thought the fury was after me and there wasn't a train for half an hour.

'That's why I've never married and why I never leave Paris.'

CEMETERY WALKERS

THE five friends were finishing dinner, five middle-aged, well-off men about town, three married and two bachelors. They met like this once a month in memory of their young days, and after dinner they talked on till two o'clock in the morning. Their early friendship had lasted and they enjoyed one another's society, so that this gathering was probably the pleasantest evening in their lives. The conversation ranged over all the topics that interest and amuse Parisians; in their case, as with most salons anyway, it amounted to a re-hash in spoken form of the morning's newspapers.

The life and soul of the party was Joseph de Bardon, a bachelor who lived the life of a man about town in its fullest and most irresponsible form. He was neither a debauchee nor a degenerate but a man interested in everything, who enjoyed life to the full, being still young, for he was hardly forty. A man of the world in the broadest and most charitable sense of the word, he was intelligent but shallow; he had read widely if superficially, and had a butterfly mind which never bothered to get to the bottom of any subject. But his observation and his adventures, everything he saw, his contacts and his discoveries furnished him with a fund of stories at once amusing and reflective and of humorous comment, which gained him a great reputation in town as a wit.

He was always the chief speaker at the dinner. It was always assumed that he would have a story to tell every month. He started on it without waiting to be asked.

Smoking, with his elbows on the table, a half-empty glass of brandy in front of his plate, relaxed in the atmosphere of tobacco scented with the aroma of coffee, he seemed quite at home, as some people are absolutely at home in certain places and at certain times, for example a penitent in a chapel or a goldfish in its bowl.

He said between two puffs of smoke:

'An odd thing happened to me not long ago.'

Everyone cried simultaneously: 'Do tell us about it!'

He went on:

'Right you are. You know I often roam about Paris like collectors who are always searching the shop-windows. What I look for is incidents, people, everything that passes by, everything that happens.

'Well, about the middle of September we had a spell of lovely weather and one afternoon I went out, not knowing where I was going. One always has a vague desire to call on some pretty woman or other. One runs through one's picture-gallery, mentally comparing one with another, weighing the interest each arouses and the charm each exerts; and one's final choice depends on the whim of the day. But, when the sun is shining and the air is balmy, visits of this kind have no attraction.

'The sun was shining and the air was balmy. I lit a cigar and wandered aimlessly along the outer boulevard. Then, as I was strolling on, it occurred to me to go on as far as the Montmartre cemetery and go in.

'I am very fond of cemeteries; they induce a restful melancholy feeling which responds to some need in me. Moreover, there are good friends there, friends one can no longer visit; I still go there from time to time.

'Now it happens that this Montmartre cemetery recalls a love affair of mine, a mistress who meant a great deal to me and of whom I was genuinely fond, a charming little lady, whose memory, though very painful, rouses in me longings ... for all sorts of things ... And I go to dream at her grave ... All is over for her now.

'I am also fond of cemeteries, because they are gigantic towns with huge populations. Just think of all the dead contained in this little space, of all the generations of Parisians housed here for ever, cave-dwellers for all time confined in their tiny vaults and holes in the earth, covered with a stone or marked by a cross, while the living occupy so much space and make such a commotion, fools that they are.

'Moreover, there are almost as many interesting monuments in cemeteries as in museums. Cavaignac's tomb has reminded me, though it is not in the same class, of Jean Goujon's masterpiece, the

effigy of Louis de Brèze, lying in the crypt of Rouen Cathedral.
All so-called modern realistic art derives from it, gentlemen. This
representation of the body of Louis de Brèze is truer, more terrifying, more alive, though carved in stone, still in the convulsions
of his death-agony, than all the tortured contorted bodies on the
tombs of to-day.

'But in the Montmartre cemetery one can still admire the impressive
monument to Baudin; there are also those of Gautier and Murger
on which I saw recently a poor wreath of faded immortelles, put
there, by whom, I wonder? Perhaps by the last shop-girl of his
time, now a very old woman, perhaps a caretaker somewhere close
by. There is an attractive statuette of Millet, uncared for and in a
state of decay. May thy paean of youth never be forgotten, Murger!

'So you must picture me going into the Montmartre cemetery,
suddenly conscious of a surge of melancholy, not entirely painful,
the kind of melancholy that makes you think, when you are in
perfect health yourself: "This place is a bit depressing, but I shan't
be here for a good while yet!"

'The autumnal tang in the air, the warm dampness with the smell
of dead leaves and the pale anæmic sunlight increased the feeling
of loneliness and the transitoriness of human life, which pervaded
the place with its odours of decay, while sublimating it into the
realm of poetry.

'I walked slowly between the rows of graves, where neighbours
have no opportunity for neighbourliness and no longer make love
or read the papers. And I began to read the epitaphs, one of the
most entertaining occupations in the world, I assure you. Neither
Labiche nor Meilhac have ever made me laugh as much as the
language of the ordinary tombstone. Paul de Kock's books never
cause half the amusement of those marble slabs and crosses, on
which the relatives of the deceased advertise their grief, their
prayers for the bliss of the departed in the next world and their
hopes to be with them again soon – not meaning a word of it!

'But the most attractive spot in this cemetery is the disused
portion, full of great yews and cypresses, the old domain of those
long dead, which will soon be used again; they will cut down the

leafy trees, fertilized by human bodies, in order to lay the corpses of to-day in neat rows beneath little marble slabs like so many slabs of gingerbread.

'When I had wandered long enough to cure my melancholy, I realized that I was beginning to get bored and that I must offer my faithful tribute of remembrance at the last resting place of my little friend. As I approached her grave, I was genuinely affected. Poor darling . . . she was so appealing, so passionate, so white, so fresh . . . and now, if one opened the grave . . .

'Leaning on the iron railing, I whispered my grief, which of course she could not hear, and I was just moving away when I noticed a woman in black in full mourning, kneeling at a tomb quite close. Her crape veil was raised, revealing a pretty head with fair hair. It was coiled round the head and shone as if with the rays of the rising sun under the black of her hat. I stayed where I was.

'She was obviously in deep grief. She had buried her face in her hands, oblivious of everything in her sorrow, rigid like a praying statue; no doubt she was recalling tragic memories behind the double curtain of hands and closed eyes, like a nun telling her beads, and she seemed like a dead woman herself, thinking of the dead. Suddenly I saw that she was going to cry by a little movement of the shoulders, like the shiver of wind in a willow. At first she wept silently, then more violently, so that her neck and shoulders shook. All at once she took her hands away from her eyes. They were full of tears and very appealing, like the eyes of a mad woman, as she looked about her, as one does on waking from a nightmare. She saw that I was watching her and seemed ashamed, covering the whole of her face with her hands. Her sobs became convulsive and her head bent slowly forward towards the marble slab. She rested her forehead on it and her veil, spreading out round her shoulders, draped the white corners of the tomb she loved like another pall. I heard her groan and she collapsed with her face on the slab and lay motionless and unconscious.

'I ran towards her, slapped her hands and blew on her eyelids, at the same time reading the simple epitaph: "Here lies Louis Théo-

dore Carrel, Captain of Marines, killed in action in Tonkin. Pray
for his soul."

'The date of the death was only a few months before. I was moved
to tears and redoubled my efforts, which were at last successful, and
she came to. I was looking very concerned – I'm not such a bad-
looking chap and still on the right side of forty. I knew instinctively, as soon as she opened her eyes, that she knew her manners
and would be grateful. She behaved as I expected, still in tears, as
she told me her story in broken sentences between convulsive sobs;
how the officer had been killed in Tonkin after they had been married only a year, a love match, for she was an orphan without father
or mother and had only just got the dowry demanded by Naval
regulations.

'I consoled her and comforted her, raising her to her feet and
supporting her. Then I said:

' "You mustn't stay here; come away."

'She murmured:

' "I'm incapable of walking."

' "I'll give you an arm."

' "Thank you so much; it's most kind of you. You had come to
mourn the dead too?"

' "Yes."

' "A woman?"

' "Yes."

' "Your wife?"

' "No, but someone I loved."

' "One may love someone else as much as a wife; love knows
no law."

' "That is quite true."

'We walked away together along the cemetery paths, she leaning
so heavily on my arm that I was almost carrying her. When we got
ouside, she murmured in a weak voice:

' "I think I'm going to faint."

' "Would you like to go and get something to drink?"

' "Yes, I should."

'I saw a restaurant, one of those places where the friends of the deceased go to cheer themselves up, when the funeral is over. We went in and I made her drink a cup of very hot tea, which seemed to pull her together. A faint smile came to her lips and she told me about herself. It was so depressing and wretched to be all alone in life, all alone at home day and night, not to have anyone left to whom to give one's affection, one's confidences, one's secrets.

'It all sounded genuine and charming as she said it. I became quite emotional. She was very young, perhaps not more than twenty. I paid her some compliments, which seemed to please her. Presently, as time was getting on, I suggested driving her home. She accepted and in the cab we sat so close together, shoulder to shoulder, that we were conscious of the heat of each other's bodies through the clothes – and that is the most exciting thing in the world.

'When the cab stopped at her house, she murmured: "I shan't be able to get upstairs alone, I live on the fourth floor. You have been so kind, I wonder if you would give me an arm up to my flat?"

'I accepted with alacrity. She went up the stairs slowly, getting much out of breath. When we reached her door, she added:

' "Do come in for a minute and let me thank you."

'Of course, I went in.

'It was a modest flat, even suggesting poverty, but everything was in good taste and well arranged.

'We sat down side by side on a little sofa and she spoke again of her loneliness.

'She rang for the maid to get me something to drink. The maid did not appear. I was delighted, supposing that she was only there in the mornings, what is called a "daily". She had taken off her hat. She really was adorable, with her blue eyes fixed on me, so steady and so blue, that I succumbed to an overpowering temptation. I seized her in my arms; she closed her eyes and I kissed them wildly, passionately again and again . . . I even went a little further.

'She struggled and resisted, repeating:

' "Please don't . . . stop!"

'What did she mean? Was there a pause between the last two words? In such circumstances "please don't . . . stop" might mean at least two things. To silence her I transferred my kisses from her eyes to her mouth and assumed that by "please don't ... stop!" she meant what I wanted her to mean. She only put up a show of resistance and, when our eyes met again after this outrage to the memory of the captain who had been killed in Tonkin, there was a look of languid tender contentment on her face, which dissipated any anxiety I might have felt.

'I went on making love to her to show my sincerity and gratitude. After we had chatted for about an hour, I asked:

' "Where do you dine?"

' "In a little restaurant close by."

' "Alone?"

' "Yes, of course."

' "Will you come and dine with me?"

' "Where?"

' "At one of the big restaurants in the fashionable quarter."

'At first she refused but soon yielded to my insistence, satisfying her qualms of conscience with the argument: "I do get so bored all alone"; then she added: "I must put on something a little less depressing." And she retired to her bedroom.

'When she came back she was in half-mourning, charming, elegant and slim in a very simple grey frock. She obviously kept different clothes for the cemetery and the town.

'Dinner was a friendly meal. She drank champagne, became gay and animated, and I went back with her to her flat.

'The affair which had started in the cemetery lasted about three months. But one gets tired of everything, especially women. I left her with the excuse that I had to leave Paris. I made it well worth her while, when I went away, and she was duly grateful. She made me promise, even swear to come back to her on my return; she really seemed quite fond of me.

'I transferred my affections elsewhere, and a month passed without the desire to see my little cemetery friend again becoming too strong to resist. But I did not forget her. The thought of her haunted me like a mysterious psychological riddle, one of those unsolved problems one feels one must unravel.

'I don't know why, but one day I felt that I should find her in the Montmartre cemetery again, and I went there.

'I walked for a long while without meeting anyone except the usual types of us, the people who have not yet severed all emotional connection with those they have loved and lost. The grave of the captain killed in Tonkin had no mourner that day; there were no flowers or wreaths on the marble slab.

'But as I was wandering in another quarter of this labyrinthine city of the dead, I suddenly saw at the far end of a narrow avenue of crosses a couple coming towards me, both in full mourning. To my amazement, as they approached, I recognized the woman. It was she!

'She saw me and blushed; and, as I brushed against her as we passed, she gave me a tiny signal, just a flicker of the eyelid, which meant: "You mustn't recognize me," but also conveyed: "Come and see me again, darling!"

'The man was a gentleman of distinguished appearance, well dressed and an Officer of the Legion of Honour, about fifty.

'He was giving her his arm, just as I had done when we were leaving the cemetery.

'I walked on nonplussed, wondering what was the meaning of what I had just seen, to what species of the human race this woman belonged, who hunted among the tombs. Was she a common prostitute, a woman who had had the bright idea of picking up in the cemetery men who were sad, haunted by the memory of some woman, wife or mistress, and unable to forget the happiness they had lost? Was she the only one or are there several of them? Is it a recognized branch of the profession? Do they walk the cemeteries as they walk the streets? Are there regular cemetery walkers? Or was she the only one who has had this brilliant idea, showing a profound grasp of psychology, of exploiting memories of those loved and lost, made suddenly more poignant by these surroundings?

'And I should have liked to know whose widow she was that day!'

MISS HARRIET

THERE were seven of us in the brake, four women and three men, one on the box seat beside the driver, and the horses were making their way up the steep hill by the zigzag road at a walk.

Having left Etretat at dawn for a visit to the ruins of Tancarville, we were still half asleep, drowsy in the keen morning air. The women especially, unaccustomed to getting up at the hour at which men go out shooting, were continually letting their eyes close and their heads fall forward or yawning, blind to the beauty of the sunrise.

It was autumn. On both sides of the road stretched bare fields, yellow with the stubble of the oats and wheat already cut which covered the ground like a bristly beard. A light mist lay over the earth like smoke. Larks were singing in the sky and other birds twittering in the bushes.

At last the sun rose in front of us, fiery red as it topped the horizon, and as it climbed, brighter every minute, the countryside seemed to wake up with a smile and shake itself, putting off its night garment of white mist like a girl getting out of bed.

The Comte d'Etraille who was sitting on the box cried: 'Look, there's a hare!' pointing to a patch of clover on the left. The animal was moving almost hidden by the grass, only its long ears showing; presently it dashed across a ploughed field, stopped, went off again at full speed, changed direction, stopped again, nervously on the look out for danger, uncertain which way to go; finally it started off again with great leaps of its hind-quarters and disappeared in a broad patch of beet. All the men roused themselves to watch the animal's course.

René Lemanoir commented: 'We've forgotten our manners this morning,' and looking at his neighbour, the little Baronne de Sérennes, who was struggling against sleep, whispered to her: 'You're thinking of your husband, Baronne. Don't worry, he won't be back till Saturday; you've got four days more.'

She answered with a sleepy smile: 'Don't be silly!' And, shaking off her drowsiness, she added: 'Now tell us something to amuse us. You are always supposed to have more luck than the Duc de Richelieu, Monsieur Chenal; tell us the story of one of your love affairs, anything you like.'

Léon Chenal, an old painter, who had been a very strong, good-looking man, exceedingly proud of his physique and very successful with women, stroked his long white beard and smiled; then, after a moment's thought, he became serious again.

'It won't be an amusing story, ladies; I'll tell you about the most tragic affair in my life. I hope no friend of mine may ever inspire such a passion.'

I

I was twenty-five at the time and was making a sketching trip along the Normandy coast.

By sketching trip I mean wandering about from inn to inn with one's luggage on one's back, pretending to be doing studies from nature and landscapes. This unplanned vagabond life is the best I know. You are absolutely free of all restraint, with no anxieties, no worries, no need even to take thought for the morrow. You take any road that attracts, following the whim of the moment, in search of nothing but beauty. You stop because a stream appeals to you or because the smell of fried potatoes at the door of some inn is good. Sometimes it was the scent of clematis that decided your choice, sometimes a barmaid's welcoming smile. Don't despise these country affairs. These girls have souls and passions too, firm cheeks and fresh lips; and their rough kisses are intoxicating and sweet as wild fruit. Love is always worth while, wherever it comes from. A heart that beats quicker when you appear, an eye that sheds a tear at your departure are things so rare, so sweet, so precious that they should never be despised.

I have known trysts in ditches covered with primroses, behind the shed where the cows were asleep, on the straw in barns still warm with the sun's heat. I have memories of coarse grey linen on firm strong bodies and a longing for simple natural caresses, more

thrilling in their honest clumsiness than the sophisticated pleasure
to be obtained from the charms of society ladies.

But what is most attractive in such random wanderings is the
countryside, the woods, the sunrise, the gloaming and the moonlight. They are the painter's honeymoon with the earth. You are
alone, very close to her in a long, peaceful lovers' tryst. You lie
down in a meadow on a bed of daisies and poppies, and before
closing your eyes in the blazing sunshine you look at the little
village in the distance with its pointed clock-tower striking
twelve.

You sit down beside a spring at the foot of an oak in a tangle of
tall feathery grass, gleaming and alive. You kneel and bend down
to drink the cool water which wets the moustache and nose, drinking with a sense of physical enjoyment as if kissing the spring, lip
to lip. Sometimes you find a pool in one of these tiny streams and
you dive in, naked, feeling as it were a deliciously cool caress, as the
gentle current strokes the body like a thing alive.

On a hill-top you are cheerful, melancholy beside a pond,
thrilled when the sun sets in a sea of blood-red clouds, reflected
crimson in the rivers. And in the evening under a moon sailing in
the zenith you have a thousand strange dreams which would never
enter the mind in the blazing heat of the day.

Well, as I was wandering like this over the very country where
we are this year, I came one evening to the tiny village of Bénouville, on the cliff between Yport and Etretat. I was coming from
Fécamp along the coast, that high straight coast-wall with its out-
crops of chalk, which plunge sheer into the sea. Since morning I
had been walking on the short turf, fine and springy as a carpet,
which grows up to the cliff edge under the salt sea wind. Singing at
the top of my voice as I strode along, watching now the slow
sweeping flight of a gull, with the white curve of its wings silhouetted against the sky, now the brown sail of a fishing-boat
against the jade-green of the sea, I had spent a day of unalloyed
happiness without a care in the world.

I was directed to a small farm-house, where travellers could
put up, a sort of inn kept by a peasant-woman; it stood in the

centre of a Normandy courtyard surrounded by a double row of
beeches.

So, leaving the cliffs I made my way to the hamlet in the shelter
of its tall trees and knocked at Mother Lecacheur's door.

She was an old peasant-woman, wrinkled and unsmiling, who
always seemed annoyed and distrustful at the sight of a visitor.

It was May at the time; apple-trees in bloom shaded the courtyard with a roof of scented blossom, raining down on the grass or
those who passed beneath them a shower of pink petals.

I asked: 'Well, Madame Lecacheur, have you got a room for
me?' Surprised at my knowing her name, she replied: 'That
depends; I'm full up. But we might manage something.'

In five minutes everything was fixed up and I put down my
rucksack on the earth floor of a primitive room, whose furniture
consisted of a bed, two chairs, a basin and a table. It opened off the
large smoky kitchen, where the guests had their meals with the
farm-hands and their mistress, who was a widow.

I washed my hands and came out again. The old woman was
frying a chicken for dinner in the open fire-place, where hung a
smoke-blackened pot-hook.

'So you've got other guests,' I said.

'We's got one middle-aged lady from England; she be in t'other
bedroom,' she answered crossly.

For an extra sixpence a day I secured the right to have my meals
alone in the courtyard when it was fine.

So my place was laid just outside the door and I began to dis-
member the skinny Normandy chicken with my teeth, washing it
down with golden cider and munching the coarse white bread, four
days old but still excellent.

Suddenly the wooden garden gate on to the road opened and a
strange figure advanced towards the house. She was very thin, very
tall and swathed so tightly in a red tartan shawl that one would have
thought she had no arms, had not one long hand been visible on the
level of her hips, holding the typical tripper's sunshade. Her face
resembled a mummy's, framed in grey sausage curls which bobbed
up and down as she walked, and for some reason reminded me of a

kipper tied up with curl papers. She walked rapidly past me with lowered eyes and disappeared into the cottage.

This strange apparition amused me; it was obviously the middle aged Englishwoman of whom my hostess had spoken.

I did not see her again that day. Next morning, when I had settled down to paint at the bottom of the charming valley you all know which runs down to Etretat, I suddenly looked up and saw a strange figure standing on the top of the cliff like a dressed flag staff. It was she. When she saw me, she disappeared.

I went back at midday for lunch and sat down at the common table in order to make the acquaintance of this old eccentric, but she made no answer to my advances, taking no notice of my atten tions. I kept her glass filled with water and passed her the dishes with persistent politeness. A slight, almost imperceptible nod and a word in English, murmured so low that I couldn't catch it, were all the thanks I got.

I gave up the struggle, though she intrigued me.

Three days later I knew as much about her as Madame Lecacheur herself.

Her name was Miss Harriet. Looking for a quiet village in which to spend the summer, she had stopped at Bénouville six weeks before and seemed to have no intention of moving on. She never spoke at meals, eating quickly and reading a little Protestant tract. She made a habit of distributing these pamphlets to all and sundry. The village priest himself had received four delivered by a little boy to whom she had given a penny for his trouble. Sometimes, without any introduction, she would say to our hostess in her bad French: 'I love the Lord above everything; I adore him in all His creation. I worship Him in all nature, I always carry Him in my heart.' And she handed the woman, who didn't know what to say, one of the booklets intended to convert the world.

They didn't like her in the village; the schoolmaster had called her an atheist, so that she was under a cloud of disapproval. Madame Lecacheur consulted the priest, who replied: 'She is a heretic, but God desireth not the death of a sinner and I believe her to be a person of strict morals.'

The words 'atheist' and 'heretic', the precise meaning of which they did not know, made everyone suspicious of her. It was alleged besides that she was rich and had spent her life travelling about the world, because her family had turned her out. Why had they turned her out? Of course, because of her impiety.

In fact she was one of those fanatically obstinate Puritan spinsters, so common in England, who haunt the hotel dining-rooms of Europe, spoil Italy, poison Switzerland and make the charming Mediterranean towns impossible, taking everywhere with them their strange crazes, the morals of a fossilized Vestal Virgin, their indescribable clothes and a kind of smell of india-rubber, as if they were put away at night in an indiarubber bag.

Whenever I caught sight of one, I used to run away like a bird at the sight of a scarecrow.

But this woman seemed such an unusual type that I was actually attracted.

Madame Lecacheur, instinctively disliking everything not of peasant origin, felt a kind of hatred in her prejudiced mind for the old maid's fanatical enthusiasms. She had found a word to describe her, a word obviously meant to express contempt – I don't know how she knew it or what confused mysterious mental process coined it. She used to say: 'She's a demoniac possessed.' This expression applied to this austere sentimental woman struck me as irresistibly comic. I always called her 'the demoniac' and took an unaccountable pleasure in saying the word aloud, whenever I saw her.

I used to ask Mother Lecacheur: 'Well, what's our demoniac been doing to-day?' And the peasant woman answered in a shocked tone of voice: 'Would you believe it, Sir? She's been an' picked up a toad what's 'ad its leg crushed, an' took it to 'er room an' stuck it in 'er basin an' puts bandages on it as if it was a 'uman. It's a real scandal, it is!'

Another day, as she was walking at the foot of the cliff, she had bought a big fish, just caught, simply in order to throw it back into the sea. And the fisherman, though well paid, had sworn violently at her, angrier than if she had stolen money out of his pocket. A month later he still could not speak of the incident without losing his temper and using bad language. Yes, Miss Harriet was really a demoniac, and it was an inspiration on Madame Lecacheur's part to have given her the name.

The stable-boy, known as Sapper, because he had done his military service in Africa as a youth, had other views about her. He would say with a wink: 'I believe the old thing's got a past!'

If only 'the old thing' had known!

Céleste, the little servant, didn't like doing things for her, I don't quite know why. Perhaps just because she was a foreigner, of another race, another language, another religion. In a word, she was a demoniac!

She spent her time wandering over the countryside, looking for God and worshipping Him in nature. I found her one evening on her knees in a bush. Seeing something red through the leaves, I pushed back the branches and Miss Harriet got up confused at having been seen like this, staring at me with frightened eyes like an owl surprised in the daylight.

Sometimes, when I was working among the rocks, I suddenly caught sight of her on the edge of the cliff like the arm of a semaphore. Her passionate gaze was fixed on the expanse of ocean, shimmering like gold, and the sky crimson in the sunset. Sometimes I saw her at the bottom of a valley, walking fast with an Englishwoman's springy stride, and I went towards her, somehow attracted, just to see the ecstatic look on her face, a hard, nondescript face but tranquil with some deep inward joy.

Often, too, I came upon her at the corner of a farm, sitting on the grass in the shade of an apple-tree, with her little holy book open on her knees, gazing vaguely into the distance.

For I, too, had no thought of going away, drawn to this peaceful country-side by a thousand bonds of love for its wide open spaces. I was happy in this secluded farm, far from everything, near the earth, the good wholesome green, beautiful earth, which we shall ourselves fertilize with our bodies. And perhaps, I must admit, a spark of curiosity kept me at Mother Lecacheur's; I wanted to get to know this enigmatic Miss Harriet a little and find out what

goes on in the lonely souls of those elderly peripatetic English
spinsters.

II

We got to know each other in an odd way. I had just finished a
study, which I thought audacious – and not without reason; it was
sold for 10,000 francs fifteen years later. It was simpler than two
and two makes four, and broke all the academic rules. The whole
of the right side of my canvas showed a rock, a huge rough rock,
covered with seaweed, brown, yellow and red, and the sunlight was
pouring over it like oil. The sun was out of the picture, behind me,
but its light, falling full on the rock, made it shine like fiery gold.
That was all. A foreground of dazzling light, flaming, magnificent.

On the left the sea, not blue or slate grey but the colour of jade,
greenish, milky, steely as if under a leaden sky.

I was so pleased with my work that I was walking on air, as I
brought it home. I wanted the whole world to see it straightaway.
I remember showing it to a cow by the side of the path, shouting:
Look at this, old lady; you won't often see the like of this!'

When I got to the door, I shouted to Mother Lecacheur at once,
at the top of my voice: 'Hullo! Come here, Mother Lecacheur, and
have a squint at this.'

The peasant woman came and looked uncomprehendingly at my
work, seeing nothing and not knowing whether it represented a
bullock or a house.

Miss Harriet was coming in and she passed behind me at the very
moment when I was holding out the canvas at arm's length to
show to my hostess. The demoniac could not avoid seeing it, for I
took care to hold it so that it must catch her eye. She stopped short,
dumbfounded, speechless.

It turned out to be her own particular rock, on to which she used
to climb in order to dream undisturbed.

She uttered an English 'Oh!' with such flattering emphasis that I
turned with a smile, saying: 'This is my latest study, Miss Harriet.'

She murmured ecstatically with a naïveté that was quite moving 'Oh! Sir, your understanding of nature is quite thrilling!'

Believe it or not, I blushed at the compliment, more moved than if it had been uttered by a queen. I was her slave; she had made a complete conquest. I could have kissed her, I assure you!

I sat next her at dinner as usual. For the first time she talked following the train of her thought aloud: 'Oh! I do love nature so!

I plied her with bread, water, wine. To-day she accepted my attentions with a mummy-like smile. And I began to talk landscapes.

After the meal, rising at the same moment, we walked together across the courtyard; then, attracted no doubt by the astonishing blaze of light kindled by the setting sun on the sea, I opened the gate leading out on to the cliff and we walked on side by side like two people understanding one another fully for the first time.

It was a warm, soft evening, one of those evenings when body and spirit both have a sense of well-being. One is completely happy, everything is perfect. The warm-scented air, full of the fragrance of grass and seaweed, rises pleasantly to the nostrils with its wild perfume and the tang of the sea, lapping the spirit with its penetrating sweetness. We were walking now on the edge of the cliff, above the boundless ocean, whose waves looked tiny as they broke three hundred feet below. With mouth open and chest expanded, we breathed the fresh air from the sea, which caressed the skin gently, salty from the long kiss of the waves.

Tightly wrapped in her tartan shawl, her prominent teeth bared to the breeze, the Englishwoman watched the great sun sinking towards the sea, like one in ecstasy. In front of us, far below, near the sky-line a three-masted schooner under full sail was silhouetted against the flaming sky, and, nearer, a steamer was passing, leaving behind an endless trail of smoke across the whole horizon.

The crimson ball was sinking slowly. Soon it touched the sea, just behind the motionless ship, which stood out against its flaming orb, as if framed in fire. It sank slowly into the gulf of the ocean. We watched it touch the water, diminish in size and finally disappear. It was all over. Only the silhouette of the little boat was still visible against the golden background of the sky.

Miss Harriet gazed at the fiery sunset with passionate eyes; she must have felt a wild longing to embrace the sky, the sea, the whole horizon.

She whispered: 'Oh! I love . . . I love . . . I love,' and I saw a tear in her eye. She went on: 'I wish I were a little bird to fly away into the sky.'

And she stood there, as I had often seen her, erect on the cliff, as red as her crimson shawl. I wanted to draw her in my sketch-book; she looked for all the world like a caricature of ecstasy!

I turned away to avoid smiling.

Then I talked painting to her as I would have talked to a fellow-student, using technical terms about tones, values, high lights and so on. She listened attentively, understanding and trying to guess the meaning of the obscure words and follow my train of thought. From time to time she interjected: 'Oh! I see. It's frightfully thrilling!'

We went back.

Next day, when she saw me, she came up quickly and shook hands. We were friends at once.

She was a good honest creature, with a soul as it were on springs, always ready for a burst of enthusiasm. She was unbalanced like all unmarried women of fifty. She seemed inhibited with an innocence that had gone sour but she had kept in her heart something that was very young and easily stirred. She loved nature and animals with a passionate love, which had fermented like wine kept too long, a sensual love which she had never given to a man.

Certain it is that the sight of a bitch suckling her puppies, a mare with foal at foot in a field, a bird's nest full of twittering fledglings, with open beaks, exaggerated heads and unfeathered bodies, made her tremble with unnatural excitement.

You poor lonely souls, straying sadly through hotel dining-rooms, poor, ridiculous, pathetic figures, I love you all, since I have known Miss Harriet!

I soon sensed that she wanted to say something but did not dare,

and her timidity amused me. When I started out every morning
with my paint-box on my back, she would come with me as far as
the end of the village, silent but obviously worried, searching for
words to begin. And suddenly she would leave me and walk away
quickly with her jerky gait.

At last one day she plucked up courage: 'I should so like to see
you paint. Will you let me? I'm very curious to know.' And she
blushed as though she had made a risky suggestion.

I took her to the bottom of the Little Valley, where I was beginning a large-scale study.

She stood behind me following my every movement with concentrated attention. Then suddenly, perhaps because she was afraid
of being in the way, she said: 'Thank you,' and was gone.

But it was not long before she became more at ease, and she took
to coming with me every day with obvious pleasure. She always
brought her own stool under her arm, never letting me carry it, and
sat by my side. She stayed there for hours, not moving or speaking,
watching every movement of my brush. When I obtained the right
effect unexpectedly with a large splash of colour applied quickly
with the knife, she uttered involuntarily a little 'Oh!' of excitement,
joy and admiration. She had a sentimental respect for my canvases,
an almost religious respect for this human copy of a small part of
the divine creation. My studies were like sacred pictures in her eyes,
and sometimes she spoke to me of God in an attempt to convert
me.

Her God was a strange being indeed, a sort of village sage, without great resources or much power, for she always pictured Him
as distressed by the acts of injustice perpetrated in His sight – as if
He were unable to prevent them.

Moreover she was on intimate terms with Him, with a knowledge
apparently of His secrets and worries. She used to say: 'It is God's
will' or 'it is not God's will', as a sergeant might say to a private:
'That's C.O.'s orders.'

She was deeply distressed at my ignorance of the divine intentions, which she was eager to reveal to me; and every day in my
pockets, in my hat if I left it on the ground, in my paint-box, in the

newly cleaned shoes at my bedroom door in the morning, I used to find those little tracts, which she received no doubt straight from Paradise.

I treated her as an old friend with frank cordiality. But I soon sensed a slight change in her manner. At first I paid no heed.

When I was working either at the bottom of my valley or in some sunken road, I would suddenly see her appear with her fast jerky walk. She sat down, out of breath as if she had been running or was under the influence of violent emotion. She was very red in the face, red as only English women can get; then for no apparent reason she would blanch with an earthy pallor and seemed about to faint. But gradually she recovered her normal appearance and began to talk.

Soon, however, breaking off abruptly in the middle of a sentence, she would get up and go away so quickly and so strangely that I wondered if I had done something to displease or offend her.

Finally I came to the conclusion that this was only her normal behaviour, which she had no doubt somewhat modified in my honour at the beginning of our acquaintance.

When she came back to the farm-house after walking for hours on the wind-swept cliffs, her long side curls had often come down and were hanging as if a spring had given way in them. Before she had not bothered about it and had come in to dinner without any embarrassment, with her hair all out of curl by the action of her sister, the wind.

But now she always went to her room to tidy what I called her 'lamp chimneys', and when I said with a gallant friendliness which always shocked her: 'You are as lovely as a star to-day, Miss Harriet', she used to blush like a girl of fifteen.

Then all of a sudden she became distant and gave up coming to watch me painting. I thought: 'It's only a phase, it will pass'; but it did not pass.

Now, whenever I spoke to her she replied with studied indifference or curt irritability. And she became rude, impatient, nervy. I saw her only at meals and we hardly spoke. I really thought I must have offended her somehow; and one evening I asked her: 'Why

have you changed towards me, Miss Harriet? What have I done 1
annoy you? You are making me very unhappy.'

She replied in an angry tone that was quite comic: 'I haven'
changed; it's a lie, it's not true'; and disappeared into her room.

Sometimes she looked strangely at me. Since then I have ofte
thought that it was the look which men condemned to death giv
to those who come to tell them that their last hour has com
There was madness in her eye, the madness of the fanatic about 1
do some act of violence; and there was something else, too, a feve
of exasperated frustration, impotently desiring some unrealize
and unrealizable dream. She seemed to be struggling against som
mysterious power within her, which she was striving to repress
and perhaps there was something else too ... I wonder ..
I wonder.

III

The explanation came as a shock.

I had been working from dawn every morning for some time a
a picture with the following subject:

A deep valley, shut in and dominated by two banks of reeds an
trees, stretched away into the distance, deserted, blanketed by th
whitish mist like cotton-wool, which sometimes fills such valley
at daybreak. And behind this curtain of fog, at once thick an
transparent, one saw, or rather sensed, the approach of two figures
a girl in a man's close embrace, she with her head back looking u
at him and he bending down towards her their lips meeting in a
kiss.

The first rays of the sun, shining through the branches, pierce
the dawn mist, casting a pink light behind the country lovers and
imparting a silvery radiance to their undefined shapes. It was a ver
successful effect, I assure you.

I was working on the slope going down to the little Etreta
valley, and that morning I happened to find just the floating mist l
wanted. A ghostly form suddenly rose in front of me; it was Miss
Harriet. When she saw me, she made as if to run away; but l

shouted to her: 'Come here, Miss Harriet, I've got a little picture for you.'

She approached as if unwillingly. I handed her my sketch. She made no comment, standing still for a long while gazing at it; and suddenly she burst into tears. Her sobs came in convulsive spasms, as with those who have struggled long against their tears but can restrain them no longer and give way, without however abandoning the effort at control.

I jumped up, moved by the sight of an emotion which I did not understand, and seized her hands with a gesture of instinctive affection, the gesture natural to a Frenchman, who always acts first and thinks afterwards.

She let her hands lie in mine for a few seconds and I felt them quivering as if every nerve were in a state of tension. Then she pulled them away quickly or rather wrenched them free.

I had recognized that quiver, for I had felt it before; there was no mistaking it. The quiver of a woman in love, whether she is fifteen or fifty, a woman of the people or a society lady, goes straight to my heart and I can never mistake it.

Her whole being, poor thing, had quivered and vibrated like a harp string and then snapped. I knew the truth. She was gone before I could say a word, leaving me dazed as if I had witnessed a miracle and remorseful as if I had committed a crime.

I did not go back for lunch. I went for a walk along the cliff, not knowing whether I wanted to laugh or cry; my position was at once comic and distressing. I recognized its ridiculous side but I realized that her unhappiness might drive her mad. I wondered what I ought to do.

I decided that I must go away and made up my mind to do so at once. After wandering about till the evening in a state of senti-mental depression, I returned for dinner.

We sat down as usual. Miss Harriet was there. She ate her food solemnly, in silence with lowered eyes. Her expression and manner were normal.

I waited till the end of the meal, then, turning to my hostess, I said:

'Well, Madame Lecacheur, I shall soon be leaving you.'

The good woman, surprised and sorry, exclaimed in her drawling accent:

'What do you mean, Sir? You're leaving us? I was just getting quite used to you!'

I was watching Miss Harriet out of the corner of my eye; her face was inscrutable. But Céleste, the little servant-girl, had looked up at me. She was a plump girl of eighteen, with a fresh ruddy complexion, as strong as a horse and clean, a rare quality in a peasant. I had sometimes given her a kiss in a corner, as one does to any chambermaid, nothing more.

So the meal ended.

I went out to have my pipe under the apple-trees, walking up and down the courtyard. All the thoughts that had passed through my mind during the day, the morning's strange revelation, this ridiculous passion I had inspired, memories awakened by this discovery, sweet exciting memories, perhaps, too, the look the servant-girl had given me, when I announced my departure, the combination of all these things stimulated me physically; I felt the prick of kisses on my lips and the stirring of the blood that drives a man to do silly things.

Night was coming on and it was getting dark under the trees when I saw Céleste come out to shut up the hen-run on the other side of the yard. I ran after her so lightly that she did not hear me coming and, as she stood up after shutting the little trap-door by which the hens got in and out, I seized her in my arms, covering her broad fat face with a hail of kisses. She struggled, laughing all the time, for this was nothing new to her.

Why did I suddenly let her go? Why did I turn round with a start? How did I sense the presence of someone behind me?

It was Miss Harriet coming in; she had seen us and was standing there stock still as if she had seen a ghost. Then she disappeared into the darkness.

I went in, ashamed and worried, more upset at having been surprised by her like this than if she had caught me committing a crime.

I slept badly, my nerves on edge, haunted by depressing thoughts. I seemed to hear the sound of weeping but I must have imagined it. Several times, too, I thought someone was moving about in the house and opening the front door.

Towards dawn I was so tired that I dropped asleep at last. I did not wake till late and only appeared for lunch, still feeling uncomfortable and not knowing how to face the situation.

Miss Harriet had not been seen. We waited for her but she did not appear. Madame Lecacheur went to her room but she was not there. She must have gone out at dawn, as she often did, to see the sunrise. No one thought anything of it and we began the meal in silence.

It was hot, very hot, one of those heavy stifling days without a leaf stirring. The table had been dragged outside under an apple-tree and from time to time Sapper went to the cellar to refill the cider jug, everyone was so thirsty. Céleste brought the dishes from the kitchen, stewed mutton and potatoes, followed by boiled rabbit and salad. Then she put on the table a plate of cherries, the first of the season.

Wishing to plunge them in water to cool them, I asked the little servant to go and draw me a bucket of very cold water.

She came back five minutes later, saying that the well had dried up. She had let out all the rope, and the bucket had touched bottom and come up empty. Madame Lecacheur wanted to see for herself and went off to look down the shaft. She came back, saying that she could certainly see something in the well, something that ought not to be there. A neighbour with a grudge against her must have thrown in a truss of straw.

I wanted to look, too, hoping to be able to make out more, and peered down over the well-head. I made out something white, I couldn't see what. Then I had the idea of letting down a lantern on the end of a cord. The yellow light flickered on the stone sides as it descended slowly. All four of us were leaning over the opening, Sapper and Céleste having joined us. The lantern came to a stop above an indistinct black-and-white object, something strange which we could not make out. Sapper cried: 'It's a horse; I can see its hoof. It must have escaped from the field and fallen in during the night.'

Suddenly I went cold all over. I had just recognized a foot, then a leg sticking up; the body and the other leg were under water.

I stammered in a hushed voice, trembling so violently that the lantern danced madly above the shoe: 'There's a woman down there; it's Miss Harriet.'

Sapper alone showed no signs of emotion; he had often seen corpses in Africa! Madame Lecacheur and Céleste uttered shrill cries and ran away.

We had to recover the body. I tied a rope firmly round the stable-boy's waist and let him down on the pulley very slowly, watching him go down into the darkness. He carried the lantern and another rope. Soon his voice, which seemed to come from the bowels of the earth, shouted: 'Stop!' and I saw him pull something out of the water; it was the other leg; presently, after tying the two feet together, he shouted again: 'Haul away!' I pulled him up, but my arms felt weak and my muscles paralysed, so that I was afraid of allowing the boy to fall back again by letting the rope slip through my hands. When his head appeared at the top, I asked him Well?' as if I expected him to give me news of the woman at the bottom.

We both stood on the stone well-head, facing each other, and leaning over the opening we began to raise the body.

Madame Lecacheur and Céleste watched us from a distance, hiding behind the wall of the house. When they saw the black shoes and white stockings of the drowned woman appear over the edge, they disappeared. Sapper seized hold of the ankles and we pulled out the poor chaste spinster in the most immodest posture. Her head was a dreadful sight, bruised and disfigured, and her long grey hair, all dishevelled, never to be tidied again, hung down, dripping and covered with mud.

Sapper remarked contemptuously: 'My God! she's a skinny one!'

We carried her to her room and, as the two women did not appear, I laid her out with the stable-boy's help.

I washed the poor disfigured face. As I did so, one eye opened a little and she seemed to be looking at me from the other world with the cold, expressionless, terrifying stare of a corpse. I tidied her dishevelled hair as best I could and arranged it clumsily over her forehead in a style it had never known before. Next I took off her soaked garments, uncovering her shoulders and breast and her long arms, as thin as match-sticks, with a feeling of shame, as if I were profaning a holy place. After that I fetched flowers, poppies, corn-flowers, daisies and fresh scented grass, to cover her bier.

I had to carry out the usual formalities, being the only person on the spot. A letter which we found in her pocket, written just before her death, asked that she should be buried in the village where she had spent her last days. It came upon me with an unpleasant shock that it was because of me that she wanted to be laid to rest here.

Towards evening the women from the village came to view the body, but I would not let anyone in; I wanted to be alone and I kept vigil all night.

I watched her by the candle-light, poor unhappy woman, who had died so tragically among strangers far from home. Had she any friends or relations anywhere? What had her childhood and her life been? Where had she come from, to wander about in this way, alone, friendless, like a dog driven from home? What secret suffering, what despair had been shut up in this unattractive body, which she had worn like a badge of shame all her life, a ridiculous uniform which had defrauded her of all affection and love?

Some people have no luck! I realized the eternal injustice of cruel Nature which had crushed that human soul. Now death had come to her and she had never known the only consolation of the dispossessed, the hope of being loved just once. Why else had she hidden herself away, flying from all human contacts? This must have been the reason why she loved all things and all living creatures except men.

I understood her belief in God; she had hoped for compensation in the next world for her unhappiness in this life. Now she would rot, to live again as a plant, which would bloom in the sun; her leaves would be pasture for cattle and her seeds be carried away by

the fowls of the air, and, after being part of their flesh, she woul
be reabsorbed into other human bodies. But what goes by the nam
of soul had perished at the bottom of the dark well. Her suffering
were over. She had given her life in exchange for other lives tha
she would help to bring into being.

The hours of my grim vigil dragged on in silence. A fain
brightness heralded the approach of dawn; soon a ray of sunshin
crept over the bed and threw a line of rosy light on sheet and hands
It was the hour she had loved. The birds awoke and began to sing
in the trees.

I flung the window wide open, drew the curtain, so that th
whole eye of heaven should see us, and, leaning over the cold body
I took the disfigured face in my hands and, without fear o
repulsion, pressed on those lips a kiss, a long kiss, the first perhap
they had ever received.

*

Léon Chenal stopped. The women were sobbing. On the box
the Comte d'Etraille was blowing his nose violently. The drive
alone was dozing and the horses, no longer feeling the whip, ha
slowed down and were hardly moving. The brake seemed almos
to stop, as if suddenly weighed down with a load of sorrow.

THE POOL

'Assault and Battery, resulting in Manslaughter.' Such was the indictment on which Léopold Renard, upholsterer, appeared before the Assize Court.

Round him were the principal witnesses, Madame Flammèche widow of the deceased, Louis Ladureau, cabinet-maker, and Jean Durdent, plumber.

Near the accused was his wife, in black, a small ugly woman, who looked like a monkey dressed up as a lady.

This is Léopold Renard's account of the incident:

'God knows, it was all an accident, it wasn't my fault, I didn't mean it. The facts explain themselves, m' Lud. I'm an honest man, a working man, an upholsterer; I've lived in the same street for sixteen years, well known and liked, looked up to and respected by everybody, as the neighbours have said in evidence, even the caretaker, who's not given to flattering people. I like my work, I like saving money, I like honest people and honest amusements. That's what caused the trouble, bad luck to it! But it wasn't intentional, so I've no reason to be ashamed of myself.

'Well, every Sunday for the last five years my wife, here present in court, and I have been going down to Passy for the day. We get an airing and besides we're both mad keen on fishing; I caught the bug from Mélie, damn her! she's crazier about it than me, blast her eyes! for she's at the bottom of all this trouble, as you'll see from what happened.

'Me, I'm a strong good-tempered sort of chap without a ha'porth of spitefulness in me; but she, my goodness, she's not much to look at, she's small and skinny but she's more vicious than a weasel. She's got her good points. I admit; sure she has, and they're ones that are very useful to a man in business. But she's got a temper, you just ask the neighbours, or even the caretaker who has just given evidence in my favour – she'll tell you a thing or two!

'Every day she used to be at me for my mildness: "I wouldn't let people do me down like this; I wouldn't let people do me down like that." If I'd listened to her, I'd have had at least three fights with fists a month on my hands . . .'

Mme Renard interrupted him:

'You can say what you like; he laughs best who laughs last!'

He turned to her good-temperedly:

'Well, I can say what I like against you; you're not in the dock.'

And, turning to the Judge, he went on:

'Now I'll go on with the story. We used to go to Passy every Saturday evening so as to start fishing at dawn next day. It's got quite a habit with us, almost a second nature, as you might say. I'd found a place, three years ago this summer, a marvellous place, under trees, eight feet of water at least, perhaps ten, a pool with holes running in under the bank, swarming with fish, a fisherman's paradise. This pool, m'Lud, I considered my own private property, having discovered it, as Christopher Columbus discovered America. Everyone in the district knew it and nobody contested my claim; nobody else would have come there, not even M. Plumeau, who's well known – no offence meant – for poaching on other people's preserves.

'Well, knowing I could reckon on the place, I used to go back to it every time, as if I owned it. As soon as we arrived on the Saturday I went on board the *Delilah* with my wife. The *Delilah* is my skiff; I had her built at Fournaise's and she's light but steady. I say, we went on board the *Delilah* and set off to bait the pool. There's nobody knows how to bait like me and all my pals know it. You'll be wanting to know what bait I use. I can't tell you that. It's got nothing to do with the accident; I can't tell you, it's my secret. More than two hundred people have asked me that question. I've been offered drinks, fried fish and stewed fish, to make me blab. But you should just come and see the way the chub come along. Yes, they've even tried force to get my recipe out of me . . . My wife's the only one who knows it, and she won't tell any more than me. Isn't that true, Mélie?'

The Judge interrupted:

'Come to the point as soon as you can.'

The accused went on: 'I'm coming to it, I'm coming to it! Well, on Saturday, July 8th, we took the 5.25 train and went out even before our dinner to do the baiting, as we do every Saturday. The weather seemed promising. I said to Mélie: "It looks pretty good for to-morrow," and she replied: "Not too bad." That's all the conversation there ever is between us.

'After that we went back to dinner. I was in good spirits and I was thirsty. That was the cause of it all, m'Lud. I says to Mélie: "Look here, Mélie, the weather's good; suppose I have a nightcap." It's a cheap white wine we call that, because, if you drink too much of it, it acts like a nightcap and prevents you sleeping, see?

'She answers: "You can do as you like, but it'll upset you again and you won't be able to get up in the morning." That was quite true, it was right, it was prudent, it was sensible, I admit. But I couldn't resist the temptation and I had my bottle. That was the beginning of everything.

'Well, I couldn't sleep. It kept me awake till two o'clock in the morning, that wretched alcoholic nightcap. And then I suddenly dropped off and slept so sound that the last trump wouldn't have woken me.

'To come to the point; my wife woke me at six. I jumped out of bed, threw on my trousers and sweater; I just gave a lick to my face and we got into the *Delilah*. We were too late. When I got to my pool, it was occupied; such a thing hadn't happened, m'Lud, for three years. I felt as if I was being robbed under my own nose. I said: "Damn, blast, damn!" And my wife started being nasty: "What about your nightcap now? What did I say, you miserable tippler? I suppose you're pleased with yourself, you great dolt!"

'I had nothing to say; it was all true.

'All the same I landed near the place to try for the leavings. And the fellow might not catch anything and go away after all.

'He was a skinny little chap in white ducks with a big straw hat. He'd got his wife with him, too, a great hulking woman, who was doing embroidery behind him.

'When she saw us settling down close to them, she started to murmur under her breath:

' "I suppose this is the only place on the river?"

'And my old woman, who was furious, retorted:

' "Those what knows their manners enquire about local customs before they squat in reserved places."

'As I didn't want trouble, I said to her:

' "Shut up, Mélie. Don't worry, don't worry; we'll see what happens."

'Well, we'd run the *Delilah* in under the willows and landed, and we began fishing, elbow to elbow, Mélie and me, alongside the other two.

'Here, m'Lud, I must go into details.

'We'd been there about five minutes when my neighbour's float bobbed two or three times and he pulled out a chub as big as my thigh, p'raps not quite so big but nearly! My heart began to thump and the sweat broke out on my forehead, and Mélie said to me: "Look there, you old drunkard, did you see that one?"

'At this moment, M. Bru, the grocer at Poissy, a devotee of the gentle art himself, went by in a boat and shouted to me: "Somebody's snaffled your place, M. Renard." I replied: "Yes, M. Bru, there are some folks don't know what's done."

'The little man in ducks pretended not to hear and so did his wife, a great elephant of a woman.'

The Judge interrupted again:

'Be careful. You are being insulting to the widow Flammèche, who is present in court.'

Renard apologized: 'I'm sorry, I got carried away!

'Well, a quarter of an hour hadn't passed before the little man in ducks caught another chub, and another almost on top of that and a fourth five minutes later.

'I could have cried with vexation and I knew Mélie was boiling; she kept on nagging at me: "Look, you miserable creature, don't you see him stealing your fish, don't you see him? You won't get a bite, not even a frog, not a blinking thing. It makes me hot all over, the idea of it!"

'I was thinking: "Let's wait till twelve o'clock; he'll go away for lunch, that poacher fellow, and then I'll get my own place back."

'ou see, m'Lud, I always have a picnic lunch on the spot on undays; we bring our food in the *Delilah*.

'There was twelve o'clock striking! He'd got a chicken in a iece of newspaper and, while he was eating, he caught another hub.

'Mélie and me had our snack, too, only a mouthful, we didn't feel ke eating.

'Afterwards, to digest my lunch, I picked up my paper. Every unday I read *Gil Blas*, there in the shade on the bank. You know 's the day Columbine has her article in *Gil Blas*. I'd been in the abit of teasing Mme Renard by pretending I knew this Columbine; isn't true, I don't know her. I've never seen her, but that doesn't natter; she writes well, and what she says is very much to the oint, considering she's only a woman. Anyhow, I like her, there ren't many who write as good an article as she does.

'Well, I began to pull my wife's leg, but she lost her temper traightaway, real violently she did. So I stopped.

'At this moment M. Ladureau and M. Durdent, our two witnesses ere present in court, arrived on the other side of the river. We new each other by sight.

'The little man had gone on fishing. He caught so many I didn't now how to contain myself. And his wife started to say: "This is a hundering good spot; we'll always come here, Désiré."

'I felt a shiver down my spine. And Mme Renard went on at me: 'You're not a man, you've got no guts, you're a chicken-hearted oward!"

'I suddenly said to her: "Look here, I'd best go away; I might o something I'd be sorry for."

'And she whispered in my ear, as if she was holding a red-hot oker under my nose: "You're not a man; now you're running way and surrendering the place, you cowardly traitor!"

'That got me on the raw but I didn't bat an eyelid.

'Then the other fellow pulled out a bream; I've never seen such fish, never!

'At this my wife began talking, sort of thinking aloud – you can ee her malice aforethought. She said: "This is what you might call stealing fish, seeing as how we'd baited the place ourselves. They might at least pay us what we spent on the bait."

'At that the little man's fat wife started to say:

' "Is it us you're referring to, Madame?"

' "I'm referring to people who steal fish, taking advantage of the money other folks have spent.'

'You're saying we are stealing fish?"

'After that came explanations and strong language. My word, there's not much you can teach women, the blighters, in the way of swear words. They were shrieking at each other so loud that our two witnesses on the other bank shouted out derisively: "Hullo, over there! Not so much noise or you'll prevent your husbands fishing!"

'The fact is, the little man in ducks and me, we sat on stock still, as if we didn't hear.

'But, my God, we did hear; I should just think we did! "You're a liar"; "You're a slut"; "You scum"; "You whore," and so on and so on, worse and worse. A sailor couldn't have done better!

'Suddenly I heard a noise behind me. I turned round. There was that great hulking woman going for my wife with her sunshade. Swish! Swish! Mélie got two proper ones! But she's got a temper, too, has Mélie, and when she sees red, she can use her fists. She seized the fat woman by the hair, and bang! crash! bang! she was boxing her ears and raining blows on her head, like ripe plums falling off a tree.

'I would have left them to it; women against women and men against men, I say, you mustn't mix the sexes. But the little man in ducks jumped up like a devil and was going for my wife. That won't do, my fine friend! I met him with my fist, the blackguard. Thud! Thud! one punch on his nose and one in the stomach. Up went his arms and up went his legs and he fell backwards, plump into the river, right in the pool!

'I'd have fished him out at once, I promise you, m'Lud, if I'd had time at the moment. But the big woman was getting the best of it and was pommelling Mélie like mad, and that was the last straw. I know I oughtn't to have gone to her rescue, while he was having a long drink in the water. But I never thought he'd drown. I said to myself: "It'll cool him off a bit."

'So I ran to separate the women. I got it myself from fists, nails and teeth. My God! What devils women are!

'To make a long story short, it took me five minutes, perhaps ten, to separate those two furies.

'I turned round. There was nothing to be seen. The river was as calm as a duck-pond and the men on the other side were shouting: "Fish him out, fish him out!"

'It's all very well to say that but I can't swim, much less dive, on my honour, I can't.

'At last the weir-keeper came along and two men with gaffs; that was a good quarter of an hour later. They found him at the bottom of the pool, in eight feet of water, as I told you, but he was there all right, the little fellow in ducks.

'That's how it happened, so help me God! I plead "not guilty", on my honour.'

The witnesses confirmed his account and the accused was acquitted.

PRISONERS OF WAR

SILENCE reigned in the forest save for the faint whisper of the snow as it fell upon the trees. It had been falling since midday in fine flakes, which coated the branches with a film of powdery snow and covered the dead leaves of the undergrowth with a delicate mantle of silver; it spread a great fleecy white carpet over the roads and intensified the boundless silence of this vast expanse of trees.

Before the door of a forester's hut a girl with bare arms was cutting wood on a stone with an axe. She was tall, slim and strongly built, the very picture of a forester's daughter or wife.

A voice from inside shouted:

'We're all alone this evening, Berthine; better come in, it's getting dark and there'll likely be Prussians and wolves prowling round.'

The girl replied as she went on splitting a log with powerful strokes, her breast lifting with every movement of her upraised arms:

'I've just finished, Mother; I'm all right, don't get the wind up; it's still light.'

She carried in her faggots and logs and stacked them round the fireplace, came out again and closed the huge solid oak shutters; finally, going in again, she shot the heavy bolts of the door.

Her mother was spinning by the fire, a wrinkled old woman, grown nervous in her old age.

'I don't like it', she said, 'when your father's out. Two women ain't no good.'

The girl replied:

'Oh! I'm quite capable of killing a wolf, or a Prussian, as far as that goes,' and she glanced at a big revolver hanging up above the fireplace.

Her husband had been called up for the army in the early days of the Prussian invasion and the two women had been left alone with the father, the old forest warden, Nicolas Pichon, usually called

Spindleshanks, who had stubbornly refused to leave his house and move into the town.

The nearest town was Rethel, once a walled fortress perched on a rock. They were patriotic Frenchmen there and the shopkeepers had decided to resist the invaders, to shut the gates and stand a siege in accordance with the traditions of the place. Twice already, in the reigns of Henri IV and Louis XIV, the citizens had won fame by their heroic defence. Damn it all! they would do the same again or see the town burnt over their heads!

So they had acquired some artillery and rifles, equipped a volunteer force, formed battalions and companies, and they used to drill every day on the barrack square. Everyone, bakers, grocers, butchers, notaries, lawyers, carpenters, booksellers, even chemists took it in turns at fixed times to parade under the command of M. Lavigne, once an N.C.O. of dragoons, now a haberdasher, having married the daughter and inherited the business of M. Ravaudan, Senior.

He had assumed the rank of Town Commandant and, as every man of military age had gone, he had enrolled all the rest, who were now training to defend themselves. Those who were fat always moved about the town at the double to get down their weight and improve their wind; those who were weaklings carried heavy loads to develop their muscles.

And they waited for the Prussians. But the Prussians did not appear. They were not far away, however. Twice already their patrols had pushed through the forest as far as the forester's hut, where Nicolas Pichon, alias Spindleshanks, lived.

The old warden, who could run like a fox, had gone to warn the town. The guns were laid but the enemy never appeared.

Spindleshanks' hut was used as a forward observation post in the forest of Aveline. The forester went in twice a week to get provisions and kept the shopkeepers in the town informed of what was going on outside.

*

That day he had gone off with the news that a small German

infantry detachment had stopped at his house two days before at about two o'clock in the afternoon, moving on almost immediately. The N.C.O. in charge spoke French.

When the old man went off like this, he always took with him his two dogs, two great bull-dogs with jowls as powerful as a lion's, for fear of the wolves which were beginning to get dangerous, and he left the two women behind, warning them to barricade themselves in the house at nightfall.

The girl did not know what fear was 'but the old woman was in a continual state of nerves and kept on repeating:

'I'm sure something's goin' to happen – you see if it don't.'

That evening she was even more jumpy than usual.

'D'you know what time your Dad'll be back?' she said.

'Oh! not before eleven anyway. When he has dinner with the Major, he's always late home.'

She was hanging up the pot over the fire, when suddenly she stopped, listening to a faint sound which came down the chimney.

She whispered:

'There's people in the wood coming this way, seven or eight of 'em at least.'

Her mother stopped her spinning-wheel in a panic and stammered:

'Oh God! and Dad's not here!'

She hadn't finished speaking when a violent banging made the door shake.

As the women remained silent, a loud guttural voice shouted:

'Oben de toor!'

Then after a moment's pause the same voice went on:

'Oben de toor or I'll pash it in!'

Berthine slipped the big revolver over the chimney-piece into the pocket of her skirt and, putting her ear close to the door, she asked:
'Who are you?'

The voice replied:

'We're the patrol that was here a day or two back.'

The girl answered:

'What do you want?'

'I've been lost in the forest since this morning with my batrol. Oben de toor or I'll pash it in.'

The girl had no choice; she quickly slid back the ponderous bolt and opening the heavy door she saw in the dim half-light from the snow six men, six Prussian soldiers, the same ones that had been there before. She spoke in a determined tone of voice:

'What do you want here at this time of night?'

The N.C.O. repeated in his guttural French:

'I'm lost, hopelessly lost; I've had noting to eat since preakfast, no more have my men.'

Berthine replied:

'I'm here all alone with Mother this evening.'

The soldier, who seemed a good sort, went on:

'That toesn't matter; I shan't to you any harm but you must give us something to eat. We're starving and dead peat.'

The girl stood back:

'Come in,' she said.

They came into the house, plastered with snow; the soft film of powdery snow on their helmets made them look like meringues, and they were obviously tired, at the end of their tether, in fact.

The girl pointed to the wooden benches on both sides of the big table:

'Sit down,' she said. 'I'll make you some stew; you do look done in.'

And she bolted the door again.

She put some more water in the pot and added another lump of butter and some potatoes and, unhooking a side of bacon that was hanging in the chimney, she cut off half of it and threw it into the soup.

The six soldiers followed her every movement with the hungry eyes of starving men. They had stacked their rifles and helmets in one corner and waited like well-behaved children on their benches in a school.

The old woman had gone back to her spinning with frequent timid glances at the invaders. The only sounds were the gentle

purring of the spinning-wheel, the crackling of the fire and the
bubbling of the boiling water.

Suddenly a strange noise made everybody start, a sort of throaty
snuffling at the bottom of the door, the loud hoarse breathing of
some animal.

The German N.C.O. had leapt towards the rifles. The girl
stopped him with a gesture, smiling:

'Wolves!' she said. 'They're like you, they prowl about and
they're hungry!'

The man was incredulous and wanted to see for himself, and, as
soon as the door was opened, there were two great grey forms
disappearing at a fast loping trot. He went back to his seat, murmuring:

'Well, I wouldn't have pelieved it!'

And he waited for the stew to be ready.

They ate ravenously, their mouths gaping from ear to ear so as
to admit the maximum amount of food; their eyes opened wide in
time with their jaws and a noise like the gurgling of water in a
gutter-pipe issued from their throats as they guzzled.

In silence the two women watched the rapid movement of the
full red beards, into which the potatoes seemed to be sucked as the
hirsute apertures opened and closed.

As they were thirsty, the girl went down into the cellar to draw
them some cider. She was some time down there; it was a small
vaulted cellar which during the Revolution had been used as a
prison and as a hiding place, too, it was said. Access was by a narrow
winding stair, closed by a trap-door at one end of the kitchen.

When Berthine returned, she was chuckling quietly to herself as
if at some private joke, as she handed the jug of cider to the
Germans. Then she ate her own supper with her mother at the
other end of the kitchen.

The soldiers had finished their food and were all beginning to
doze round the table. From time to time a head would fall with a
thud on to the table and its owner would wake with a start and
sit up.

Berthine said to the N.C.O.:

'You can lie down in front of the fire; there's heaps of room for all the lot of you, Lord knows. Mother and I are going up to our room.'

And the two women went upstairs. The Germans heard them lock their door and walk about for a bit; afterwards there was silence.

The Prussians lay down on the stone floor with their feet to the fire and their heads resting on their rolled-up greatcoats. Soon all six were snoring in impressive concert in six different keys from treble to bass.

*

They must have been asleep for some time, when a shot rang out, so loud that one would have said it had been fired quite close to the walls of the house. The soldiers sprang up. But two more shots were heard, followed by three others.

The door of the first floor room burst open and the forester's daughter appeared barefooted, in her chemise and petticoat, holding a candle, with an air of consternation. She stammered:

'The French are here – two hundred of 'em at least! If they find you, they'll burn down the house. Get down into the cellar as fast as you can and keep quiet. If you make a sound, we're lost.'

The N.C.O., thoroughly frightened, murmured:

'Right ho! Right ho! Where's the way town?'

The girl hurriedly lifted the small square trap-door and the six men went down the narrow winding stair and disappeared into the bowels of the earth, going backwards in order to feel each step with their feet.

But, when the spike of the last helmet had gone, Berthine dropped the heavy oak trap-door, which was thick as a wall and tough as steel, held in place by hinges and a regular prison cell lock, and, as she gave a double turn to the key, she began to laugh quietly to herself, so pleased that she wanted to indulge in a wild dance of joy above the heads of her prisoners.

They didn't make a sound, enclosed as it were in a solid stone box, with only an iron-barred ventilation hole.

Berthine immediately lit the fire again and put on the pot to make some more soup, murmuring:

'Dad'll be tired to-night.'

Then she sat down and waited.

The regular tick of the pendulum of the grandfather clock was the only sound in the stillness.

From time to time the girl glanced at the clock impatiently, as if to say:

'Time's going mortal slow.'

But soon she thought she heard the murmur of voices under foot. Low faint whispering came to her through the vaulted stone roof of the cellar. The Prussians were beginning to guess her trick and soon the N.C.O. came up the narrow stair and hammered on the trap-door with his fist. Once more he shouted:

'Oben de toor!'

She went over to the opening in the floor and said, imitating his German accent:

'What to you want?'

'Oben de toor.'

'Not on your life!'

The man lost his temper:

'Oben or I'll pash in the door!'

She began to laugh:

'Bash away, lad, bash away!'

He began to batter at the oak trap over his head with his rifle butt. But it would have stood up to the blows of a battering ram.

The forester's daughter heard him go down again, and presently the soldiers came up one after the other to try their strength and examine the fastening. But, no doubt, realizing that their efforts were in vain, they all went down again into the cellar and began talking among themselves.

After listening for a time the girl went and opened the outside door and strained her ears for any sound in the darkness.

At last she heard a bark in the distance. Immediately she gave a hunter's whistle and almost at once two huge dogs emerged from the darkness and gambolled round her. She seized them by the

scruff of the neck and held them quiet. Then she shouted as loud
as she could:

'Hullo! Dad!'

A voice, still some distance away, answered:

'Hullo! Berthine!'

She waited a minute or two and called again:

'Hullo! Dad!'

The voice, now quite near, replied:

'Hullo! Berthine!'

The girl went on:

'Don't pass in front of the ventilation hole; the cellar's full of
Prussians.'

Suddenly the tall figure of a man was silhouetted between two
tree-trunks on the left, standing still. He asked anxiously:

'Prussians in the cellar? What on earth are they up to there?'

The girl began to laugh again:

'They're yesterday's lot. They got lost in the forest. I put 'em to
cool their heels in the cellar.'

And she told her story, how she had scared them with revolver
shots and shut them up in the cellar.

The old man, practical as always, asked:

'Well, what d'you want me to do with 'em now?'

She replied:

'Go and fetch M. Lavigne with his men. He can take 'em
prisoner. He'll be as pleased as Punch!'

And old Pichon answered with a smile:

'You bet he will.'

His daughter went on:

'Here's your soup; eat it up quick and get a move on.'

The old warden sat down and began to eat his soup after putting
down on the floor two full plates for his dogs.

The Prussians, hearing voices, kept quiet.

A quarter of an hour later Spindleshanks set off again. And
Berthine waited, her head in her hands.

*

The prisoners were beginning to move about again. They shouted and called, banging angrily on the unyielding trap-door with their rifle butts. Next they started firing out of the ventilation hole, hoping no doubt to attract the attention of any German patrol in the neighbourhood.

The forester's daughter didn't stir; but all this noise irritated her and got on her nerves. A wave of cold anger came over her; she could have murdered the lot of them, the blighters, just to make them keep quiet!

Finally, with growing impatience, she kept her eyes on the clock, counting the minutes.

Her father had been gone an hour and a half; he must have reached the town by now. She imagined him telling his story to M. Lavigne, who went pale with excitement and rang for his servant to bring his uniform and his arms. She seemed to hear the drummer hurrying along the streets. Frightened heads were thrust out of the windows. Now the citizen-soldiers were coming out of their houses, hardly dressed, out of breath, fastening their belts, making their way at the double to the Major's house.

Soon the detachment, with Spindleshanks at their head, would march off in the darkness through the snow in the direction of the forest. She looked at the clock:

'They should be here in an hour.'

Nervous impatience was getting the better of her. Every minute seemed an hour.

The time would never pass!

At last the hands of the clock pointed to the hour she had fixed in her mind for their arrival. And she opened the door again to listen. She saw a dim figure walking carefully. She cried out in terror. It was her father.

He said:

'They've sent me on to make sure nothing's changed.'

'No, nothing.'

Thereupon he gave a long shrill whistle in the darkness. And soon a dark mass became visible, moving slowly among the trees; it was the reconnoitring section of ten men.

Spindleshanks kept repeating:

' Don't go in front of the ventilation hole.'

And the early arrivals pointed out the dangerous spot to the late comers.

At last the main body appeared, two hundred men in all with two hundred cartridges apiece.

M. Lavigne, fussing about excitedly, posted them so as to surround the house completely, leaving a broad space unoccupied in front of the little dark hole on ground level which admitted air to the cellar.

After that he went into the house to obtain details of the strength and attitude of the enemy, who were now so quiet that they might have disappeared and melted into thin air through the ventilation hole.

M. Lavigne stamped on the trap-door and shouted:

'The Prussian Officer in command!'

No answer from the German.

'The Prussian Officer in command!'

But it was no good. For twenty minutes he called on this officer, who remained dumb, to surrender with arms and equipment, promising him and his men their lives and the honours of war. But he could elicit no sign either of consent or hostile intentions. The situation was getting awkward.

The citizen soldiers were stamping their feet in the snow, swinging their arms like cab-drivers to keep warm, and they could not take their eyes off the ventilation hole, conscious of an increasing childish desire to pass in front of it.

At last one of them took a chance, a man called Potdevin who was very fast. He took a run and dashed across like a stag. His venture was successful. The prisoners gave no sign of life.

A voice shouted:

'I don't believe there's anybody there!'

And another soldier bolted across the empty space in front of the dangerous aperture. So it became quite a game. Every minute someone sped across from one side to the other like children playing Prisoners' Base, throwing up clouds of snow as he ran at full speed. To keep warm they had started big fires of dead wood which lit up the running figure of each National Guard as he rapidly transferred himself from the party on the right to that on the left.

Somebody shouted:

'Your turn, Maloison!'

Maloison was a portly baker, the size of whose stomach was a permanent source of jokes to his friends.

He hesitated. They taunted him. Finally he made up his mind and went off at a slow dignified double, being short of breath, his great belly wobbling from side to side.

The whole company were convulsed with laughter. They encouraged him with shouts:

'Well done, Maloison!'

He had got about two-thirds of the way across when there was a flash of swift red flame from the ventilation hole; a shot rang out and the huge baker pitched forward on his nose with a scream of terror.

*

No one went to his assistance. Presently they saw him dragging himself along in the snow on all fours and when he got across the dangerous area he fainted.

He had got a bullet high up in the fat part of the thigh.

After the first shock of surprise and terror they began to laugh over the incident.

But Major Lavigne appeared at the door of the forester's hut. He had at last decided on his plan of campaign. He gave his orders in ringing tones:

'Planchut and his plumber's mates this way!'

Three men stepped forward.

'Take down the gutter-pipes from the house!'

In a quarter of an hour they had brought twenty yards of piping to the Major.

Next, with infinite precautions, he had a small hole made in the edge of the trap-door, and after rigging up a pipe-line from the pump to this aperture he announced with the air of a man supremely pleased with himself:

'Now we'll stand our friends the Germans a little drink!'

A wild cheer expressed everyone's admiration of this happy idea, followed by shouts of joy and roars of laughter. The Major organized working parties to relieve each other every five minutes and at last gave the order:

'Pump away!'

When the iron pump-handle had begun to work, a gurgle was heard inside the pipes and soon water began to fall into the cellar, from step to step, splashing like a miniature waterfall in a goldfish pond. They waited.

An hour passed, then two, then three.

The Major stamped up and down the kitchen in a state of feverish excitement, putting his ear to the floor from time to time in an attempt to guess what the enemy were doing, wondering if they were going to surrender.

At last they began to move about. They could be heard shifting the barrels, talking and splashing about.

Finally about eight o'clock in the morning a guttural voice was heard from the ventilation hole:

'I want to sbeak to the French Officer in command.'

Lavigne answered from the window, being careful not to put his head too far out.

'Do you surrender?'

'Yes, I surrender.'

'Pass out your rifles.'

Without a moment's delay a rifle was pushed out of the hole, followed by a second and a third, till they were all there lying in the snow.

And the same voice said:

'That's the lot; make haste; I'm trowned.'

The Major gave the order:

'Stop pumping!'

The pump-handle dropped motionless. After packing the kitchen with men, with rifles at the ready, he gingerly raised the oak trap-door.

Four heads appeared, soaked, four fair heads with tow-coloured hair, and they saw the six Germans climb out one after the other, shivering, dripping, terrified.

They were seized and bound, and at once, fearing a possible surprise attack, the Frenchmen started back in two parties, one escorting the prisoners, the other carrying Maloison on a mattress supported on poles.

M. Lavigne was awarded a decoration for capturing a German patrol and the portly baker got the Military Medal for a wound received in action.

MONSIEUR BUSH

OING down the main staircase of his club, which was centrally
ated to the temperature of a greenhouse, the Baron de Mordiane
d left his fur coat open; the result was that when the massive
ont door closed behind him he felt an icy shiver, one of those
dden painful shivers, which affect the spirits like the shock of
ief. Besides, he had lost money and he had been having trouble
ith his digestion for some time and had to be careful what he ate.

He was going home and suddenly the thought of his great empty
t, of his manservant dozing in the hall, of the bathroom, where
e water for his evening bath would be singing gently in the
ater, of his antique bed, broad and solemn as a mortuary couch,
nt another shiver to the bottom of his heart and the marrow of
s bones, even more painful than that of the icy air.

For some years he had been conscious of the oppression of
neliness which sometimes affects elderly bachelors. Before, he had
en strong, active and cheerful, spending all his days in sport and
l his nights in amusements. Now he was putting on weight and
sing the power of enjoyment. Exercise tired him, suppers and
en dinner-parties were bad for him, and women now bored him
much as they had amused him in his youth.

The monotony of evenings like this, with the same friends whom
always found in the same chairs at the club, the same game with
runs of good and bad luck, which always provoked the same
mment, the same jokes on the same subjects made by the same
en, the same scandal about the same women, all this sickened him
such an extent that he sometimes actually thought of suicide.
e could not go on following this empty routine, so common place,
frivolous and at the same time so tedious, and he longed for
me kind of peace and quiet, something comforting, without
owing exactly what.

He did not think of marriage, he was quite certain on that point;
had not the courage to condemn himself to the boredom and the
avery of the married state, to the hateful existence in which two

people, always living together, get to know each other so well th
it is impossible for one to say anything that the other does not kno
in advance, or to have an idea, a desire, an opinion, not alread
guessed by the other. He held that it can be interesting to see
woman again only when one knows her slightly, while there is still i
her something inscrutable and unknown, while she remains to som
extent intriguing and mysterious. So he would have needed a famil
that was not a family, where he could have spent only a part of h
life! And again the memory of his son haunted him.

For a year this son had never been out of his thoughts; he wa
conscious of a desire that gave him no peace to see him and kno
him. He had had the child in his young days as the result of
dramatic love affair. The baby had been sent to the South an
brought up near Marseilles in ignorance of his father's name.

The latter had first paid a nurse's wages, then school fees, the
a young man's extravagances, and finally he had provided mone
to enable him to make a sensible marriage. A discreet solicitor ha
acted for him in the matter without giving away his secret.

The Baron de Mordiane, therefore, knew only that a son of h
blood was living somewhere not far from Marseilles, that he wa
considered intelligent and well educated, that he had married th
daughter of an architect-contractor, to whose business he ha
succeeded. He was also said to be doing very well.

Why shouldn't he go and see this unknown son, concealing h
identity, in order to make a preliminary investigation and se
whether he might later on, if necessary, find a haven of refuge wit
this family?

He had done things handsomely, giving his son a large sum o
money, gratefully accepted, to enable him to set up house. So h
was certain not to find himself up against excessive pride; and th
thought, this desire to go South was never out of his consciousnes
like some itch. He was drawn there, too, by a strange egotistica
sentiment of self-pity at the idea of this cheerful sunny house o
the sea, where he would find his daughter-in-law, young an
pretty, his grandchildren welcoming him with open arms, and hi
son, who would remind him of his short-lived happiness in th

affair of long ago. He was only sorry that he had given him so much money and that the young man had made such good use of it that he could no longer appear in the role of benefactor.

He was walking along thinking of all this, with his fur collar turned up; and he suddenly made up his mind. A cab was passing; he hailed it and drove home and, when his manservant had woken up and opened the door, he said:

'Louis, we shall be starting to-morrow evening for Marseilles. We may be away for a fortnight; make all the necessary arrangements.'

The train was running by the side of the muddy Rhône and on across a dusty plain with smiling villages, a country of extensive views, bounded in the distance by bare mountains.

The Baron de Mordiane, waking up after a night in his sleeping compartment, looked sadly at himself in the small mirror he carried in his dressing-case. The hard Southern light showed him wrinkles which he had not realized were there; he had aged without being aware of it in the half-light of Paris flats.

As he looked at the crowsfeet round his eyes and the sagging lids and saw how the hair was receding from his temples and forehead, he thought:

'Good God! I've not only lost my youth; I'm an old man.'

And his longing for peace suddenly became acute, with a vague desire he had never felt before to dandle his grandchildren on his knee.

About one o'clock in the afternoon he arrived in an open carriage hired in Marseilles, in front of one of those country houses one finds in the South, which are so white, at the end of a drive of plane-trees, that one is dazzled and involuntarily closes the eyes. He smiled, as he walked up the drive, thinking:

'Upon my word! this is a jolly spot!'

Suddenly a child of five or six appeared from behind a shrub and stood on the edge of the drive, gazing wide-eyed at the gentleman.

Mordiane went up to him:

'Good afternoon, my boy!'

The boy did not answer.

The Baron bent down and picked him up to kiss him, but he was met by a suffocating smell of garlic, which seemed to exhale from his whole person, and put him down again quickly, murmuring:

'Oh! he must be the gardener's son.'

And he went on towards the house.

Washing was drying on a line in front of the door, shirts, napkins, cloths, aprons and sheets, while rows of socks on strings one above the other filled a whole window, like sausages hanging up in front of a pork-butcher's shop.

The Baron called.

A servant appeared, a typical Southern servant, dirty and slatternly, with unbrushed hair falling over her face; her skirt, darkened by an accumulation of stains, still showed traces of its original gaudy colour, reminiscent of a clown at a country fair.

He asked:

'Is M. Bush at home?'

He had given his son this name long ago, with a libertine's cynical levity, to make it clear that he had been found under a gooseberry bush.

The maid repeated:

'Do you want M. Bush?'

'Yes.'

'Well, he's in his room, drawing plans.'

'Tell him that M. Merlin wants to speak to him.'

She replied in astonishment:

'Well, come in, if you want to see him.'

And she shouted:

'M. Bush, a visitor!'

The Baron entered, and in a large room, darkened with half-closed shutters, he was dimly conscious of people and things in a general atmosphere of dirt.

Standing at a table covered with every kind of litter, a short bald man was drawing on a large sheet of paper.

He stopped his work and stepped forward.

His waistcoat open, his trousers unbuttoned and his shirt-sleeves

olled up indicated that he felt the heat and his muddy shoes
howed that it had rained some days before.

He asked with a strong Southern accent:

'Whom have I the honour of addressing?'

'Monsieur Merlin . . . I've come to consult you about buying a
building site.'

'Ah! Excellent!'

And Bush, turning to his wife, who was knitting in the semi-
darkness, said:

'Clear a chair, Joséphine.'

Mordiane now noticed a young woman, already looking elderly,
for women in the provinces age at twenty-five, for want of care
and daily baths, all the little precautions, all the little cleansing
treatments, all the little attentions of the beauty parlour, which
preserve the freshness of youth and prolong charm and beauty
almost up to the age of fifty. She had a shawl over her shoulders
and her hair was twisted into a knob anyhow; it was beautiful hair,
thick and black, but one guessed that it rarely saw the brush; as she
reached out towards a chair her hands were those of a charwoman;
she picked up a child's garment, a knife, a piece of string, an empty
flower-pot and a dirty plate, that had all been left on the chair, and
offered it to the visitor.

He sat down and noticed on Bush's work-table, besides books
and papers, two freshly pulled heads of lettuce, a basin, a hair-
brush, a napkin, a revolver and several dirty cups.

The architect saw his expression and said with a smile:

'You must excuse us! The drawing-room is a bit untidy; it's
because of the children.'

And he brought his chair up to talk to his client.

'So you're looking for a site not far from Marseilles?'

His breath, though from a distance, carried to the Baron the
whiff of garlic which all Southerners exhale as naturally as a flower
exhales its scent.

Mordiane asked:

'Was it your son I met under the plane-trees?'

'Yes! Yes! The second.'

'You've got two?'

'Three, Sir, one a year.'

And Bush seemed very proud of the fact.

The Baron was thinking: 'If they all smell as strong, their room must be a regular hothouse!'

He went on: 'Yes, I'm looking for a nice site, near the sea, with a little private beach.'

Bush plunged into details. He had ten, twenty, fifty, a hundred places of this sort, at all prices, to suit all tastes. Words flowed from him like water from a tap; he had a self-satisfied smile and kept nodding his bald round head.

And Mordiane remembered a little fair woman, slim, with a hint of sadness in her soft voice, saying 'My own darling love'; even the memory of that voice stirred the blood in his veins. She had loved him passionately, wildly, for three months; then she had become pregnant, her husband being away as a colonial governor; and she had run away and hidden herself, out of her mind with despair and fear, till the child was born, whom Mordiane had taken away one summer evening and whom they had never seen again.

She had died three years later of consumption, having gone to join her husband in his distant colonial governorship. Now this was their son in front of him; he accented his final syllables like the clang of a bell, as he said:

'This plot, Sir, is a unique bargain . . .'

Mordiane remembered that other voice, as soft as the whisper of the breeze, murmuring:

'My darling love, we'll never part.'

And he recalled the melting depths of those blue loving eyes, as he looked at the expressionless goggle eyes, blue also, of this absurd little man, who was yet like his mother.

Yes, he was getting more and more like her every minute; he had her intonation, her gestures, all her little ways; he was like her as a monkey can be like a human being; he was her son, he had inherited from her a thousand little points of likeness, but, though unmistakable, they were caricatured, irritating and horrible. The Baron was miserable, suddenly haunted by this revolting likeness

ore obvious every minute; it was maddening, exasperating, it
ortured him like a nightmare, like remorse.

He stammered: 'When could we inspect this site?'

'Oh! to-morrow, if you like.'

'Yes, to-morrow. What time?'

'One o'clock.'

'Right!'

The child he had met on the drive appeared at the open door and
awled: 'Fayther!'

Nobody answered him.

Mordiane was standing up, his legs quivering with the desire to
un away and escape. The child's 'fayther' had struck him like a
ullet. It was his son who was being addressed, his son, who stank
f garlic, a typical Southern 'fayther'. How sweet had been the
cent of his lover's body long ago!

Bush showed him to the door.

'Is the house yours?' said the Baron.

'Yes, Sir, I've just bought it. And I'm proud of it. I'm nobody's
hild and I don't forget it; I'm proud of it. I owe nothing to
nyone. I'm a self-made man; I owe everything to my own
fforts.'

The child, who had stayed near the door, shouted again, but
rom further away, 'Fayther.'

Mordiane, trembling and panic-stricken, fled as one flees from
ome great danger.

'He'll guess who I am and recognize me,' he thought. 'He'll
hrow his arms round my neck and call me "fayther" too and give
e a garlic-scented kiss!'

'See you to-morrow, Sir.'

'Yes, to-morrow at one o'clock.'

The open carriage was bowling along the dusty road:

'Drive to the station!'

He could hear the two voices, one far off and soft, the weak, sad
oice from the dead, saying 'My darling love', and the other
aucous, drawling, terrifying, bawling 'fayther', as one shouts
Stop thief!', when a burglar is running away down the street.

The next evening, as he went into the club, the Comte d'Etreil
said to him:

'We haven't seen you for three days. Have you been ill?'

'Yes, I've been a bit off colour. I get headaches from time t
time.'

LOOKING BACK

'Now, darlings,' said the Comtesse, 'it's bed-time.'

The three children, two girls and a boy, got up and went across to kiss their grandmother.

After that they went to say good-night to the Curé, who had been dining at the castle, as he always did on Thursdays.

The Abbé Mauduit took the two girls on his knee, put his long arms in the black-sleeved cassock round their necks and, drawing their heads towards him with a fatherly gesture, he pressed a long affectionate kiss on each forehead.

Then he put them down and the little things left the room, the boy in front and the girls behind.

'You are fond of children, M. le Curé?' said the Comtesse.

'Very fond, Madame.'

The old lady raised her eyes to the priest's face:

'And don't you ever find it hard living alone?'

'Yes, sometimes.'

He fell silent and after a pause he went on: 'But I was never made for everyday life.'

'What do you know about it?'

'Oh! I know well enough. I was made to be a priest. I have followed my vocation.'

The Comtesse was still looking at him.

'Come, M. le Curé, tell me about it; tell me how you made up your mind to renounce all that makes the rest of us love life, all that comforts and consoles us. What decided you not to follow the normal path of marriage and family life? You are neither a mystic nor a fanatic, neither a kill-joy nor a pessimist. Was it something that happened, a great sorrow, that made you take life vows?'

The Abbé Mauduit got up and went to the fire, holding out the heavy shoes of a country priest to the flames. He still seemed to hesitate about answering.

He was a tall, white-haired old man, who had been the parish priest of Saint-Antoine-du-Rocher and the neighbourhood for twenty years. The peasants always said of him: 'He's a real good sort.'

He was a good man, kindly, good-tempered, accessible and, above all, generous. He would have divided his cloak like Saint Martin. He was ready to laugh and equally ready to cry, like a woman, which lowered his reputation a little in the eyes of the dour peasants.

The old Comtesse de Saville, who had retired to her castle at Rocher to bring up her grandchildren after the deaths in close succession of her son and daughter-in-law, was very fond of her curé and used to say of him: 'He's got a good heart.'

He came every Thursday and spent the evening at the castle, and he and the Comtesse had become close friends with the genuine, open-hearted friendship possible only to the old. They were so much of a mind that they hardly needed to put their thoughts into words, being both good souls with the simple goodness of unsophisticated kindly folk.

She insisted: 'Now, M. le Curé, it's time for *you* to make your confession to *me*.'

He repeated: 'I was not born for ordinary life. Fortunately I discovered it in time and I have very often had cause to know how right I was.

'My parents, who were wholesale haberdashers at Verdiers and quite well off, were very ambitious for me. They sent me to a boarding-school very young. People do not realize how unhappy a boy can be at school simply from loneliness and being away from home. The routine life without affection is good for some but disastrous for others. Children are often more sensitive than people think, and, if they are shut up in this way too early away from those they love, excessive sensitiveness, which plays havoc with their nerves, may develop and become pathological and dangerous.

'I hardly played any games; I made no friends and was violently home-sick all the time; I cried in bed at night and was always trying to recall memories of home, trivial memories of little insignificant things and happenings. I could not get out of my mind all I had

eft behind me. I gradually became a nervous wreck, for whom
rifling difficulties assumed the proportions of acute misery.

'The result was that I remained morose and self-centred, inhibited and friendless. The process of increasing mental strain went
on subconsciously but surely. Children's nerves are easily affected;
great care ought to be taken to avoid any disturbance in their lives,
until they are practically mature. But who realizes that for some
boys at school an undeserved imposition may cause as much
mental anguish as the death of a friend will later on? Who really
appreciates that something quite trivial may cause in certain im-
mature minds an emotional upset which may in a very short time
inflict incurable damage?

'This is what happened in my case; home-sickness developed in
me to such an extent that my whole life became one long agony.

'I told no one and said nothing about it. My natural sensitiveness
gradually increased till it became pathological and my mind was
one open wound. The slightest touch produced twinges of pain and
agonizing repercussions which did me permanent harm. Happy
indeed are those to whom nature has given a thick skin and the
armour of stoicism!

'I reached the age of sixteen. The fact that everything hurt me
made me abnormally shy. Knowing that I had no defence against
the blows of chance or fate, I shrank from all contacts, all advances,
all the activities of school life. I was continually on the defensive,
as if constantly threatened by some unknown but always anticipated misfortune. I dared not speak or act in public. I was obsessed
with the idea that life was a battle, a frightful struggle, in which
one received terrible blows and wounds not only painful but
mortal.

'Instead of hopes of happiness for the morrow, such as normal
people have, I was conscious only of an undefined terror and I
wanted to hide and avoid the struggle, in which I was bound to be
defeated and killed.

'When I had finished my studies, I was given six months' holiday
in which to choose my career. A very simple incident suddenly
enabled me to understand myself and revealed to me my unhealthy

psychological condition; I realized my danger and made up m
mind to avoid it.

'Verdiers is a small town in flat country with woods all round i
My parents' house was in the main street. I now spent my tim
away from the home I had missed and longed for so much.
wandered over the countryside, day-dreaming, by myself, so th
my dreams could develop without interruption.

'My father and mother, wrapped up in their business and anxiou
about my future, could talk of nothing but their sales and th
careers open to me. They loved me like hard-headed practic
people with their head rather than their heart. I lived in the priso
of my own thoughts, never free from the terrors of anxiety.

'Well, one evening after a long day out, as I was walking fast i
order not to be late home, I saw a dog running at full spee
towards me. He was a sort of red spaniel, very thin, with long curl
ears.

'He halted ten yards from me; I stopped too. He began to wa
his tail and came slowly towards me with timid movements of hi
whole body, cowering down as if begging and moving his hea
gently from side to side. I spoke to him. Then he began to craw
towards me on his belly, looking so humble, so miserable, s
appealing that tears came into my eyes. I went towards him but h
ran away; he soon came back and I knelt down on one knee an
spoke kindly to him, enticing him to come closer. At last he wa
within reach of my hand and I stroked him very gently, takin
great care not to frighten him.

'He became bolder, gradually stood upright, put his paws on m
shoulders and began to lick my face. He followed me home.

'This was the first living creature I had ever loved passionately
because he returned my affection. My love for the animal was, n
doubt, exaggerated and ridiculous. I had a vague idea that in som
way we were brothers, both lost in life, both lonely and defenceless
He never left me, slept at the foot of my bed, was fed in the dining
room in spite of my parents' protests and he came with me on m
solitary walks.

'I often stopped on the edge of a ditch and sat down on the grass

Sam immediately ran to me and lay down by my side or on my knee, nosing at my hand to make me stroke him.

'One day towards the end of June, as we were on the road to Saint-Pierre-de-Chavrol, I saw the bus from Ravereau coming. It was travelling fast with the four horses at full gallop; it had a yellow body and a black leather tilt over the seats on the top like a cap. The driver was cracking his whip and a cloud of dust rose under the wheels of the heavy vehicle and drifted away behind.

'Suddenly, just as it reached me, Sam, perhaps frightened by the noise and wanting to get to me, dashed in front of it. The hoof of one of the horses knocked him over; I saw him roll, summersault, get up and fall again amid the forest of legs; the whole bus gave two great bumps and I saw behind it something writhing in the dust. He was almost severed in two; his belly was torn open and his entrails were hanging out, spouting blood. He tried to get up and walk, but he could only move his fore legs, which scrabbled at the ground; his hind quarters were already dead. And he was howling pitiably, mad with pain'.

'In a minute or two he was dead. I cannot describe my feelings and how much I was affected. I could not leave my room for a month.

'One evening my father, who was furious with me for making such a fuss over such a little thing, cried: "What will you do when you have a real sorrow, if you lose a wife or children?"

'In a flash I began to understand myself. I realized why little everyday troubles assumed catastrophic proportions in my eyes; I saw that I was so constituted that I felt everything over-keenly and was hyper-susceptible to painful impressions, which were intensified by my abnormal sensitiveness; and a paralysing fear of life gripped me.

'I was without physical desires or ambition; so I decided to sacrifice the possibility of happiness to the certainty of suffering. "Life is short; I will devote myself to the service of others; I will soothe their sorrows and rejoice in their happiness," I said to myself. "As I shall not feel either myself directly, I shall experience these emotions only with diminished intensity."

G 2

'And if you only knew how suffering still tortures me and wring my heart! But what would have been intolerable agony in my own case has been sublimated into sympathy and pity.

'I could never have endured the sorrow with which I come into contact every day had it been my own. I could not have seen a child of my own die without dying myself. And, in spite of everything, I still have such an undefined, subconscious fear of something happening, that the sight of the postman coming to my door sends a shiver down my spine, though now I have nothing to fear.'

The Abbé Mauduit fell silent. He was looking into the fire in the great fireplace, as if seeking to read there all the mysteries and secrets of the life he might have lived, if he had faced suffering more bravely. He went on in a lower voice:

'I was right; I am not made to live in this world.'

The Comtesse said nothing; at last, after a long silence, she commented:

'As for me, if I had not got my grandchildren, I don't think I should have the courage to go on living.'

The Curé got up without another word.

As the servants in the kitchen were asleep, she took him herself to the door into the garden and watched his tall, slow-moving shadow in the light of his lantern plunge into the darkness.

Then she went back and sat down by the fire, and thought of many things that do not occur to the young.

THE WITHERED HAND

ABOUT eight months ago a friend of mine, Louis R . . . , had invited some old school friends in one evening; we were drinking punch and smoking, as we talked literature and painting, with a funny story from time to time, the usual sort of young men's party. Suddenly the door burst open and one of my best childhood friends came in like a hurricane. 'Guess where I've come from,' he cried as he entered: 'I bet it's the Mabille night-club,' suggested one of the party. 'No, you look too cheerful; you've been borrowing money, burying your aunt or taking your watch to your uncle's,' opined another. 'You've been getting tight,' interjected a third, and, when you scented Louis' punch, you came up to go on with the process.' 'You're all wrong, I've just come from P... in Normandy, where I've been staying for a week, and I've brought back a friend of mine, a noted criminal, whom I beg leave to introduce to you.' With these words he took out of his pocket a withered hand; it was a terrifying object, blackened, shrivelled, with very long fingers, like the claw of a bird of prey; the muscles were amazingly powerful and were tied, inside and out, with a leather thong the colour of old parchment. The narrow yellow nails were still on the ends of the fingers; one could sniff the criminal a mile off.

'Picture to yourselves,' explained my friend, 'the sale the other day of the effects of an old wizard, well known in the district; he attended the Sabbat every Saturday night on a broom-stick, practised both white and black magic, made cows give blue milk and carry their tails like Saint Anthony's pal. Anyhow the old rascal was much attached to this hand, which he alleged belonged to a famous criminal, executed in 1736 for having thrown his legitimate wife head first into a well, which she probably deserved, and hung the priest who had married them from his own church steeple. After this double exploit he had travelled and, in the course of a life that was busy though short, he had robbed twelve travellers on the road, smoked out twenty monks in a monastery and turned a nunnery into his harem.' 'But what are you going to do with the horrible thing?' we exclaimed. 'I propose to use it as a bell-pull, by Jove, to scare away duns.' 'My friend,' said Henry Smith, a tall phlegmatic Englishman, 'I believe this hand is just a bit of pemmican, preserved by a new process, and I advise you to make it into soup.' 'Let's be serious, gentlemen,' remarked a medical student, who was half-seas over, in a matter of fact tone of voice, 'look here, Pierre, if I may offer a suggestion, you'd better give these human remains Christian burial, for fear of the owner coming to demand his own back; moreover, possibly this hand has contracted bad habits – you know the proverb "once a murderer always a murderer."' 'And once a toper always a toper,' replied our host, pouring out a big glass of punch for the student, who tossed it off and rolled under the table dead drunk. A roar of laughter greeted this sally and Pierre, raising his glass and bowing to the hand, said: 'I drink to your owner's next visit.' Then we talked of other things and finally went home.

Next day, as I was passing his house, I went in; it was about two o'clock and I found him reading and smoking. 'Well, how are you?' I said. 'Quite well,' he replied. 'And your hand?' 'Oh, my hand, you must have seen it on my bell-pull, where I put it last night when I came home; but, by the way, fancy, some idiot, wanting no doubt to play a practical joke, came and rang the bell like mad about midnight; I enquired who was there and as there was no answer I retired to bed and went to sleep.'

At this moment there was a ring; it was the landlord, a very rude, ill-mannered fellow, who came in without taking off his hat. 'Sir,' he said to my friend, 'I must ask you to remove immediately the piece of carrion you have tied to your bell-pull; otherwise I shall have to give you notice.' 'Sir,' replied Pierre with a perfectly straight face, 'you are offering an insult to a hand which, I must inform you, belonged to a gentleman.' The landlord turned on his heel and went out as he had come in. Pierre followed him, took down the hand and attached it to the bell-pull which hung over his bed in the recess. 'This hand,' he said, 'is better than the Trappists'

'Frater, memento mori" to encourage serious thoughts every night as I go to sleep.' After an hour I left him and went home.

The following night I slept badly. I was jumpy and nervy; several times I woke with a start; I once even imagined a man had got into the room, and I got up and looked in the cupboards and under the bed; at last about six in the morning, as I was beginning to get sleepy, a loud knock at my door brought me out of bed with a jump; it was my friend's servant, half dressed, pale and trembling: 'Oh, Sir!' he cried between sobs, 'my poor master's murdered!'

I threw on my clothes and rushed round to Pierre's place. The house was full of people arguing; amid general confusion there was a continuous coming and going; everybody was talking, telling the story and giving all sorts of different accounts of what had happened. I had great difficulty in making my way to his room; the door was guarded, but I gave my name and was admitted. Four policemen were standing in the centre of the room with note-books; they were taking notes, whispering from time to time and writing; two doctors were conversing near the bed, on which Pierre was lying unconscious. He was not dead but he was a ghastly sight. The eyes were staring; it was as if the dilated pupils were fixed on some horrible uncanny sight in panic terror, the hands were clenched. The body from the chin down was covered with a sheet, which I raised. On his neck were five finger-prints, driven deep into the flesh, and there were a few drops of blood on his night-shirt. At this moment one thing struck me; I happened to look at the bell in the recess, the withered hand had disappeared. No doubt the doctors had removed it, so that those who came into the wounded man's room should not have a shock, for the hand was really terrifying. I didn't discover what had happened to it.

I now give the story of the crime from the next day's paper, with all the details which the police had been able to find out. This is the account:

'A brutal assault was committed yesterday on a young man, M. Pierre B . . ., a law student, who belongs to one of the best families in Normandy. This young man had got home about ten o'clock in the evening; he dismissed his servant, one Bonvin, saying that he was tired and was going to bed. About midnight this man was woken by his master's bell ringing violently. He was alarmed, struck a light and waited; the bell stopped for about a minute and then began to peal again so furiously that the servant, terrified out of his wits, rushed out of his room and went to rouse the porter, who ran to call the police; they arrived about a quarter of an hour later and broke open the door.

'A grim sight met their eyes; the furniture had been overturned, and everything pointed to a desperate struggle between the victim and his assailant. In the centre of the room, on his back lay young Pierre B . . . as if dead, his body rigid, his face livid and his eyes staring horribly; on his neck were five deep finger-prints. The report of Dr Bourdeau, who was immediately summoned, states that the assailant must have been a man of unusual strength, with an abnormally long and sinewy hand, for the fingers, which had left five marks like bullet holes in the neck, had almost met through the flesh. There is no clue to the motive for the crime nor to the identity of the perpetrator.'

Next day the same paper reported:

'M. Pierre B . . ., the victim of the murderous assault, of which we gave an account yesterday, recovered consciousness after two hours of unremitting attention from Dr Bourdeau. His life is not in danger but grave fears are entertained for his reason. There is no trace of the assailant.'

In fact, my poor friend was insane; for seven months I went to see him every day in the mental home but he never recovered a glimmer of reason. He talked strangely in his ravings and, like all madmen, he had a fixed idea and always imagined he was being pursued by a ghost. One day they came to summon me in a hurry, telling me that he was worse, and I found him dying. For two hours he remained perfectly quiet, then, suddenly getting out of bed in spite of our efforts he waved his arms and screamed, with all the symptoms of panic terror:

'Take it away! Take it away! He's strangling me! Help! Help!' He staggered twice round the room shrieking, and fell forward, dead.

As he was an orphan, it fell to my lot to convey the body to the little village of P . . . in Normandy, where his parents were buried. He had come from there on the evening when he had found us drinking punch at Louis R . . .'s and introduced us to the withered hand. His body was placed in a lead coffin and four days later I was walking sadly with the old Curé, who had given him his first lessons, in the little cemetery, where his grave was being dug. It was a lovely day, the cloudless blue sky was bathed in sunlight and birds were singing in the brambles on the bank, where the two of us as children had often come to eat the blackberries. I could still picture him slinking along the hedge and worming his way through the little hole I knew so well over there, on the far side of the plot, where paupers are buried; and then we used to go home, our cheeks and lips blackened with the juice of the fruit we had eaten; I looked at the bushes and they were covered with fruit; I picked a blackberry mechanically and ate it; the priest had opened his breviary and was muttering prayers, and at the end of the path I could hear the shovels of the men digging the grave.

Suddenly they shouted to us; the Curé closed his book and we went to see what they wanted. They had come on a coffin. With one blow of the pick-axe they removed the lid and we saw the skeleton of an abnormally tall man, lying on his back; his empty eye-sockets seemed to be looking defiantly at us. I felt quite uncomfortable; I don't know why, but I was almost frightened. 'Hullo!' cried one of the men, 'look here! This fellow had one hand cut off at the wrist; here's the hand.' And he picked up from the side of the body a great withered hand, which he held out for us to see. 'My goodness!' said the other, laughing, 'he looks as if he'd got his eye on you and was just going for you to make you give back his hand!' 'Come along, my friends,' said the priest, 'leave the dead in peace and close the coffin again; we'll dig poor M. Pierre's grave somewhere else.'

Next day it was all over and I was on my way back to Paris, leaving fifty francs with the old priest for masses for the repose of the soul of the man whose grave we had desecrated.

THE QUESTION OF LATIN

THIS question of Latin, which has been discussed lately till every-one is sick of it, reminds me of an incident which happened when I was a boy.

I was finishing my secondary-school course at a cramming establishment in one of the large towns in Central France, the Robineau Institute, which had a great reputation in that part of the country for the excellence of its Latin teaching.

For the last ten years in all competitive examinations the Robineau Institute had defeated the Imperial High School in the provincial capital and all the Secondary Schools in the smaller towns, and its run of successes had been due, it was said, to a mere uncertificated teacher, M. Piquedent, or rather Daddy Piquedent.

He was one of those grey-haired men of uncertain age, no longer young, whose life-story was obvious at first sight. Having taken a post as an uncertificated teacher in the first private school that offered, in order to be able to continue his own studies for a University degree, with the possibility of a doctorate later, he had found himself so deeply involved in this depressing job that he had remained an uncertificated teacher all his life. But his love of Latin had never left him, holding him in its grip like some depraved passion. He went on reading the poets, prose writers and historians, explaining them and writing notes with a pertinacity which amounted to an obsession.

One day it occurred to him to make the whole class answer his questions entirely in Latin; and he went on with this until they could keep up a conversation with him as if they were speaking their mother tongue.

He listened to them as a conductor listens to his orchestra at rehearsal, and he was always banging on his desk with his ruler and saying:

'Lefrère, Lefrère, you're making a howler! Don't you remember the rule? . . .' 'Plantel, that turn of phrase is completely French, not

Latin. You *must* get the feeling for the genius of the language. Just listen to me . . .'

The result was that at the end of the year boys from the Robineau Institute won all the prizes for Latin Composition, Unseen and Declamation.

The following year the proprietor, a cunning little man with the physique and facial contortions of an ape, inserted in his prospectus and advertisements and painted up over the door of the Institute:

'Special attention to Latin. – All five classes in the School have gained first prizes.

'Two special prizes in the examination open to all the Public and Secondary Schools in France.'

For ten years the Robineau Institute had had an unbroken series of successes. So my father, attracted by this performance, sent me as a day-boy to this Robineau whom we called Robinetto or Robinettino and made me take private lessons with Daddy Piquedent at five francs an hour, of which the teacher got two and the proprietor three. I was eighteen at the time and in the Sixth.

These private lessons took place in a small room with a window on the street. Instead of talking Latin to me Daddy Piquedent began to tell me all his troubles in French. Having no relations or friends, the poor fellow took a fancy to me and poured out his sorrows.

For ten or fifteen years he had never spoken to a soul alone.

'I am like an oak-tree in the desert,' he would say, 'sicut quercus in solitudine.'

He didn't hit it off with the other teachers and he had no friends in the town, because he was too busy to have time for social contacts.

'It's just as bad or worse at nights, my boy. I've always dreamt of a room with my own furniture, my own books, my own possessions which no one else could touch. As it is, I have nothing I can call my own, nothing except my trousers and my frock-coat, not even my own mattress or pillow. I haven't got a room to shut myself up in, except when I come to this room to give a lesson. Do you realize what that means? A man who spends his whole life without the right or the time to shut himself up alone, no matter where, to think, to meditate, to work, to dream. My dear boy, a key, the key of a door that one can lock, that spells happiness, the only happiness in life!

'Here all day I invigilate Preparation among these fidgety kids and at night I sleep in a dormitory with the same kids snoring all round me. I sleep in a bed without any privacy at the end of two rows of other beds, responsible for the discipline of all these little blighters. I can never be alone, never! If I go out, the streets are crowded, and, when I am tired of walking about, I go into a café full of men smoking and playing billiards. I tell you, it's hell!'

'Why don't you do something else, Sir?' I asked.

'But what, my dear boy?' he cried, 'What? I'm not a boot-maker, a carpenter, a hatter, a baker or a hairdresser. I know nothing but Latin and I've got no degree, so I can't demand a big salary. If I'd got my doctorate, I could ask a hundred francs for what I now have to give for five; and no doubt my lessons wouldn't be half as good, for the letters after my name would be enough to keep up my reputation.'

Occasionally he would say:

'The only peace I have in my life is the hours I spend with you. Don't be afraid; you shan't be the loser; I'll make it up in class by getting you to talk twice as much as the others.'

One day I plucked up my courage and offered him a cigarette. First of all he looked at me in consternation; then he glanced at the door:

'But suppose somebody came in, my dear boy!'

'Very well, let's smoke out of the window,' I replied.

So we went and leant with our elbows on the window-sill over the street, cupping our hands to conceal the thin rolls of tobacco.

Opposite was a shop where they did ironing; four women in loose white overalls were pressing the linen spread out before them with heavy irons, the heat raising a cloud of steam. Suddenly a fifth girl, carrying a large basket which made her bend to one side as she walked, came out on her way to deliver shirts, handkerchiefs and sheets at the customers' houses. She paused at the door as if she was already tired but, looking up, smiled when she saw us smoking and with her one free hand blew us an ironical kiss with the nonchalance of a working-class girl. Presently she walked off slowly, shuffling along in her loose slippers.

She was a girl of about twenty, short, rather thin and pallid, with a lively expression and a shock of untidy fair hair.

Daddy Piquedent was quite sympathetic and murmured:

'What a job for a woman! It's a horse's job!'

And he waxed emotional over the grim life of the workers; he had the enthusiasm of a sentimental socialist and there was a catch in his voice when he spoke of the hard lot of the working class in the style of Jean-Jacques Rousseau.

Next day as we were leaning out of the same window, the same work-girl spotted us and shouted in a shrill pert voice, cocking a snook in our direction: 'Good morning! Don't work too hard!'

I threw her a cigarette, which she immediately lit. And the four other women crowded to the door, holding out their hands for the same.

And every day there was an exchange of friendly chat between the work-girls on the pavement and ourselves who ought to have been working in the school.

Daddy Piquedent was as good as a play. He was terrified of being seen, for he might have lost his job, and he made grotesque, shy gestures like an actor making love on the stage, to which the girls responded with a hail of kisses.

An idea that I ought to have been ashamed of was beginning to take shape in my head. One day as I entered the room I whispered to the old beak:

'You won't believe it, Sir, but I've met the little laundry-maid – you know, the one with the basket – and I've had a talk to her.'

He was somewhat intrigued by my air of secrecy:

'What did she say to you?'

'She said . . . well, she said . . . she rather liked you. As a matter of fact . . . I think . . . she's a bit gone on you.'

I saw him turn pale and he answered:

'Nonsense, she's laughing at me. This sort of thing doesn't happen at my age.'

'Why not?' I replied without a smile: 'You're not so bad-looking!'

I saw that my lie had made an impression and said no more.

And every day I told him I had met the girl and talked to her about him. The result was that in the end he believed me and in all seriousness sent the laundry-maid passionate kisses.

Well, one morning on my way to school I really did meet her. I spoke to her without hesitation, as if I had known her ten years.

'Good morning; how are you?'

'Quite well, Sir, thank you.'

'Have a cigarette?'

'Oh! No, not in the street.'

'You can take it home.'

'Right ho! I'd like one.'

'Look here, d'you know . . .?'

'What, Sir?'

'The old man, my teacher . . .'

'You mean, Daddy Piquedent.'

'Yes, Daddy Piquedent. So you know his name?'

'Of course! Well . . .?

'Well, he's in love with you.'

She burst out into hysterical laughter and cried:

'You're joking!'

'Not a bit, I'm dead serious. He talks about you all our lessons. I bet he means to marry you.'

She stopped laughing. The word 'marriage' makes any girl serious. Then she repeated incredulously:

'You're joking.'

'I swear it's true.'

She picked up the basket which she had put down at her feet:

'Well, we'll see,' she said.

And off she went.

As soon as I got to school I took Daddy Piquedent aside:

'You must write her a letter; she's madly in love with you.'

And he wrote her a long passionate love-letter, full of phrases and periphrases, of metaphors and similes, the sort of love-letter one would expect from a philosopher or a university don, a masterpiece of flowery exaggeration, which I undertook to deliver to the girl.

She read it with a grave face, obviously impressed, and murmured:

'How beautifully he writes! You can see he's an educated man. Will he really marry me?'

'Of course he will,' I answered brazenly, 'he's mad about you.'

'Well, he'd better invite me to dinner on Sunday at the Isle of Flowers.'

I promised that the invitation would be sent.

Daddy Piquedent was deeply moved by all I told him about her. I added:

'She's in love with you, Sir, and I believe she's an honest girl. You mustn't seduce her and then desert her.'

He replied with emphasis:

'I'm an honest man, too, my dear boy.'

I admit I had no serious intention. It was all a schoolboy joke, nothing more. I had guessed how easy it would be to take advantage of the old schoolmaster's innocent gullibility. I was just having a bit of fun and I never asked myself what would come of it. I was eighteen and had been known at school for years as a confirmed practical joker.

So it was arranged that Daddy Piquedent and I would take a cab to the Queue-de-Vache ferry, where we would pick up Angèle, and I would take them in my boat, for I did a lot of rowing in those days. I would row them to the Isle of Flowers, where we would all dine together. I had inflicted my company upon them in order to enjoy my triumph, and the old man, by accepting my suggestion and so risking his position as principal actor, showed clearly that he really was a little mad.

When we reached the ferry, where my boat had been moored since the morning, I saw in the grass, or rather sticking out above

the tall grass on the bank, a huge crimson sunshade like an enormous poppy. Under the sunshade the little laundry-maid was
waiting for us in her Sunday best; she was quite charming, though
a little pale, and had nice manners, though there was something a
bit suburban about her.

Daddy Piquedent took off his hat to her with a bow. She held
out her hand and they looked at one another in silence. Then they
got into my boat and I took the sculls.

They sat side by side on the stern seat.

The old man was the first to speak:

'What a perfect day for a trip on the water!'

'Yes, isn't it?' she murmured.

She let her hand trail in the water, just touching its surface with
her finger-tips, setting up tiny transparent wavelets, delicate as a
sheet of glass, which broke against the side of the boat with a gentle
splash.

When we reached the restaurant she found her tongue and
ordered dinner, fried fish, chicken and salad. After that she took us
for a stroll round the island, which she knew well.

By this time she was in high spirits, amusing and quite ready to
poke fun at us.

The question of love was not mentioned till dessert. I had stood
champagne and Daddy Piquedent was slightly drunk; she was well
away herself and kept calling him:

'M. Piquenez.'

Suddenly he said:

'Mademoiselle Angèle, I think M. Raoul has informed you of my
sentiments.'

At once she was as serious as a judge:

'Yes, M. Piquedent.'

'Do you reciprocate them?'

'A girl never answers a question like that!'

He was breathless with emotion and went on:

'Do you think you could ever love me?'

She smiled:

'You old silly! You're awfully sweet!'

'Well, Mademoiselle Angèle, do you think that some day we might . . .'

She hesitated a moment and said with a quiver in her voice:

'You mean you'll marry me? Nothing doing otherwise, you know.'

'Of course, Mademoiselle Angèle.'

'Well, I don't mind if I do, M. Piquenez!'

So these two innocent creatures got engaged all through a schoolboy's practical joke. I didn't take it seriously and perhaps they didn't either. Suddenly she hesitated:

'You know, I haven't got anything, not a brass farthing.'

He stammered, for he was as tight as Silenus:

'I've got five thousand francs in the Savings Bank.'

She exclaimed triumphantly:

'Then we can set up in business, can't we?'

He was puzzled:

'But what sort of business?'

'Oh! I don't know; we'll see. One can do a lot with five thousand francs. You don't expect me to come and live in your school, do you?'

He hadn't looked as far ahead as that and he stuttered with perplexity:

'Set up in what? It's not so easy. I know nothing but Latin.'

She began to consider the problem, running through all the occupations she had ever hankered after:

'You couldn't be a doctor, I suppose?'

'No, I've got no degree.'

'Nor a chemist?'

'No, that's just as hopeless.'

She uttered a cry of joy; she'd had an inspiration:

'I know, we'll buy a grocer's shop. That'll be fine, we'll buy a grocer's shop; in quite a small way, of course; one can't do much with five thousand francs.'

He reacted violently:

'No, I can't be a grocer . . . I'm . . . I'm too well known in the place . . . and I don't know anything but Latin!'

But she stopped his mouth with a glass of champagne. He drank it and said no more.

We got back into the boat. It was a dark night, pitch dark; but I could see their arms round each other's waist and they kissed several times.

Then a dreadful catastrophe occurred. Our escapade was discovered and Daddy Piquedent lost his job; and my father, furious, sent me to the Ribaudet Academy to finish my last year.

Six weeks later I passed my Matriculation and went to Paris to read Law. I didn't go back to my home town for two years.

Round a corner in the Rue du Serpent a shop caught my eye, with a sign: Piquedent's Imported Canned Goods Store, and underneath for the benefit of the uneducated: Groceries.

I quoted aloud:

'Quantum mutatus ab illo!'

Piquedent looked up and, deserting his customer, ran towards me with outstretched hands:

'Ah! My dear young friend, you here! What luck! What luck!'

A good-looking woman, very plump, hurriedly left the cash-desk and threw herself into my arms. I hardly recognized her, she had put on so much weight.

I asked:

'How are things going?'

Piquedent had gone back to his scales:

'Oh! fine, very well indeed! I've cleared three thousand francs this year!'

'And what about the Latin, Sir?'

'Latin! Good Heavens, Latin! One can't live on Latin!'

MONSIEUR PARENT

I

LITTLE George on all fours was making castles in the sand on the path. He picked up handfuls of it, built a pyramid and then stuck a chestnut leaf on the top.

His father, sitting on an iron seat, kept a fond gaze fixed on the child, with eyes for no one else in the crowded public garden.

All along the circular path running round the grass plots in front of the fountain and Trinity Church other children were similarly busy at their games like little puppies, while their bored nurse-maids stared blankly into space or their mothers gossiped together, keeping a watchful eye on their young.

Wet-nurses walked about solemnly in pairs, with the long brightly coloured ribbons of their bonnets streaming out behind them, carrying shapeless white masses wrapped up in lace, while little girls in short skirts with bare legs held serious confabulations in the intervals of running races with their hoops; and the garden attendant in his green uniform strolled about through the masses of children, threading his way carefully so as not to destroy the sand castles or tread on little hands and interfere with these fasci-nating human insects, all working as busily as ants.

The sun was nearly setting behind the roofs of the Rue Saint Lazare and cast its long slanting rays over the animated throng of youngsters and well-dressed grown-ups. A golden light shone upon the chestnuts and the three fountains in front of the great west door of the church were streams of liquid silver.

Monsieur Parent watched his son sprawling in the dust, follow-ing his every movement with loving gaze, as though he wanted to kiss the child across the intervening space as he played.

Suddenly looking up at the church clock, he discovered that he was five minutes late. He got up, took the child by the arm, shook the dust out of his clothes, cleaned his hands and hustled him off towards the Rue Blanche. He was in a hurry to get home before his

wife returned; and the little fellow, unable to keep up, trotted along
by his father's side. Presently he picked the child up and, increasing
his pace, breasted the slope in spite of shortness of breath. He was
a man of forty, already grey and somewhat portly, with a nervously
apologetic air as if ashamed of the comfortable paunch he had
developed.

A few years before he had married a young wife whom he adored
and who had him completely under her thumb and bullied him
incessantly. She was continually nagging at him alike for sins of
omission and commission, with venomous comments on everything
he did, his habits, his simple pleasures, his tastes, the way he walked,
his gestures, his increasing girth and his good-tempered unruffled
way of talking.

But he was still fond of her and he adored George, the child she
had given him, who was now three years old and had become his
father's greatest joy and interest. He had a little money of his own
and he lived without working on his income of 20,000 francs a
year; his wife, whom he had married without a dowry, was always
furious with him for having no occupation.

At last he reached home, put the child down on the bottom step
of the staircase, mopped his brow and started to go up.

On the second floor he rang the bell.

An elderly woman, who had been his nurse, one of those
masterful servants who rule the family with a rod of iron, came to
the door; he enquired anxiously:

'Is the mistress home?'

The servant shrugged her shoulders:

'Have you ever known the mistress in by half-past six?'

He replied awkwardly:

'All right, so much the better; I shall have time to change, I'm
very hot.'

The woman gave him a look of mingled pity, annoyance and
contempt. She growled:

'Oh! I'm not blind; you're in a muck sweat, Sir, you've been
running and I expect you've been carrying the child, all for the
pleasure of waiting for the mistress till half-past seven. You

wouldn't catch me being so punctual. I'm getting dinner ready for eight o'clock, and if I'm kept waiting, so much the worse; a joint spoils if it's over-cooked.'

Monsieur Parent pretended not to hear; he murmured:

'All right, all right! George's hands want washing, he's been making mud pies. I'm going to change; tell the housemaid to see that the child is clean.'

And he went to his room. As soon as he got there he bolted the door; he wanted to be alone, quite alone, absolutely alone. By now he was so used to being slanged and abused that he was never happy unless the door was locked; he dare not even sit down to think quietly by himself, unless he felt safe under lock and key. Throwing himself into a chair, to rest a bit before changing, he realized that Julie was developing into a new danger in the house. She hated his wife, that was obvious; and her feelings were especially bitter against Paul Limousin, who had been the closest friend of his bachelor days and had remained on terms of intimate friendship in the house after his marriage, a thing which does not often happen. It was Limousin who oiled the wheels and acted as a buffer between Henriette and himself, and who defended him, sometimes with spirit, sometimes even roughly, against undeserved reproaches, painful scenes and all the daily worries of his life.

But during the last six months Julie had always been going out of her way to make cutting remarks and ill-natured criticisms of her mistress. She was always down on her and would say twenty times a day: 'If I was you, Sir, I wouldn't let myself be bullied like this. But it's none of my business; that's all there is to it, everybody must go their own way.'

One day she had actually been rude to Henriette, who had said nothing at the time, but in the evening she had remarked to her husband:

'Look here, next time that woman gives me a bit of her lip, I'm going to chuck her out.' But, though she was otherwise entirely fearless, she seemed nevertheless afraid of the old servant; and Parent attributed this mildness to consideration for the woman who had been his nurse and had closed his mother's eyes.

Now the crisis had come; things could not go on as they were any longer; and he was terrified when he thought of what was going to happen. What could he do? The idea of giving Julie notice appeared such an appalling decision that he dared not dwell on it. It was equally impossible to side with her against his wife; and before a month was out the situation between the two women would become intolerable.

He remained sitting in the chair, his arms hanging down limply, vaguely trying to find some solution to the problem but without success. Then he murmured to himself: 'Luckily I've got George: without him I should be utterly miserable.'

Presently it occurred to him that he might consult Limousin and he made up his mind to do so; but immediately he remembered the animosity between the servant and his friend and was afraid that the latter would advise him to give her notice; and again he was lost in an agony of doubt and indecision.

The clock struck seven. He started. Seven o'clock and he had not changed! Terrified and breathing hard, he undressed, washed, put on a clean shirt and dressed again hurriedly, as if someone was waiting for him in the next room for a very important appointment.

This done, he went into the drawing-room with a feeling of relief. He glanced at the paper, went and looked out of the window, and came back and sat down on the sofa, as the door opened and his son came in smiling, clean and tidy. Parent took him up in his arms and kissed him passionately. First he kissed his hair, then his eyes, his cheeks, his mouth, his hands. Then he lifted him in the air right up to the ceiling as high as he could reach. After that he sat down exhausted by the exertion and putting George on his knee made him 'ride a cock-horse'.

The child was delighted and laughed and waved his arms, crowing with joy, while his father roared with laughter, too, completely happy, his fat stomach quivering, enjoying it all even more than the child.

This weak, resigned, bullied husband loved his son with all his honest heart. He loved him with all the uncontrolled passion, with the wildly extravagant caresses and all the shamefaced tenderness, which had always been repressed and had not been able to come out and expand even in the early days of his married life, for his wife had been unemotional and discouraging from the first.

Julie appeared at the door, her face pale and her eyes flashing, and announced in a voice quivering with rage:

'It's half-past seven, Sir.'

Parent glanced at the clock with anxious resignation and murmured:

'Yes, it is half-past seven.'

'Well, my dinner is ready.'

Foreseeing the approaching storm, he did his best to stave it off:

'But didn't you tell me, when I came in, that you wouldn't have it ready till eight?'

'Eight! Well I never! You wouldn't give the child his dinner at eight, would you? I said 'eight', I know, but of course I didn't mean it. It would ruin the child's digestion to feed him at eight. I wouldn't mind, if there were only his mother to consider. A fat lot she cares about the child. What sort of a mother is she, anyhow? A mother like her's a disgrace.'

Parent, trembling with anxiety, realized that he must cut short this threatening scene somehow.

'Julie,' he said, 'I won't have you talk about your mistress in this way. You understand and don't you forget it in the future.'

The old servant, dumbfounded, turned on her heel and left the room, banging the door so violently that all the glass of the chandelier tinkled.

For several seconds there was a faint undefined carillon of little invisible bells, echoing in the still air of the drawing-room.

George, first of all surprised, began to clap his hands with joy and puffing out his cheeks made a loud plop with all the force of his lungs to imitate the bang of the door.

Then his father told him stories, but he was so preoccupied that he was continually losing the thread, and the child, unable to follow, opened his eyes wide in astonishment.

Parent kept his eyes on the clock; he seemed to see the hands moving. He wished he could stop the clock and make time stand still, till his wife came in. It was not that he was annoyed with Henriette for being late, but he was frightened of her, frightened of Julie, frightened of everything that might happen. Ten minutes more would be enough to cause an irreparable catastrophe, recriminations, a violent scene which he dared not even imagine. At the mere thought of the quarrel, the raised voices, the reproaches hurtling through the air like bullets, the two women glaring at one another face to face, flinging abuse, his heart beat faster and his mouth went dry, as if he had been walking in the sun; he became limp as a rag, so weak that he could not even pick up his son and jog him up and down on his knee.

Eight o'clock struck; the door opened and Julie appeared again. Her fit of temper had passed but she wore an air of bitter, cold resolution that was even more terrifying.

'I served your mother, Sir,' she said, 'to her dying day and I have looked after you from your birth till to-day. I think I can say I have been a faithful servant of the family . . .'

She waited for an answer.

Parent stammered:

'But of course, my dear Julie.'

She went on:

'You know I have never considered the question of money but only your interests; I have never deceived you or lied to you; you've never had cause to find fault with me . . .'

'But of course, my dear Julie.'

'Well, Sir, this can't go on any longer. It's out of consideration for you that I've said nothing; but things have gone too far, you are the laughing-stock of the neighbourhood. You can do what you like, but it's common knowledge; I must tell you at long last, though I hate telling tales. If Mistress comes in like this at any old hour, it's because she's doing unmentionable things.'

He stood there dazed; he could only stammer:

'Not another word . . . you know I forbade you . . .'

She interrupted him, determined not to be cut short:

'No, Sir; now I must tell you everything. Monsieur Limousin has been her lover for a long time. I've seen them myself dozens of imes kissing behind doors. Why, Mistress would never have married you if Monsieur Limousin had had any money. If you remembered, Sir, how the marriage was arranged, you'd understand the whole thing . . .'

Parent got up, livid with rage, stammering:

'Stop, not another word . . . or . . .'

She went on:

'No, I'm going to tell you the whole truth; mistress married you for your money and she was unfaithful from the very start. Of course, it was an understood thing between them; you've only got to think for a minute to see it all. Then, because she didn't love you, she made life hell for you; it made my heart bleed for you, as I watched it all . . .'

He took two steps forward with clenched fists, repeating: 'Be quiet . . . stop . . .'; there was nothing else he could say.

The old servant stood her ground; she was obviously determined to go through with it.

At this moment George, who had been scared at first, now terrified by the angry voices, began to scream. He was standing behind his father, howling, his face contorted and his mouth open.

His son's cries exasperated Parent, overcoming his timidity and making him see red. He rushed at Julie with both hands raised ready to strike her and shouting:

'You wretch, you'll drive the child out of his mind.'

He was already close to her when she flung in his face:

'Hit me, if you like, me that brought you up, but that won't alter the fact that your wife is unfaithful and the child isn't yours!'

He stopped short, his hands dropped to his side and he stood in front of her so dazed that he didn't know where he was. She added:

'You've only got to look at him to see who the child's father is. He's the spit and image of Monsieur Limousin, God knows! You've only got to look at his eyes and his forehead. A blind man could see it . . .'

But he had seized her by the shoulders and was shaking her with all his might, stammering:

'You snake . . . you snake . . . get out of the house, you viper; get out or I'll kill you; out with you, get out . . .'

And exerting all his strength he hurled her into the next room. She fell on the table which was already laid, upsetting and breaking the glasses; quickly picking herself up, she put the table between herself and her master, and while he was chasing her to get hold of her again, she spat in his face the terrible words:

'You've only got to go out . . . to-night . . . after dinner and come back again at once . . . and you'll see if I've told a lie. Just try . . . and you'll see.'

She had got to the kitchen door and escaped. He ran after her, but she ran up the back stairs to her servants' bedroom, where she shut herself in and slammed the door:

'You'll leave the house this minute!'

She answered through the door:

'Don't worry, Sir; I shall be gone in an hour.'

He went slowly down the stairs, clutching the banisters to avoid falling, and returned to the drawing-room, where George was sitting on the floor in tears.

Parent collapsed on to a chair and looked dully at the child. He did not understand, his brain refused to work; he felt stupid, dazed, semi-conscious, as if he had just fallen on his head; he hardly remembered the horrible things the servant had told him. But gradually, like ruffled water, his brain grew calm again and cleared and the awful truth began to come home to him.

Julie had spoken so definitely, so emphatically, with such conviction and certainty that he did not doubt her sincerity, but he clung to the hope that she might be mistaken. She might be wrong, blinded by her devotion to him and deluded by her instinctive hatred of Henriette. But, as he tried to reassure and convince himself, a thousand little things came back to him, words his wife had used, the way Limousin had looked, a mass of trifles unnoticed at the time, how they had gone out late and been away at the same time; even gestures, insignificant in themselves but hard to explain, which he had not observed or understood at the time but were now full of meaning, made it clear that there was an understanding

etween them. Everything that had happened since his engagement
uddenly came back to him in his present overwrought state of
mind. He went over everything, an intonation that was hard to
xplain, a suspicious attitude; and to the mind of the poor man, so
lacid and kindly by nature, now in an agony of uncertainty, what
might still have been only suspicions appeared as proven truth.

In obstinate desperation he went back over the five years since
is marriage, trying to recall everything month by month, day by
ay; and every disquieting occurrence which he discovered was
ike a wasp's sting in his heart.

He forgot George, who had stopped crying and was squatting
n the carpet. But seeing that no one was taking any notice of him
he child began to cry again.

His father ran to him, picked him up and rained kisses on his
ead. At any rate he still had his son! Nothing else mattered. He
eld him tightly in his arms, burying his face in his fair hair, com-
orted and relieved, stammering: 'George ... George darling, my
wn little George ...' But he suddenly remembered what Julie had
aid ... Yes, she had said that he was Limousin's child. That was
nthinkable, of course it wasn't true, he could never be in doubt
or a minute. It was one of those vile lies which originate in a
ervant's obscene imagination! He repeated: 'George, darling
George!' The child had stopped crying under his caresses.

Parent felt the warmth of the little body through the clothes.
t revived his love, his courage, his happiness. The warmth of the
hild's body was like a kiss, giving him strength and something to
ive for.

Then he held the lovely curly head a little away from him to be
ble the better to fix his passionate gaze upon it. His eyes devoured
t with desperate intensity, as if the sight intoxicated him, and he
ould only repeat over and over again: 'Oh! my darling ... my
arling little George!'

Suddenly the thought flashed across his mind: 'But supposing he
s really like Limousin after all!'

He felt a strange sharp pain, a stabbing, paralysing sensation of
old all over his body, as if every bone in his body had suddenly

turned to ice. Suppose he really was like Limousin! . . . and he kept his eyes fixed on the child, who was now laughing. He looked at him with a dazed blank stare of bewilderment, scanning his fore-head, nose, mouth, cheeks, searching in every feature for some likeness to Limousin.

His mind began to wander as in the early stages of insanity; and the child's face seemed to change as he looked, assuming strange forms and fantastic likenesses.

Julie had said: 'A blind man could see it.' So there must be some-thing striking, something about which there could be no doubt. Was it perhaps the forehead? Perhaps that was it. But Limousin had a rather narrow forehead. What about the mouth? Limousin wore a full beard; how could one compare the child's podgy chin with this man's bearded one?

Parent thought: 'I can't see anything there, anyway not now, I'm too upset to recognize any likeness . . . I must wait; I must have a good look at him to-morrow, when I'm getting up.'

He thought: 'If he was like me, I should be saved, everything would be all right.'

And he took two strides across the room in order to examine the child's face by the side of his own in the glass.

He perched George on his arm, so that their faces were quite close, and he was in such a state of excitement that he said out loud: 'Yes, we've got the same nose . . . the same nose . . . but have we? I'm not sure . . . and the same expression . . . no, we haven't, he's got blue eyes . . . So . . . oh! my God! my God! . . . I'm going mad . . . I won't look any more . . . I'm going mad ! . . .'

He rushed away from the glass to the other end of the drawing-room, threw himself into an arm-chair, put the child on another and broke down. His tears came in great convulsive sobs. George, frightened by his father's tears, immediately started to scream.

The door-bell rang. Parent jumped as if he had been shot. He said:

'There she is . . . what am I going to do?' And he ran and shut himself in his bedroom, in order to have time at least to dry his eyes. But a few seconds later another peal at the bell made him jump again; at once it occurred to him that Julie had gone without telling the housemaid. So no one would go to open the door. What was to be done? He went to the door himself.

Suddenly his mind was made up; he felt brave, ready to act a part and full of fight. The frightful shock had matured him in a flash. And besides he wanted to know the truth, he wanted it with the desperation of timidity, the determination of a good-natured man goaded beyond endurance.

But he found himself shaking all over. Was he afraid? Was he still frightened of her? He wondered. No one knows what a coward will not dare when driven to desperation.

He crept to the door and stopped behind it to listen. His heart was beating so violently that he could hear nothing else, only the pounding of his blood and George's continued screaming in the drawing-room. Suddenly the pealing of the bell above his head startled him like an explosion; he seized the knob and, breathing hard, almost fainting, he turned it and opened the door.

His wife and Limousin were facing him on the staircase.

She remarked, annoyance mingled with surprise:

'Have you taken to answering the door? Where on earth is Julie?'

His throat was dry and he was panting; he tried to answer, but he couldn't utter a word.

She went on:

'Have you lost your tongue? I asked you where Julie was.'

At last he managed to stammer:

'She's . . . she's . . . gone . . .'

His wife was beginning to lose her temper:

'What do you mean "gone"? Where's she gone? Why has she gone?'

He was gradually recovering himself and was conscious of a surge of hatred against the shameless woman in front of him:

'Yes, gone for good . . . I've sacked her . . .'

'You've sacked her . . . Julie? You must be mad.'

'Yes, I've sacked her for impertinence and for . . . for ill-treating the child.'

'Julie?'

'Yes, Julie.'

'What was she impertinent about?'

'About you.'

'About me?'

'Yes, because her dinner was burnt, and you weren't in.'

'What did she say?'

'She made ... well, rude remarks about you, things I couldn't and wouldn't listen to ...'

'What sort of things?'

'There's no good repeating them.'

'But I insist on knowing.'

'Well, she said it was hard lines for a man like me to be married to a woman like you, unpunctual and untidy, careless and a bad housekeeper, a bad mother and a bad wife.'

The young woman had come into the hall, followed by Limousin who took no part in this unexpected scene. She slammed the door, threw her cloak on a chair and advanced on her husband, stuttering with rage:

'You say ... you say ... that I'm ...'

Very pale but quite calm, he replied:

'I say nothing, my dear; I'm only telling you at your own request what Julie said. May I remind you that it was because of what she said that I turned her out of the house?'

She felt such a violent desire to tear out his beard and scratch his face that she was trembling all over. She sensed his revolt in the tone of his voice and his whole attitude. But there was nothing she could say; she tried to regain the offensive by a frontal attack that would hurt him.

'You've had dinner?' she said.

'No, I waited.'

She shrugged impatiently:

'It's silly to wait after half-past seven. You might have guessed that I had been kept and that I was busy shopping.'

Then suddenly she was conscious of a desire to explain how she had spent the time and she told him in curt supercilious sentences that she had been looking for some things she needed for the house a long way away, right on the other side of the town in the Rue de Rennes; she had run into Limousin after seven in the Boulevard Saint-Germain on her way home and had asked him to take her to a restaurant to get a snack, not liking to go by herself, though she was almost fainting with hunger. That was how she had dined with him, if you could call it dinner; they had only had some soup and a bit of chicken, in their hurry to get home.

Parent answered simply:

'A very sensible thing to do; I'm not making any complaints.'

At this point Limousin, who had so far said nothing, came forward and, holding out his hand, murmured:

'Are you all right?'

Parent took the proffered hand and shook it perfunctorily:

'Yes, I'm all right.'

But the young woman seized on a word in her husband's last sentence:

'Complaints . . . why do you talk of complaints? It sounds as if you meant something.'

He defended himself:

'No, not at all; I was only trying to tell you that I hadn't worried over your being late and wasn't blaming you.'

She took him up sharply, determined to pick a quarrel:

'My being late? One would think it was one o'clock in the morning and I had been out all night.'

'Not at all, my dear. I said "late", because there's no other word I could use. You were to be in by half-past six and you come back at half-past eight. That's being late! I quite understand; I'm not . . . I'm not even surprised. But . . . well, I don't see what else I could have said.'

'You talk as though I had been out all night . . .'

'Not at all . . . not at all . . .'

She saw that he did not mean to stand up to her and she was just going to her room when she noticed at last that George was screaming and asked, suddenly anxious:

'What's the matter with the child?'

'I told you Julie had been a bit rough with him.'

'What did the horrible woman do to him?'

'Oh! nothing much, she gave him a push and he fell down.'

She wanted to see the child and rushed into the dining-room,
but stopped short in front of the table, which was covered with
spilt wine, broken decanters and glasses and salt-cellars upset.

'What's the meaning of this wreck?'

'It's Julie who . . .'

But she interrupted him furiously:

'This is a bit too much! Julie calls me a shameless hussy, knocks
my child about, breaks my glass, turns the house upside down, and
you seem to regard it all as perfectly natural.'

'But I don't . . . after all I did turn her out.'

'Yes, you turned her out . . . you ought to have had her arrested,
the police ought to be called to deal with this sort of thing.'

'But . . . my dear . . . I really couldn't do that . . . there was no
ground . . . I assure you it was all very difficult . . .'

She shrugged her shoulders with infinite contempt:

'Of course, you'll never be anything but a spineless rotter, a poor
white, a creature with no will, no decision, no guts. Your precious
Julie must have laid it on pretty thick to make you turn her out.
I wish I'd been here to listen even to a minute of it.'

Opening the drawing-room door, she ran to George, picked him
up and hugged him, kissing him all the time: 'Georgie, dear, what's
the matter, Mummy's own precious darling?'

He stopped crying under his mother's caresses. She repeated:
'What's the matter?'

He replied, his eyes filling with tears as he remembered his fright:
'Zulie hit Daddy.'

Henriette turned to her husband, first of all in amazement.
After a moment the glint of laughter showed in her eye, her soft
cheeks quivered, her lip curled, her nostrils dilated, and finally a
loud explosion of mirth burst from her mouth, a cascade of laughter
echoing merrily like the trill of a bird's song. She kept repeating,
showing her white teeth as she laughed, every word barbed with a
sting to wound Parent:

'Ha ha! Ha ha! so she hit you, did she? My God! that's price-lessly funny. Do you hear, Limousin? Julie hit him, she hit my husband. What a joke!'

Parent stammered:

'No, it's not true, it's a lie; on the contrary, it was I who threw her into the dining-room with such force that she upset the table. The child didn't see what happened; it was I hit Julie.'

Henriette repeated her question to the child:

'Say it again, darling. Did Julie hit Daddy?'

''Es, Zulie hit him.'

Then, suddenly changing the subject, she went on:

'But the child hasn't had his dinner, has he? You've had nothing to eat, my sweetie?'

'No, Mummy.'

She rounded angrily on her husband:

'You're mad, mad as a hatter. It's half-past eight and George hasn't had his dinner.'

He was feeling quite dazed as a result of the scene and all these explanations, but he tried to excuse himself:

'My dear, we were waiting for you; I didn't want to dine without you. You're always late getting in and I thought you'd be back any minute.'

She threw the hat she had kept on till this moment into an arm-chair and said with exasperation in her voice:

'It really is intolerable to have to deal with nitwits who can't guess a thing and can't do anything for themselves. So, if I hadn't come in till midnight, the child wouldn't have had any food at all. Mightn't you have realized, when I wasn't back by half-past seven, that something had kept me and delayed me unexpectedly?'

Parent was trembling, feeling that he was losing control of his temper; but Limousin interposed and said, turning to the young woman:

'You're being very unfair, my dear. Parent couldn't guess you'd be so late – you hardly ever are; besides, how could he have managed by himself, when he had turned Julie out?'

But Henriette, now in a violent temper, replied:

'Anyhow he'll have to do for himself now, I'm not going to help. He'd better get a move on.'

And she went straight to her room, having already forgotten that her son hadn't had his dinner.

Limousin immediately set to work like ten men helping his friend. He swept up and cleared away the broken glass all over the table, laid it again and put the child into his highchair, while Parent went to look for the housemaid and get her to serve the meal.

When she came, she was amazed, for she had been working in George's room and had heard nothing.

She brought in the soup, followed by the burnt leg of mutton and mashed potatoes.

Parent had sat down by his son, distraught, unable to grasp what had happened. He fed the child and tried to eat himself; he cut up his meat and chewed it but he had difficulty in swallowing, as if his throat was paralysed.

Suddenly he became conscious of an overpowering desire to look at Limousin, who was sitting opposite him, rolling bread pellets. He wanted to see if he was like George but he dared not raise his eyes. However, at last he plucked up courage and cast a fleeting glance at the face he knew so well, though he felt as if he had never seen it before, it looked so different from what he had expected. Every few minutes he glanced furtively at this face, trying to fix in his mind its most insignificant lines, features and expression; then he quickly looked back at his son, pretending to be feeding him.

Two words kept echoing in his ear: 'His father, his father, his father!' They reverberated in his brain with every heart-beat. Yes, perhaps this man, sitting quietly opposite him at table, was his son's father, his darling George's father. Parent stopped eating, he couldn't swallow another mouthful. A stabbing pain, which made him want to scream, grovel on the ground and tear at the furniture with his teeth, was gnawing at his vitals. He wanted to seize his knife and plunge it into his stomach; that would give him relief and put him out of his agony; it would be the end of everything.

Could he go on living now? How was he to carry on, get up in the morning, eat his dinner, go out into the street, go to bed at night and sleep, always with the thought piercing like a dentist's drill, 'Limousin George's father'. No, he would never have the strength to go for a walk, get dressed, think or talk to anyone. Every day, every hour, every minute he would be trying to find out, to guess, to solve this ghastly problem. And every time he saw his beloved child, there would be this agony of uncertainty tearing at his heart, torturing every fibre in his body. He would have to go on living in the same house with the child he loved and hated at the same time; for he knew that he would come to hate him in the end. It was agony. If he knew that Limousin was the father, perhaps he would manage to keep sane and sleep in spite of his misery and his pain. It was not knowing that was unbearable. Not knowing he would be always on the watch, always in torment, every time he kissed the child who perhaps was another's. When he took him out for a walk, when he had him in his arms, when he felt the caress on his lips of the silky hair, he would adore him but at the back of his mind there would always be the thought 'Perhaps he's not mine.' Wouldn't it be better never to see him again, to give him up, to lose him in the streets, or to run away himself, so far away that he would never hear the child mentioned at all?

He started as he heard the door open. His wife came in.

'I'm quite hungry,' she said, 'aren't you, Limousin?'

Limousin replied with some hesitation:

'Yes, I am too.'

And she had the mutton brought back.

Parent wondered: 'Did they really have dinner? Or did they get late because they had been making love?'

Anyhow they both made a good meal. Henriette, now quite calm, laughed and joked. Her husband watched, glancing at her and quickly turning his eyes away.

She was wearing a pink dressing-gown trimmed with lace; and this attractive scented garment showed off her fair hair, her white neck and her plump hands, like a shell with a fringe of foam. What had she been doing all day with this man? Parent saw them in each other's arms, whispering words of love. Why couldn't he know, why couldn't he guess the truth, when he had them sitting side by side opposite him?

How they must be laughing at him, if they had really been deceiving him ever since his marriage! Was it possible that anyone could make such a fool of a man, an honest man, just because his father had left him a little money? Why can't one look into people's hearts and see the truth? How was it that the scoundrel's trickery could be hidden from the honest man, why was the voice the same to tell lies or to make love, why was the treacherous glance intended to deceive the same as the look of sincerity?

He watched them closely, waiting for a gesture, a word, an intonation.

Suddenly a thought struck him: 'I'll catch them out to-night.' And he said:

'My dear, as I've got rid of Julie, I must do something to-day about finding another servant. I'm going out now to get hold of someone for to-morrow. I may be a little late home.'

She replied:

'All right; I'm staying where I am. Limousin will keep me company. We'll wait for you.'

And, turning to the maid, she said:

'Put George to bed; after that you can clear away and go up to your room.'

Parent had got up; he felt dizzy and his knees were knocking together so that he could hardly stand. He murmured: 'So long!' and he got to the door, supporting himself against the wall, for the floor seemed to be heaving like the deck of a ship.

The maid had taken George out of the room in her arms. Henriette and Limousin went into the drawing-room. As soon as the door was shut the latter exclaimed:

'You know, you're mad to bully your husband like this.'

She retorted:

'Look here, I'm beginning to find this recent habit of yours of holding up Parent as a martyr a bit tiresome.'

Limousin threw himself into an arm-chair and, crossing his legs, said:

'That's the last thing in the world I want to do, to hold him up as a martyr, but in our position it's absurd to nag at him from morning to night.'

She took a cigarette from the mantelpiece, lit it and answered:

'But I don't nag at him; on the contrary it's his stupidity that annoys me; I only treat him as he deserves.'

Limousin retorted impatiently:

'I think you're behaving like a fool. But all women are the same. The position is this; here is an honest man, too honest; he's so confiding and good-natured that he's a fool; he doesn't bother us, he never suspects anything, we are completely free to do as we like in peace; and you do everything you can to irritate him and spoil our life.'

She turned to him:

'You make me tired. You're a coward like all men; you're afraid of this idiot.'

He jumped up angrily:

'I like that! I should like to know what he has done to you and why you've got your knife into him. Does he make you unhappy? Does he knock you about? Is he unfaithful? No! It's a bit thick to make his life a hell just because he's too good-hearted, and get your knife into him just because you're deceiving him.'

She went up to Limousin and looking him straight in the eye she hissed:

'And who are you to reproach me with deceiving him, I should like to know? You must be a pretty dirty dog.'

He defended himself rather shamefacedly:

'But I'm not reproaching you, my dear girl, I'm only asking you to use a little tact with your husband, because we can't either of us afford to rouse his suspicions; you must see that.'

They were standing quite close to one another; he was tall and dark, with Dundreary whiskers, in a slightly common way quite a good-looking young man and very conscious of the fact; she was small and fair, with a pink and white skin, a typical Paris girl, a mixture of prostitute and middle-class respectability. She had been born in the room behind a shop, had grown up on the door-step learning to give the glad eye to passers-by, and she had been married to a good-hearted man, whom she had chanced to pick up in this way and who had fallen in love with her after seeing her every day at her door, as he went out in the morning and came home at night.

She was saying:

'You don't understand, you big fool, that I hate him just because he married me or rather bought me, and because every word, every act, every thought of his gets on my nerves. He exasperates me every minute of the day by his stupidity – what you call his good-nature – and by the slowness of his mind – what you call his confiding disposition; above all I hate him because he is my husband instead of you. I am always conscious of him between us, though that doesn't cramp our style much. And there's one other thing; he's too much of a fool to suspect anything; I should like him to be just a bit jealous. There are moments when I could scream: "Can't you understand anything, you great booby? Don't you see Paul is my lover?"'

Limousin began to laugh:

'Meanwhile you'd better keep quiet or you'll upset the apple-cart.'

'Oh! don't worry about that! There's nothing to be afraid of with that imbecile. No, but it's incredible that you don't understand how I hate him and how he gets on my nerves. You always seem so friendly and shake hands with him with such an innocent air. Sometimes men surprise me.'

'There are times when deception is unavoidable, my dear.'

'It's not a question of deception, my dear man, but of decent feeling. When one man deceives another, he seems to feel more friendly towards him; but as soon as a woman deceives a man, she immediately hates him.'

'I can't see why one should hate a good fellow just because one is his wife's lover.'

'You don't see . . . you don't see . . . You men have none of you a spark of decency in you. How shall I put it? There are some things one feels and can't or rather mustn't say. But it's no good, you wouldn't understand. Men have no nice feeling.'

And smiling with the good-humoured contempt of a woman of the world, she put both hands on his shoulders and held out her mouth to be kissed; he bent down towards her putting his arms round her and their lips met. As they were standing in front of the mirror behind the mantelpiece, there was an exact reflection of their embrace in the glass behind the clock.

They had heard nothing, neither the sound of the key turning in the lock nor the creak of the door; but Henriette suddenly pushed Limousin away with both hands, uttering a shrill cry, and they saw Parent watching them, livid with rage, with fists clenched, without his shoes and his hat slipping forward over his eyes.

He was standing stock still watching them, only his eyes darting from one to the other. He seemed to have gone mad; then suddenly without a word he threw himself upon Limousin, seized him in an iron grip as if to throttle him and pushed him towards the corner of the room with such force that Limousin, losing his balance and sawing the air wildly with his arms, crashed the back of his head against the wall.

But when Henriette realized that her husband was going to murder her lover, she fell upon Parent, seized him by the throat and, digging her slender delicate fingers into his flesh, gripped him so fiercely with all the nervous strength of a desperate woman that blood spurted under the pressure of her nails. And she fixed her teeth in his shoulder as if she wanted to tear him in pieces. Parent, half strangled and suffocating, let go of Limousin in order to shake off his wife, who was clinging to his neck; and seizing her round the waist he hurled her with one push right across the room.

Then his anger began to cool, for the violence of a weak, good-natured character is always short-lived, and he stood there between the two, panting, exhausted, not knowing what to do. His blind rage had spilled over in this effort like the froth when a bottle of wine is uncorked; and this unaccustomed burst of energy left him breathless.

As soon as he could speak, he stammered:

'Leave the house . . . both of you . . . at once . . . get out!'

Limousin was standing motionless in the corner of the room, leaning against the wall, still too frightened to understand anything or move a finger. Henriette, leaning on a small round table, her fists clenched and her head thrust forward, her hair dishevelled and her torn bodice showing her naked breast, was waiting like a wild beast about to spring.

Parent went on in a more determined tone:

'Leave the house at once, both of you; get out!'

Seeing that his first fit of anger was passing, his wife recovered herself, stood up straight, took two steps towards him and said in almost her usual insolent tone:

'Are you out of your mind? What's come over you? What's the meaning of this monstrous assault?'

He turned on her and, threatening her with upraised fist, he stammered:

'This is the last straw . . . it's too much . . . I've heard everything . . . everything, you understand . . . you wretch . . . you're both of you blackguards . . . Leave the house . . . both of you . . . this minute or I'll kill you . . . get out!'

She realized that there was nothing to be done, that he knew the truth, that she could not pretend innocence and had got to give in. But she had recovered all her self-assurance, and her hatred of this man, now coming to a head, gave her courage to defy him out of pure bravado.

She said in level tones:

'Come along, Limousin; as I'm being put into the street, I'm coming to you.'

But Limousin made no move. Parent, his anger boiling up again, shouted:

'Go away, leave this house . . . you wretches . . . or else . . . or else . . .' and he seized a chair and swung it round his head.

At this Henriette walked rapidly across the room, took her lover by the arm, pulled him away from the wall to which he seemed to be glued and dragged him towards the door, exclaiming:

'Do come, my dear, come along ... you can see the man is insane ... come along.'

As she went out she turned to her husband, wondering what she could do, what she could find that would really hurt him, before she left the house. Suddenly an idea occurred to her, one of those ideas full of deadly poison distilled from a woman's treachery.

She said in a determined tone of voice:

'I want to take my child with me.'

Parent, aghast, stammered:

'Your ... your child ... you dare ask for your child ... after ... after ... Oh! this is too much. How have you the face? Get out of this house, you bitch! Get out!'

She came back a few steps towards him, the ghost of a smile on her lips at the thought that now she had got her revenge, and she faced him, standing quite close to him:

'I want my child ... and you have no right to keep him, because he isn't yours ... you understand what I'm saying ... he's not yours, he's Limousin's.'

Dumbfounded, Parent shouted:

'That's a lie ... that's a lie ... you wretch!'

But she went on:

'You fool! Everybody knows it except you. I tell you, there's his father. You've only got to use your eyes to see it.'

Parent staggered back. Suddenly he turned, seized a candle and rushed into the next room.

He came back almost at once with little George in his arms, wrapped up in his cot blankets. The child, woken up with a start, was crying with fright. Parent thrust him into his wife's arms and without a word pushed her roughly out of the door towards the staircase, where Limousin was prudently waiting.

He shut the door again at once, double locked and bolted it. He had hardly got back into the drawing-room when he crashed full length on the floor unconscious.

II

Parent now lived alone, entirely alone. For the first few weeks after
the separation the novelty of his changed life prevented him from
thinking. He resumed his bachelor habits, lounging about the
streets and taking his meals in a restaurant as he used to do. Wishing
to avoid any scandal, he paid his wife an allowance through his
solicitor and hers. But gradually memories of the child began to
haunt his imagination. Often when he was alone at home in the
evening he suddenly thought he heard George calling 'Daddy'.
His heart immediately started to beat faster, and he got up quickly
and opened the door on to the staircase to look, in case the child
had come back. Yes, he might have come home as dogs and pigeons
do. Why should a child have less homing instinct than an animal?

Finding he was mistaken, he went back to his arm-chair and
began to think about the child. He thought about him for hours
and days at a time. It was not only a mental obsession, but also, and
even more, a physical obsession, a longing of his senses and his
nerves to hold him tight and hug him, to fondle him, to take him
on his knee and jog him up and down and turn him head over heels.
The memory of past caresses put him in a fever and drove him
mad. He felt the little arms round his neck, the little mouth pressing
a big kiss on his beard, the silky hair tickling his cheek. The longing
for the love play that was no more, for the soft skin, warm and
delicate, offered to his kiss, made him mad like desire for a woman
loved and lost.

Suddenly in the street tears would come into his eyes as he
thought that he might have had his tubby little George trotting at
his side and be taking him for his walk as he used to do. And he
would go home and sob till it got dark, with his head in his hands.

Twenty, a hundred times a day he asked himself the question:
'Was he or wasn't he George's father?' But it was chiefly at night
that he went over and over again the arguments for and against
either solution of the problem. Hardly had he gone to bed when the
interminable consideration of the pros and cons drove him to
desperation.

Immediately after his wife's departure he had had no doubts; of course the child was Limousin's! But gradually uncertainty began to creep in. Clearly Henriette's assertion carried no weight; she had defied him merely in order to exasperate him. If one considered the probabilities dispassionately, it was quite likely that she had lied.

Limousin was the only one who might have told the truth. But how could he find out for certain, how could he cross-examine his former friend and force him to confess?

Sometimes he got up in the middle of the night, determined to go and find Limousin and throw himself on his mercy, offering him anything he liked, in order to put an end to this ghastly uncertainty. Then he went to bed again in despair – of course his wife's lover would lie too! In fact, he would be sure to lie, to prevent the child's real father getting his son back.

There was absolutely nothing he could do.

He bitterly regretted his hasty action, due to thoughtless impatience; he ought to have had the sense to bide his time and lie low for a month or two in order to get ocular proof. He should have concealed his suspicions and let them betray themselves naturally. By watching the other man as he kissed the child he could have drawn his inferences and discovered the truth. A friend's kiss is quite different from a father's. He could have spied on them from behind doors. Why hadn't he thought of that? If Limousin, left alone with the child, had not immediately picked him up and hugged and kissed him passionately, if he had let him go on playing, indifferent, without taking any interest, all doubt would have been cleared up. It would have been obvious that he was not his father and knew it and had none of a father's feelings.

In that case he, Parent, having got rid of the mother, would have kept his son and been happy, completely happy.

He tossed about in bed, bathed in perspiration and miserable, trying to recall Limousin's manner with the child. But he could remember nothing, not a gesture, not a glance, not a word, not a caress that had been suspicious. Moreover the child's mother had never shown any interest in him. If her lover had been the father, she would surely have been fonder of him.

So they must have taken away his son out of motives of revenge and cruelty, in order to punish him for having found them out.

And he made up his mind to go to the magistrates the first thing in the morning and make application for the return of his son.

But he had hardly taken this decision when the opposite conviction swept over him. As Limousin had been Henriette's lover from the beginning, she must have given herself to his embraces with the passionate ardour of self-surrender that enables a woman to become a mother, while her coldness in all her intimate relations with himself must surely have prevented her conceiving a child in his arms.

So, if he claimed the child and obtained custody of him, he would always be bringing up and looking after another man's son. He wouldn't be able to look at him, kiss him, or hear him say 'Daddy' without the thought striking him and poisoning his joy: 'He's not my child.' He would condemn himself to a life of utter misery and never-ending torture. No, it was better to remain alone, to live, grow old and die alone.

Every day, every night the ceaseless agony of these torturing doubts began again; nothing could allay them or give him peace of mind.

His worst time was when it started to get dark in the evening; the twilight brought on fits of depression. Misery descended on him like rain and a wave of despair, surging up with the darkness, swept over him and drove him mad. He was afraid of his own thoughts, as one is afraid of a criminal, and they pursued him like a hunted animal. He was afraid above all of the terrible darkness of his empty house and even of the deserted streets, only lit here and there by the gas-lamps, where one imagines a pickpocket in every solitary passer-by, as one hears his step in the distance and slows or hurries on according to whether he is coming towards one or approaching from behind.

Instinctively, in spite of himself, Parent would make his way towards the brightly lit crowded streets. The lights and the people drew him, distracted his thoughts and dulled the ache in his heart. Presently, when tired of wandering aimlessly through the back streets, as the crowds thinned and the pavements began to empty, fear of being alone in the silent streets drove him to some big café, full of people drinking and brilliantly lit. He made his way there, as a moth is drawn to a candle, sitting down at a small round table and calling for a beer. He sipped it slowly, starting every time a customer rose to leave. He would have liked to seize his arm and stop him and ask him to stay a little longer, so much did he dread the moment when the waiter would stand in front of him and say angrily: 'Time, Sir, closing time!'

Every night he was the last to leave. He saw the tables cleared away and the lights put out one by one, till only two, his own and the one over the bar, remained. He watched in despair the girl-cashier counting her cash and locking it up in a drawer; and he was finally hustled out into the street by the waiters, who mumbled under their breath: 'He's not all there; one would think he had nowhere to sleep.'

And as soon as he found himself in the dark street alone, he began to think of little George and rack his brains and worry himself silly, trying to decide whether he was or was not the boy's father.

In this way he got into the habit of spending his day in the café, where the jostling throng of drinkers surrounds you with a crowd you know by sight but never speak to, and where the heavy pipe smoke lulls your worries to sleep and the heavy beer dulls the brain and drugs the sensibility.

He lived in the café. The first thing in the morning he went there so as not to be alone, to have someone to look at and distract his mind. Soon, too indolent to move, he took his meals there. About twelve o'clock he banged with his saucer on the marble-topped table and the waiter bustled up with a plate, a glass, a napkin and the day's bill-of-fare. When he had finished his meal he sipped his coffee with his eye on the little decanter of brandy, which would give him an hour of blissful forgetfulness. First he moistened his lips with the alcohol, just to get the taste of it, savouring the flavour of the spirit with the tip of his tongue; then he poured it slowly into his mouth drop by drop, throwing his head back, and rolled the fiery liquor round his palate and his gums and the mucus in his mouth, mixing it with the fresh saliva which was stimulated by the contact of the alcohol. Finally, when it had lost some of its rawness in this way, he swallowed it meditatively, feeling it run right down his throat into his stomach.

After every meal for more than an hour he sipped three or four glasses, which gradually induced a state of torpor. Soon his head would fall forward on his chest, his eyes would close and he slept. About the middle of the afternoon he woke up and immediately stretched out his hand for the glass of beer which the waiter had put before him, while he was asleep; and after drinking it he got up from the red velvet seat, hitched up his trousers, pulled down his waistcoat to cover the white line of his shirt visible between the two, shook his coat-collar and drew down his cuffs; after that he returned to the papers, which he had already read in the morning.

He read them over again from the first line to the last, including the advertisements, situations wanted, announcements, Stock Exchange news and theatre programmes.

From four to six he strolled about the boulevards, taking the air, as he called it, and after that he came back to the place reserved for him at the café and called for his absinthe.

Later on he talked to the regular customers he had got to know. They discussed the events of the day, the items of news and the political happenings; that took him up to dinner-time. The evening was a repetition of the afternoon till closing time. That was the moment he dreaded most, when he had to go back to the darkness of his empty house, so full of painful memories, bitter thoughts and anguished torment. He had given up all his old friends and he never saw his relations or anyone who might remind him of the past.

But as his own house became a hell for him, he took a room in a large hotel on the mezzanine floor, so that he could watch the passers-by. In this vast hostelry he was no longer alone; he was conscious of swarming life all round him. He heard the sound of voices in the rooms; and, when the memories of his past misery became too cruelly acute, as he stood before his turned-down bed and by his lonely fireside, he went out into the broad passages and

walked up and down like a sentry, looking sadly at the two pairs
of shoes in front of each door, the woman's little shoes snuggling
up against the man's heavier boots; and he thought how happy all
these people were, sleeping blissfully side by side or in each other's
arms in their cosy bed.

Five years passed in this way, five depressing years, in which
nothing happened except an hour or two of love at fifty francs a
time now and then.

One day in the course of his usual walk from the Madeleine to
the Rue Drouot he saw a woman whose figure seemed familiar.
A tall man and a boy were with her. The three of them were walking
in front of him. He said to himself: 'Where have I seen those people
before?' And suddenly he recognized a gesture; it was his wife with
Limousin and his son, his beloved little George.

The beating of his heart nearly suffocated him, but he did not
stop; he wanted to see them and he followed them. They looked
like a family party, a respectable middle-class family party. Henriette had taken Paul's arm and was talking to him in a low voice
with a sidelong glance at him from time to time. Parent then had a
sight of her profile and recognized the charming line of her cheek,
the movement of her lips, her smile and the caress of her glance.
But he was most interested in the child. How tall and strong he had
grown! Parent could not see his face, only the long fair hair falling
over his coat-collar in wavy curls. It was George, this tall bare-
legged boy, walking by his mother's side like a little man.

When they stopped to look in at a shop-window, he got a view
of all three. Limousin was now grey; he had aged and shrunk. His
wife, on the contrary, had put on weight, though she was as
attractive as ever. George was unrecognizable, he had grown so
much.

They continued their walk and Parent followed them again;
then, quickening his pace, he passed them and presently turned
round so as to meet them face to face quite close. As he passed the
boy he felt a desire, a passionate desire, to throw his arms round him
and carry him off. He brushed against him as if accidentally. The
boy turned his head and looked crossly at this clumsy man. And

Parent fled, driven away by the glance which hurt him like a blow. He fled like a thief, haunted by the fear that his wife and her lover had recognized him. He ran all the way to his café and flung himself panting on to a chair.

That evening he had three absinthes.

For four months the pain of this meeting rankled in his heart. Every night he saw in imagination the three of them again walking happy and untroubled along the boulevard, father, mother and child, before going home to dinner.

This new picture obliterated the old one. It was something fresh, a different hallucination, a new agony. Little George, the child he had loved and kissed so often in the old days, was disappearing into a dim past that would never return, and he now saw a different boy, as it were the brother of the first, a little boy with bare legs, and this one did not know him. This thought caused him exquisite pain. The child's affection for him was dead; there was no longer any bond between them; this boy would not have stretched out his arms to him when he saw him. He had even given him an ugly look.

Gradually he recovered his peace of mind; his mental agony was dulled; the picture before his eyes, which had made his nights hideous, lost its sharpness of outline and haunted him less often. He began to live again like other people, like all those who have no occupation and drink their beer at marble-topped tables, wearing the seat of their trousers shiny on the shabby velvet of café benches.

He became an old man in the pipe smoke and the gas fumes made him lose his hair; his weekly bath, his fortnightly hair-cut, the purchase of a new suit or hat were the events of his life. When he entered the café in a new hat, he took a long look at himself in the glass before sitting down, put it on and took it off several times, adjusted it at different angles and finally asked his friend, the barmaid, who was an interested spectator, if she thought it suited him.

Two or three times a year he used to go to the theatre and in the summer he sometimes spent an evening at an open-air concert in the Champs-Elysées. The tunes stayed in his head and he remembered the songs for several weeks; sometimes he even hummed them over, beating time with his foot, as he sat in front of his glass of beer.

Year followed year in unbroken monotony; but the time did not seem long, because nothing ever happened.

He did not notice the passing of time. He was getting nearer to the grave sitting at a café table, doing nothing, making no effort; and only the big mirror behind his head, which was getting balder every day, reflected the ravages of time, which sweeps away frail humanity in its inexorable march.

Now he hardly ever remembered the tragedy which had made shipwreck of his life on that ghastly evening twenty years before; and the proprietor of his café, the sixth owner since he had first come to it, often said to him: 'You ought to pull yourself together, Monsieur Parent; you ought to get out into the country and have a holiday; I've noticed a great change in you in the last few months.'

And when his customer had gone the proprietor would say to his girl-cashier:

'Poor old Parent's going downhill fast; it's no good always sticking in Paris. Do try and get him to go out into the country sometimes and have fried fish for lunch; he listens to what you say. The nice weather will soon be here and it will do him good.'

And the cashier, out of kindness and pity for her most constant customer, kept saying to Parent: 'Look here, Sir, you must make up your mind to get out of town; the country is divine in good weather. If I could, I'd live in the country always.'

She confided her dreams to him, the simple romantic dreams of every girl cooped up from year's end to year's end behind a shop-window, watching the noisy artificial life of the streets flow past, while she dreams of the peaceful pleasant life of the country; she dreams of life under the trees in the clear bright sunshine which pours down on fields, thick woods, clear streams, cows dozing in the meadows and all the myriad kinds of flowers, blue, red, yellow, violet, purple, pink and white, so lovely, so fresh and sweet-smelling, all the wild flowers which nature has provided for us to make into great bunches.

She loved to talk to him of her unrealized desire, that would never be realized but which never died; and the poor hopeless old man loved to listen. He soon got into the habit of coming to sit close to the bar so as to talk to Mlle Zoé and discuss the country with her. Later on he gradually began to want to go and see just for once, if it was really as delightful as she said outside the walls of the great city.

One morning he asked:

'Do you know a place where one can get a good lunch not too far from Paris?'

She replied:

'Oh! you ought to go to the Terrace at Saint-Germain. It's so nice!'

He had gone there once for an outing during his engagement. He made up his mind to go there again.

He chose a Sunday, for no special reason, just because it was the conventional thing to go out on Sundays, even if one had nothing to do all the week.

So one Sunday morning he set out.

It was the beginning of July, a hot sunny day. Sitting next the door of his compartment, he watched the trees and the quaint little houses in the outskirts of Paris. He felt depressed, annoyed with himself for giving way to this strange whim and breaking his routine. He was getting tired of the scenery, which was constantly changing but always remained the same. He was thirsty and at every station he would have liked to get out and sit down at the café he could see outside the station, drink a beer or two and take the first train back to Paris; moreover the journey seemed interminable. He didn't mind sitting for days on end, provided the same things, never changing, met his eye, but he found it nerve-racking and tiring to be travelling, while he remained in his seat, and watching the whole country passing by, while he never moved.

The Seine, however, interested him every time he crossed it. Under the Chatou bridge he saw the skiffs speeding past under the powerful strokes of the bare-armed rowers; he thought to himself: 'Those fine fellows must be having a great time!'

The long ribbon of the river, stretching away on both sides of the bridge at Pecq, aroused deep within him a vague longing to be walking along its banks. But the train plunged into the tunnel just before the Saint-Germain station and soon pulled up at the arrival platform.

Parent got out and, walking slowly like a tired man, made his way with his hands behind his back towards the Terrace. When he came to the iron railing he stopped to look at the extensive view. In front of him stretched the immense plain, limitless as the sea, very green and dotted with large villages as big as towns. White roads crossed this expanse of countryside, with copses here and there; the Vésinet lakes shone like silver plates, and the distant hills of Sannois and Argenteuil were faintly outlined through a shimmering, bluish haze which hid all detail. The pitiless glare of a blazing sun was pouring down on this stretch of country, which was still veiled in the morning fog; the moisture was rising from the hot earth in a thin vapour and there was a damp mist above the Seine, which curled like a snake endlessly across the plain, winding round the villages and following the line of the hills.

A gentle breeze, laden with the scent of grass and growing things, caressed the face, penetrated into the lungs and seemed to make the heart young again and stir the blood.

Surprised at a new sensation, Parent inhaled deep breaths of the fresh air, his eyes dazzled by the extent of the view; and he murmured: 'My word! It's good to be here!'

Then he walked on a few steps and stopped to look at the view again. He seemed to be aware of strange new sensations, not the landscape before his eyes, but something within him, experiences he had never had, happiness of which he had only dreamed, joys he had never tasted; a whole horizon of life, which he had never suspected, opened before him, as he gazed at this limitless expanse of country.

He realized all the ghastly drabness of his life in the brilliant light of the blazing sun. He saw the twenty years of his existence in the café, joyless, monotonous, depressing. He might have travelled like other people, gone far, far away among foreigners to unexplored lands beyond the seas; he might have taken an interest in other people's enthusiasms, in the arts and sciences; he might have tasted life in its myriad forms, life at once mysterious, delightful or painful, ever changing, ever inexplicable and exciting.

Now it was too late. He would go from glass to glass of beer till he died, without family, without friends, without hope, without interests. And a wave of utter misery swept over him, an over-powering inclination to run away and hide, to return to Paris, his café and his torpor. All the thoughts, all the dreams, all the desires, buried in the subconscious mind of those who never think, had been awakened, stirred by the sunlight on the plain before him.

He felt he would go mad if he stayed any longer where he was by himself, and he hastened to the Henri IV restaurant for his lunch; he meant to drug himself with wine and spirits and he would at least have someone to talk to.

He took a small table under the trees, commanding a view of the whole countryside, ordered his meal and asked for it to be served at once.

Other excursionists arrived and sat down at tables near him; he felt better now that he was no longer alone.

In an arbour three people were lunching. He had glanced at them several times casually, as one glances at strangers, without taking them in.

Suddenly a woman's voice sent a shiver down his spine:

The voice had said: 'George, you shall carve the chicken.'

And another voice answered: 'Right you are, Mother!'

Parent looked up; he realized, he knew by instinct at once who they were.

He certainly would not have recognized them. His wife had gone quite white and had lost her figure; she was now an old woman, dignified and respectable; she was eating with her head well forward to avoid spilling her food on her dress, though she had covered her front with a napkin.

George was grown up. He had got a beard, the uneven, almost colourless beard which curls round the chin of the very young. He was wearing a top-hat, a white duck waistcoat and a monocle, no doubt because it was the smart thing. Parent gazed at them dumbfounded. Was this really his son George? No! He did not recognize this young man. There was no longer any bond between them.

Limousin had his back to Parent and was eating, with his shoulders a little bent.

So the three of them looked happy and contented; they came out into the country to lunch at well-known restaurants. They had enjoyed a quiet peaceful life, a family life in a nice, cosy, well-appointed house, full of all the little things which make life pleasant; they knew the joys of family affection and were continually hearing the tender words so natural to those who love each other. And this life they owed to the money which he, Parent, had given them, after they had deceived and wronged him and wrecked his life. They had condemned him, the innocent, trusting, good-natured man, to all the bitterness of living alone, to his hateful existence between the streets and the café, to every kind of mental torture and physical discomfort. They had turned him into a miserable useless creature, lost in the crowd, a poor, joyless, hopeless old man with no one to lean on. For him life was an aching void, because he had nothing to love in the world. He might travel abroad or tramp the streets, he might go into every house in Paris, open the door of any room, but he would never find inside the well-loved face he was looking for, the face of wife or child with a smile of welcome. It was this thought that was so bitter, the thought that there was no door he could open and find behind it someone awaiting his embrace.

It was all the fault of these three wretches, his unfaithful wife, the friend who had betrayed him and this tall fair boy with the arrogant air.

His feelings were now as bitter against the boy as against the other two. He must be Limousin's son; otherwise Limousin would never have brought him up and loved him like this. Of course, Limousin would quickly have got rid of both mother and son if he had not been sure that the child was really his own. One does not bring up other people's children!

So there they were, quite close to him, the three guilty ones who were responsible for all his suffering.

Parent watched them with mounting anger, his temper rising, as he remembered all his pain, his agony, his despair. What infuriated him most was their air of placid self-satisfaction. He wanted to kill them, throw his soda-water siphon at them, and crush Limousin's skull, as he watched him bending his head down to his plate and raising it again, as he ate.

And they would go on living like this, without worries or anxieties of any kind. No! That was really too much! He would have his revenge, he would have his revenge here and now, when he had them in his power. But what was he to do? He pondered over the problem, recalling the deeds of violence perpetrated in gangster novels, but nothing practical suggested itself. And he went on drinking glass after glass to keep his anger at white heat and give himself courage, so as not to miss an opportunity that would never recur.

Suddenly an idea, a wicked idea, occurred to him. He stopped drinking to work out the details. A smile played round his lips and he murmured: 'Now I've got them. We shall see what we shall see!'

A waiter asked him:

'What would you like next, Sir?'

'Nothing but coffee and some of your best brandy.'

He kept his eyes on them, as he sipped glass after glass. There were too many people in the restaurant for what he meant to do; so he would wait for them to finish and follow them; they were sure to go for a stroll on the Terrace or in the forest. When they had gone a little way he would catch them up and have his revenge. Yes! Revenge would be sweet; and it was high time, too, after twenty-three years of suffering. They had no idea what was in store for them!

They were taking their time over their lunch, chatting unconcernedly. Parent could not hear what they were saying but their gestures revealed no anxiety. His wife's face in particular infuriated him. She had adopted the patronizing air of a portly lady devoted to good works, impervious to criticism, protected by the armour plate of virtuous principles.

At last they paid their bill and got up. Then he saw Limousin fo the first time. He looked like a retired diplomat; so impressive were his magnificent silky whiskers, now quite white, which flowed over the lapels of his frock coat.

They went out. George was smoking a cigar, his top-hat tilted over one ear. Parent immediately followed them.

First they strolled along the Terrace, admiring the view with the tranquil contentment of those who have lunched well. Presently they went into the forest.

Parent rubbed his hands and continued to follow them at a distance, keeping out of sight, so as not to attract attention too soon.

They went on slowly, enjoying the beauty of the forest and the warmth of the air. Henriette had taken Limousin's arm and was walking by his side, holding her head high like a wife proud of the dignity of her position. George was slashing the leaves with his cane, now and then leaping the ditches across the path like a spirited young stallion eager to gallop off through the trees.

Parent gradually came nearer and nearer to them, panting with excitement and fatigue, for he had lost the habit of walking. Soon he caught them up, but he was seized by a sudden fear of something he could not define or explain, and he passed them, meaning to turn and face them later.

He walked on with beating heart, conscious of them all the time behind him, and he kept saying to himself: 'Now's the moment; pull yourself together, don't be a coward; now's the time!'

He turned round. They had sat down, all three of them, at the foot of a big tree and they were still talking.

In a flash he made up his mind and walked rapidly back. He stopped in front of them, standing in the middle of the path, and without preamble he stammered in a voice quivering with emotion:

'It's me, here I am! You didn't expect me, did you?'

The three of them gazed in surprise at this seeming madman.

He went on:

'One would think you didn't recognize me. Look again! I'm Parent, Henri Parent. Ah! you didn't expect to see me. You thought it was all over and done with, that you would never see me again; but I've come back, and we are going to have a little explanation.'

Henriette, terrified, hid her face in her hands, murmuring: 'Oh! my God!'

Seeing this unknown man apparently threatening his mother, George had got up, ready to seize him by the coat-collar.

Limousin, struck dumb, was gazing with terror in his eyes at this ghost, who after breathing hard for a minute, went on:

'Now we're going to have a little explanation. The time has come. You deceived me, you condemned me to a convict's life and you thought I should never find you again.'

But the young man seized him by the shoulders and cried, as he pushed him away: 'What do you want? Are you mad? Clear out and be quick about it or I'll horsewhip you!'

Parent answered:

'What do I want? I want to tell you the truth about these two people.'

But George, losing his temper, was shaking him and was on the point of striking him. Parent went on:

'Hands off, young man! I'm your father ... Look, these two wretched creatures know well enough now who I am.'

Frightened, the boy let go and turned to his mother.

Parent, released from his grip, advanced towards her:

'Well! You tell him who I am; tell him my name is Henri Parent and that I'm his father, because his name is George Parent and you are my wife and all three of you are living on my money, on the allowance of ten thousand francs that I've been making you since I drove you out of my house. Tell him, too, why I drove you out of the house. Because I found you with this scoundrel, your lover. Tell him how you married me, an honest man, for my money and how you were unfaithful from the beginning. Tell him who you are and who I am ...'

He stammered and panted with the violence of his rage.

The woman cried out piteously:

'Paul, Paul, stop him, make him be quiet and say no more! Don't let him say these things before my son!'

Limousin at last got up and murmured in a very low voice:

'Shut up! Don't say any more! Don't you realize what you are doing?'

Parent went on in a furious temper:

'Yes, I know perfectly well what I'm doing. But this is not all. There's one thing I want to know, something that has been torturing me for twenty years.'

And turning to George, who was leaning against a tree in bewilderment, he went on:

'I want you to listen to this: when she left my house she wasn't satisfied with having deceived me; she wanted to drive me mad. You were my one comfort. Well, she took you away, swearing that he was your father, not I. Was that a lie? I don't know. For twenty years I've been trying to find out.'

He went close up to her, a tragic, terrible figure, and, tearing away the hands that covered her face, he went on:

'I insist on your telling me to-day which of us is the boy's father, he or I, your husband or your lover. Come on, out with it!'

Limousin threw himself upon him but Parent pushed him back and, snarling with rage, cried:

'Oh! you're brave enough to-day, a good deal braver than the way you hid on the stairs, because I was going to kill you. Well, if she won't answer, you answer. I suppose you know as well as she does. Tell me, are you this boy's father? Come along, out with it!'

He went back to his wife:

'If you won't tell me, at least tell your son. He's a man now. He has a right to know who is his father. I've never known, never; so I can't tell you, my boy.'

He was losing all control and his voice rose to a shriek; he was waving his arms like a man in an epileptic fit:

'Now then . . . answer . . . she doesn't know . . . I bet she doesn't know . . . of course she doesn't . . . she went to bed with both of us . . . what a joke! . . . nobody knows, nobody at all . . . how can anyone know such a thing? . . . you'll never know either, my boy, you'll never know any more than I do, never . . . Well . . . ask her . . . ask her . . . you'll find she doesn't know . . . and I don't know

... he doesn't know ... you don't know ... so nobody knows ..
you can choose ... yes, you can choose ... him or me ... mak
your choice ... good evening! ... that's all. If she makes up he
mind to tell you, you'll come and tell me, won't you, at th
Continental Hotel; I'd like to know. Good evening ! ... and th
best of luck!'

He went away gesticulating, still talking to himself, under th
tall trees, through the fresh clear air, full of the scent of growin;
things. He never turned round to look at them but walked straigh
on, spurred by his anger and supported by his excitement, with onl
one thought in his mind.

Suddenly he found himself outside the station. A train was jus
starting and he got in. On the way his anger cooled and he becam
rational again and returned to Paris, amazed at his own audacity.

He felt tired, as if every bone in his body had been broken. Bu
he went to the café for his usual beer.

Seeing him come in, Mlle Zoé asked him in surprise:

'Back already? Are you tired?'

He replied:

'Yes ... yes ... very tired ... very tired ... you see ... whe
one isn't used to going out! This is the last time, I shall never g
into the country again. I should have been better here in Town.
shall never leave Paris again.'

And she couldn't get him to tell her about his trip, though sh
tried hard.

That evening for the first time in his life he got dead drunk an
had to be carried home.

GUSTAVE FLAUBERT

MADAME BOVARY

Translated by

ALAN RUSSELL

Flaubert's 'story of provincial life' in nineteenth-century Normandy has been something of a legend ever since it was first published in 1857. Or, rather, it has been two legends. The first is that of Emma Bovary, the embodiment of desires yearning beyond their inimical environment, failing to escape it, and finally breaking themselves upon it. The second is the legend of Gustave Flaubert, saint and martyr of literature, who shut himself up for over four years in his room at Croisset to make of Emma's story a novel that should be also a model of stylistic perfection.

'Style' to Flaubert was no mere pretty play with words, but a search in words for the very tone and texture of life. 'The form of a thought is its very flesh.' In that search the writer must 'become' whatever he writes of, as Flaubert 'became' not only 'the lovers in the wood' but 'the leaves, the wind, the horses' . . .

TWO SHILLINGS AND SIXPENCE

ABBÉ PRÉVOST

MANON LESCAUT

Translated by

L. W. TANCOCK

Manon Lescaut was originally an episode in a much longer novel, now forgotten by all but historians of literature. It has survived because it is one of the greatest love-stories ever written. Its author, Antoine-François Prévost, a renegade monk and at times a fugitive from justice, put into the tale of Des Grieux the brief moments of ecstasy and long hours of self-torture of a man who for the love of women had become a social failure and an outcast. In a moment of genius Prévost transmuted his own commonplace experience into an imperishable story of the warfare between the flesh and the spirit common to all mankind. For Manon young Des Grieux sacrifices duty, career, family, and religion, deceives his best friend, and sinks into degradation. In his heart he knows that Manon is shallow and deceitful, his conscience and commonsense tell him he is wrong, but for her he plunges into ruin, and he follows her to the end.

This passionate romance is an unheroic tragedy in a setting of sordid realism – the underworld of eighteenth-century Paris. But its pitiless analysis of the human heart, its terrible logic, its clarity and economy, and above all the poignant simplicity of its final scene, have for upwards of two hundred years earned it a position among the masterpieces of French art.

ONE SHILLING AND SIXPENCE

BALZAC

OLD GORIOT

Translated by
MARION CRAWFORD

Goriot is the tale of a young man's temptation by the world, the flesh and the devil. The devil is represented by a character founded on the criminal Vidocq, who later became Chief of the Paris Sûreté; the world and the flesh by Paris in the early nineteenth century, and the lovely aristocratic women of the Faubourg Saint-Germain. It is also the tale of a working-class Lear whose daughters, to whom he had given his all, left him to die in poverty while they lived in the world of fashion. These are the chief among many threads of the story, which are intertwined through the intersecting lives of a group of people who by various chances came to live in a boarding-house in an old but obscure corner of Paris.

But the fascination of *Goriot* does not lie mainly in the story, exciting though that is, and though it is unfolded with a keen dramatic sense and enjoyment of the comedy of situation and character, but rather in the power Balzac possesses to convince us that his characters are the same flesh and blood as ourselves and intensely interesting as human beings, whatever their race, class or period, though conditioned by strange circumstances, and driven by outsize passions.

TWO SHILLINGS

THE PENGUIN MODERN PAINTERS

Edited by

SIR KENNETH CLARK

Seventeen leading contemporary painters have so far been represented in this series, of which fourteen volumes are still available at three shillings and sixpence each. These are: Henry Moore, Duncan Grant, Victor Pasmore, Edward Bawden, Ben Shahn, William Nicholson, Ben Nicholson, Frances Hodgkins, David Jones, John Piper, Paul Nash, Stanley Spencer, Paul Klee and, most recently, the American artist Edward Hopper. The volumes measure 7⅛ by 8⅝ in. and each contains 16 illustrations in four-colour half-tone, 16 black-and-white reproductions and a 16-page appreciation of the artist's work by a well-known critic. *The Listener* commented on the series: 'It continues, by dint of a carefully planned combination of good qualities, to provide the best value for money obtainable in this or, I suspect, any other country to-day.'

THE PENGUIN PRINTS

This is a new series of reproductions of famous pictures, new and old and of every school. Each is mounted in a folder 13¼ by 17 in. in size, on the inside of which appears an appreciation of the artist and the painting or drawing, and each is priced at six shillings † or five shillings and fourpence*, according to the amount of the purchase tax. The first six are: Turner's *Yacht Approaching Coast**, Paul Klee's *Landscape with Yellow Birds*†, John Piper's *View of Windsor Castle*†, Picasso's *Le Chardonneret*†, Amedeo Modigliani's *Le Petit Paysan*†, and Pieter de Hooch's *Courtyard in Delft**. They have been described by *The Listener* as 'technically accomplished, beautifully produced' and *The New Statesman* said 'they meet the demand for colour reproductions in a much more admirable fashion than comparable books'.

THE
KING PENGUINS

Edited by

NIKOLAUS PEVSNER

AND

R. B. FISHENDEN

Described by Clive Bell as 'short, illustrated monographs, edited and written by scholars,' the King Penguins were originally inspired by the Insel-Bücherei, a series published in Leipzig before the war. The sixty odd volumes cover a wide range of subjects from *Russian Icons* to *British Beetles*, from *Heraldry in England* to the recently published *A Book of Scripts*, and in each case the colour or black-and-white illustrations have been introduced by a twenty-eight to sixty-eight page essay. Special care has been taken to use the best possible methods of reproduction and the high standard of the typography is now widely recognized. They have stiff board covers attractively designed, and are priced at two shillings and sixpence or three shillings.

FROM T. D. BARLOW'S
Woodcuts of Albrecht Dürer

THE PENGUIN SCORES

This series, under the general editorship of Dr. Gordon Jacob, Professor of Theory, Composition and Orchestration at the Royal College of Music, London, has been planned to meet the needs of concert-goers and amateurs of music. The format has been carefully chosen for convenience of holding or carrying in pocket or handbag. Each has a musical introduction by the General Editor, and a special biographical note by a music critic. In number five and all later volumes, for greater ease in score-reading, the parts of the transposing instruments have been printed at actual sounding-pitch.

The first eleven volumes, with in each case the writer of the biographical note, are:

1. MOZART: *Symphony No. 40 in G minor* – F. Bonavia

2. BACH: *Brandenburg Concerto No. 3, in G* – Frank Howes

3. BEETHOVEN: *Overtures: Coriolan and Egmont* – W. McNaught

4. HAYDN: *Symphony No. 101, in D (The Clock)* – Mosco Carner

5. MENDELSSOHN: *Overtures: A Midsummer Night's Dream and Fingal's Cave* – Ralph Hill

6. SCHUBERT: *Symphony No. 8, in B minor (Unfinished)* – Eric Blom

7. BACH: *Brandenburg Concertos Nos. 1 and 2, in F* – Frank Howes

8. WEBER: *Overtures: Oberon and Der Freischütz* – Scott Goddard

9. BEETHOVEN: *Symphony No. 1, in C* – W. McNaught

10. MOZART: *Symphony No. 41, in C, 'Jupiter'* – F. Bonavia

11. TCHAIKOVSKY: *Fantasy Overture, Romeo and Juliet* – Gerald Abraham

TWO SHILLINGS AND SIXPENCE EACH